JET XII

†

Rogue State

Russell Blake

First edition.

978-1549581267

Published by

Reprobatio Limited

CHAPTER 1

Jerusalem, Israel

A throng of pedestrians worked its way along the sidewalks of a small road that led to the Yamin Moshe Park – a verdant expanse where an annual arts fair had commenced that morning. Musicians had been plying their trade throughout the day from the stage of the nearby Sultan's Pool to the delight of the crowd, and vendors sold balloons and delectables to the gathering. The afternoon was blustery and warm; a balmy breeze from the Old City favored the attendees with welcome relief from the sun, and the tops of senile trees that framed the street rustled as though quietly applauding the new arrivals.

Jet squeezed Hannah's hand and snuck a sidelong glance at her daughter. The little girl's cheeks were pink from the walk, and her eyes shone bright with excitement. Jet's heart swelled in her chest at the sight of her angel enraptured by the prospect of the event that she and Matt had been talking about for weeks. Matt seemed to sense Jet's scrutiny from beside him and leaned into her, the scent of soap and a hint of aftershave still fresh on his skin.

"Big day for our little warrior," he murmured.

She smiled and nodded once. "Hannah's pretty excited about it, too."

Matt returned the smile and ran his fingers through his hair, which had grown out more over the two months since they'd set up camp in Israel. Jet considered him momentarily, and her jade eyes sparkled behind her sunglasses. She was about to follow up her quip when the roar of a heavy truck engine echoed off the stone building façades behind her.

Jet glanced over her shoulder as a flatbed loaded with crates

1

bound with strapping tape lumbered along the winding road. The driver seemed to have difficulty choosing the right gear, the motor revving and a black trail belching from the exhaust as it trundled past them. Several pedestrians ahead stepped back onto the sidewalk in time to avoid being run down, and Matt frowned as the truck careened around a bend and disappeared from view.

"Moron," he said. "Driving way too fast with that load."

Jet instinctively drew Hannah closer. "He's lucky he didn't hit anyone. Can't believe they let him on this street with the crowds."

A yellow balloon drifted overhead, carried by the wind toward the park, from which the faint sound of live music carried. Hannah, her smile lighting the world, squealed and pointed at the orb framed against a blue so vivid it hurt the eyes.

"Look, Mama! Balloon!" she cried.

"We're almost there," Jet said. "We'll get you one of your own. Would you like that?"

Hannah nodded enthusiastically. "Please."

Matt grinned and allowed a faster-moving couple to pass them, eyeing them with a smirk. "Ah, youth. Everyone's in a hurry instead of enjoying the day."

"You sound like a grumpy old man," Jet teased.

"I should. I'm green with envy."

She chuckled and glanced at him. "I'd say you still manage pretty well."

"You're just plying me with compliments so I'll pay for everything."

Jet's eyebrows rose. "Is it that obvious?"

He laughed, and they continued on their way, the break from Tel Aviv a welcome distraction in spite of that coastal city's ample charms.

~ ~ ~

With a wooden expression, Faraj Amir wiped away the beads of sweat coursing down his face and returned to wrestling with the flatbed's gear shifter. He cursed as he over-revved on a downshift and manhandled the wheel to the left. The steering was stiff and unresponsive due to the heavy load. He stared down at the speedometer with a scowl – nothing about the piece of junk was in decent condition, and he'd been unsurprised when the speedo had barely registered movement on the drive from the warehouse where he'd stolen it.

The suspension groaned alarmingly as he passed a cluster of pedestrians ambling toward the fair, and he forced himself to concentrate – he couldn't allow himself to be distracted by the surroundings. Faraj might not survive the hour, but he wouldn't allow his sacrifice to be in vain; he would see his mission through to its conclusion. That morning he had bid his sister and his friends farewell after being honored by them in a touching ceremony, and now his heart was hammering from the adrenaline coursing through his veins. If by some miracle he survived the blow he was about to strike on behalf of his people, it would be the will of Allah – but he wasn't expecting to and had made his peace.

He barely resisted the urge to mow down the civilians he passed, but he would offer his adversaries no warning to tip them off. He had his instructions and his mission was clear: he would not flinch or vary from it.

Faraj glanced at the ancient buildings that whizzed by the passenger-side window as he picked up speed on the downgrade approach to the security checkpoint by the park. For a brief instant he felt weightless, ethereal, as though able to fly if he wished, and he took the sensation as a good omen. Allah had filled him with courage and spirit, and the righteousness of his final act would ensure his place in Paradise. After two decades of misery during his brief lifetime, he was a true believer that his path was a holy one; the scum who had invaded his homeland deserved no mercy, just as they had shown none to his people.

His jaw clenched as he rounded the final bend, and he slammed the shifter into a lower gear. Speed and momentum were now more important than any attempt at stealth. He tugged on the seatbelt that crossed his chest to confirm it was well secured, offered a final prayer, and ducked low, only his eyes and the top of his head visible over the dashboard, the truck now a juggernaut whose trajectory was set, with Faraj now just along for the ride.

~ ~ ~

Jet's head jerked back at the crack of assault rifle fire from near the park. She instinctively ducked into a nearby doorway, shielding Hannah with her body as she moved. Matt was right behind her, expression grim, staring up the street at where the panicked crowd was stampeding away from the gunfire. The intensity of the shooting increased and seemed to last forever before it suddenly stopped, replaced by alarmed shouts and screaming from terrified pedestrians.

"What the hell–" Matt started.

Jet cut him off. "Stay here with Hannah," she said, her tone cool.

"What? Where are you going?"

"To see what happened."

"Stay here, Maya. This isn't your fight."

"Maybe not, but if I can help…"

Matt could see he wasn't going to win any argument with her and nodded instead. Jet knelt in front of her daughter and looked into her wide, uncomprehending eyes.

"I'll be right back, Hannah," she whispered.

The little girl shook her head, hard. "No, Mama. Don't go."

Jet kissed her forehead and reached into Hannah's backpack. She withdrew a frayed plush toy and handed it to Hannah, trying to keep her tone light. "Keep Bunny safe. I'll only be gone for a few minutes."

"Mama–"

Jet shushed her, straightened, and looked to Matt. "If I'm not back in ten minutes, head for the station, and I'll call your cell."

Deep lines creased his forehead. "I wish you'd reconsider."

"Don't worry."

Matt watched as she took off at a sprint, her movements fluid and graceful, a tribute to her training and the morning exercise regimen that kept her in professional athlete form. He offered his hand and Hannah took it, her gaze following Jet as she ran down the street against the flow of humanity tearing in the opposite direction, the instinct to put distance between itself and danger a sensible reaction Matt knew wasn't an option for Jet. He sighed and crouched beside the little girl, ready to run if necessary, swearing silently at the stubbornness of the woman he'd committed to spending his life with.

Jet dodged between panicked groups of people who thankfully showed no signs of injury. She rounded the corner where she'd last seen the truck and slowed at the sight of an older woman lying in the middle of the street, crying out for help. Young, able-bodied men ran past the woman, their eyes wild, and Jet waited until there was a lull and then made her way to her and helped her to her feet.

"Are you okay? Can you walk?" Jet asked.

The woman stood, obviously unstable, her appendages trembling. "I... Someone knocked me down. My knee hurts...and I think I twisted my ankle."

Jet quickly inspected the knee, where a gash had rent the skin. Blood was already congealing, and Jet had no doubt the woman would live. "I'll help you over to the side," she said. "Wait there, and someone will be along."

"What do you think happened?" the woman asked in a small voice.

"Whatever it is, it's bad."

"At least the shooting stopped."

Jet supported the woman and led her to a stoop, her limp pronounced. The woman sat in the shade and Jet regarded her. "You should be okay here. Just don't move until help arrives."

"They just knocked me down like I was nothing."

Jet nodded. "It's over. I'll be back."

"Thank you."

Jet wended her way between the now sparse runners. She was nearly to the intersection that led to the park when she nearly collided with a young man who was hurrying in the opposite direction.

"What happened?" she asked.

"A big truck. Hit the guard post." He hesitated. "You're going the wrong way."

"I can help with first aid."

He studied her face with frank astonishment and then nodded. "You're going to have your hands full."

"How far is it?"

"Not much farther. I hope you have a strong stomach."

Jet continued along the street and, when she turned another corner, stopped in her tracks at the nightmare before her. Bodies littered the ground, most dressed in the distinctive uniform of the Israel Defense Forces, and the pavement in front of steel crowd control barricades was awash with blood. Smoke corkscrewed from the crushed hood of the ruined flatbed truck, the axle broken and the chassis halfway through the rubble, which had come to a stop when it smashed into a stone wall that ran along the park perimeter.

Sirens from approaching emergency vehicles wailed in the distance as a radio squawked from one of the downed men, his inert form soaked in crimson. A few unharmed soldiers stood nearby with rifles in hand, clearly in shock at the horrific scene. Jet took in the carnage and slowly raised her hands to show she was unarmed, the soldiers' expressions telegraphing hair triggers and frayed nerves. One of the nearest eyed her and motioned with the ugly snout of his Uzi.

"That's far enough," he warned.

"It's okay. I'm here to help," she said in Hebrew.

"How?"

"I can do triage. I've been trained. Do you have any medics in the area?"

"Not so fast. Stay where you are."

Jet nodded. "Okay, but some of these men might make it if they get aid fast enough."

The man said something to his companion and they approached, his weapon still trained on her. "Hold still. We're going to search you."

"I saw the truck on the way here. I thought something had to be wrong, that kind of load on a weekend."

The soldier's partner frisked Jet and she didn't resist. When he had assured himself that she was only carrying a cell phone and a wallet, he stepped back and flipped the wallet open to eye her driver's license, which was newly issued by the Mossad, identifying her as Sarah Epstein, schoolteacher. If the man suspected it as anything but genuine, he didn't show it, and after showing it to his partner, handed it back to her along with the phone.

"Ambulances are on the way," he said, his voice strained. She guessed he was in his early twenties and sympathized with his predicament – routine guard work had suddenly turned into a full-scale suicide attack. Jet glanced at the cab of the truck, the windshield shattered from rifle rounds and the sheet metal of the body riddled with holes.

"Did the driver make it?" she asked.

The soldier's young face hardened. "Not a chance. But he still did enough damage for this to be considered a win by them." He spit and swallowed hard. "Animals."

A groan emanated from the twisted body of a nearby casualty. Jet raised an eyebrow and indicated the wounded man. "Let's see if we can do some good."

The first soldier adjusted his rifle, pointing the barrel away. "I hope you know what you're doing."

"I can't promise any miracles, but at this point, anything's better than nothing."

The soldier nodded and then looked away. "We didn't stand a chance. He got at least twenty of us. And more than double that wounded. He was on top of us before we could stop him."

Jet looked around her. "I can see. Now let's help those we can. You have a first aid kit anywhere around here?"

The second man nodded. "I think I can find one."

"Good. And if you can get some rope, that will help for tourniquets. If not, belts or strips of cloth. Anything to slow the bleeding."

Jet watched as the pair moved away, their steps unsure, and she remembered when she had been in similar straits, now so many years ago it seemed like a different lifetime. She knew they would replay the horror of the assault for years in their heads, the visions coming in the dark of night long after they thought they'd processed the brutality, and she didn't envy them.

The man on the ground groaned again, and Jet moved to his ruined body, her lips a thin line, any hope of a quick return to Matt and Hannah having vanished at the sight of the wounded.

They would understand.

CHAPTER 2

Sinai, Egypt

An arid wind blew off the desert south of Rafah with steady intensity. The night sky over the Gaza Strip was black as coal, a marine layer from the sea obscuring the moon and stars. In the distance, a few lights glimmered in the beleaguered city largely bombed out of existence but still home to 140,000 Palestinians with nowhere else to go.

A band of figures trudged through the sand toward the border, the forbidden northern Sinai more than familiar to the descendants of the Bedouins who had traveled the land for eons. Now, with no way to earn more than a subsistence existence, many had turned to smuggling in a time-honored tradition that the Egyptian military largely turned a blind eye to – presuming the right palms had been greased.

The column of a dozen men toted backpacks and walked with the dogged determination of those whose destination drew near. Their long trip would soon end when they reached one of the remaining tunnels that stretched from the forbidden no-man's land near the Egyptian border into Gaza. There, the cargo would be passed to the locals, and the mules' job done and their pay collected, the Bedouins would disappear into the night like wraiths before light could bring detection – and certain death.

Most of the tunnel system had been destroyed in the last few years, but human ingenuity had defeated attempts to shut them all down, with the surviving passages more than 150 feet below the surface, reinforced with concrete and able to withstand aerial bombardment – at least, that was the hope of the unfortunates who labored twelve-hour days, round the clock, digging them. Essential to obtaining medical supplies and necessities for the population of Gaza, they were also a valuable sideline for the organized smuggling groups who plied their trade through the passages and had made many of their number millionaires in a society where the vast majority lived in abject poverty and misery.

The section of no-man's land near the border that the Bedouins were approaching was the most treacherous – a trench, sixty feet deep and thirty wide, dug by the Egyptians to prevent vehicles from bringing cargo to the mouths of the tunnels in what had once been the Egyptian side of Rafah, now a deserted wasteland following the bulldozing of all the buildings along the border to eliminate cover for the tunnel mouths. Still, even within the desolation there remained numerous hidden entrances that the smuggling networks used, although at a vastly reduced rate than in the route's heyday.

The Bedouin in the lead abruptly stopped near a small rise, and his fellows spread out at the sight of another group approaching from the coast – a procession of at least twenty men leading camels and a few mules, all laden with heavy loads. The smugglers waited in silence, there being no place to hide in the barren wilderness as the newcomers neared.

Within two minutes the groups faced off. The drovers from the coast were unfamiliar to the Bedouins – probably local Egyptians, they surmised. The leader of the Bedouins offered a traditional greeting to the Egyptians, but they didn't reciprocate, their body language belligerent.

"What are you doing here?" a bearded Egyptian snapped at the leader.

"Same as you," the Bedouin replied, his hand beneath his robe on the grip of his pistol.

"Not tonight, you aren't," the Egyptian growled. "Get out of here."

"We've got a rendezvous. We mean you no harm."

The Egyptian scanned the gloom. "The military will be on us like flies, out in the open like this. Move out. Last warning."

"Maybe you didn't understand. We've got a meeting at the border," the Bedouin said, removing his pistol from the folds of his garment and holding it easily by his side. "You're free to do what you need to do, and you have my blessing to go in peace, but we're not leaving."

The Egyptian's eyes narrowed at the sight of the gun. "What are you carrying?"

"None of your business."

"It is now."

The Bedouin stood motionless, staring the Egyptian down. After a tense standoff, the Egyptian grinned and laughed harshly. "Must be something pretty special if you're willing to die for it."

The Bedouin shrugged. "Everyone dies eventually."

"What tribe are you?"

"Al-Tirabin."

"A big tribe."

"That's right." The Bedouin paused. "Why?"

The Egyptian smiled again, revealing an uneven ridge of yellow teeth. "I like to know whose lives I have taken."

The Bedouin frowned. "It is I who have the gun. My men are armed as well. We want no trouble, just to get paid and move on."

"Perhaps we can work together. You can give us your packs, and we will meet your conduit."

The Bedouin shook his head. "That will never happen."

The Egyptian nodded, his smile still fixed in place. "I thought that's what you would say." He turned from the Bedouin, and two sound-suppressed automatic rifles cut the tribesmen down where they stood. Only a few of the Bedouins were able to get off any shots before being slaughtered. The encounter was over before it started, and the Egyptian watched the nomads die without expression. When the fallen were motionless, he motioned to two of his men.

"Let's see what they were carrying," he said.

The men moved to the Bedouin leader and unslung his pack. One of them opened it, and his eyes widened when he saw the contents.

The Egyptian squinted in the gloom. "What is it?"

His man extracted a kilo package of white powder with Chinese characters hand-painted along one edge.

The Egyptian's smile disappeared. "Damn."

"What do we do?" the man holding the brick asked, his tone unsure.

"Do?" The Egyptian glared at the man as though he were mad. "We take it and sell it, of course."

"In Rafah? There will be reprisals."

"Maybe not. We can find a middleman on this side, move it at a discount, and let him take any heat."

"Perhaps we should have left them alone."

The Egyptian frowned and shook his head. "Too late now. Stupid bastard should have said something. Just like a Bedouin to play it too close to the chest."

The arms smugglers typically avoided the drug mules, who were protected by some of the most aggressive of the Rafah predators as well as by Hamas, which operated as the government of the Gaza Strip. To interfere with the trade was a death sentence, and few were willing to take the risk – it was a small world, and such an action would carry grievous consequences.

Then again, a score like this would enable a smart man to retire for good.

And the Egyptian was a smart man.

He would find someone who could arrange a transaction that wouldn't come back to bite him, and then take an extended vacation far from the miserable stretch of desert that had spawned him.

"Let's get moving. There's no way the Army didn't hear the shots, so they'll be headed this way – doesn't matter how much we paid for them to leave us be." He gestured at the dead men. "Take their things. We'll leave the drugs somewhere until we've done our business, and worry about how to unload it later."

"Are you sure? Maybe we should let the army find it…"

The Egyptian glowered at his man. "You're not paid to think. Do as I ordered or you'll join these maggots – understand?"

The pair of smugglers exchanged a glance, and the one with the drugs in hand nodded. "I meant no disrespect."

"Then get to it. We don't have all night."

The Egyptian watched the men loot the Bedouins and considered executing them there, but decided that could wait. His brothers, cousin, and he could attend to that matter once they'd dropped off their cargo of weapons and were safely away from the border. That two-thirds of the party wouldn't make it to daybreak didn't disturb him a bit – the desert had always been a harsh mistress, and the take from this much heroin would be too large for men who weren't related to him to keep silent about. Their deaths were necessary to ensure he would live. It was simple, and he couldn't hesitate or he would bring destruction down upon his own head and that of his family.

It was either him or them, and he couldn't change what had already happened.

He cocked his head at the sound of a distant engine and snapped his fingers. "We're out of time. The army will drag their feet, but we need to be well clear of here by the time they arrive. Haji, Amir, cover our tracks so they have nothing to follow. The rest of you laggards, move."

CHAPTER 3

Bucharest, Romania

Cezar stood by the side of a hospital bed, his military uniform crumpled from a long night in a metal chair by the vital signs monitor. The only sounds in the room were the steady beeping of the pulse oximeter and his brother's labored breathing.

His brother Gavril was the oldest of four siblings, a man who'd clawed his way from modest beginnings to a position of moderate success in the government ministry, a mid-level bureaucrat who'd provided for his family and enjoyed reasonable prosperity given the turmoil his country had endured. Built like a fireplug and tall in his youth, he was now jaundiced, the parchment skin stretched over his cheekbones nearly translucent in the fluorescent light, his eyes watery and unfocused, barely able to recognize his youngest brother.

"Feeling any better?" Cezar asked, his hand over Gavril's.

"No. I'm dying. Everything's…shutting down," Gavril managed, his voice weak.

Cezar had no words of encouragement to offer; anything he could say would be a vacant platitude his brother, even in his compromised condition, would see through and call him on. That was how Gavril had always been: tough but fair, and not given to dishonesty no matter the reason.

Instead of speaking, Cezar squeezed his hand, his own eyes now moistening at the thought of a life without Gavril, struck down in the prime of his life by a curse that had come out of nowhere.

Gavril, like all the boys in the family, had never been shy about having a drink – a cultural rite of passage Romanians celebrated and some took to excessive levels. But unlike many of his peers, he had never given himself over to alcoholism, at least not as practiced by so much of the population; Romania had the fifth highest alcohol consumption rate on the planet, and with it an out-of-control substance abuse problem that affected one in every six males. By Romanian standards, Gavril was a heavy drinker, but not to the point it interfered with his work or made him violent.

When he'd learned that he was suffering from late stage cirrhosis of the liver, it had come as a shock. The best the doctors had been able to tell, he'd fallen victim to infectious mononucleosis that had weakened his liver to the point that the drinking he might have been able to tolerate when healthy had corroded his body from within and had progressed to the point his liver was no longer able to break down the toxins in his blood and expel them. He'd been placed on a list for potential organ donation, but the current wait was two years; and Gavril had weeks, on the outside, to live. Every day his blood markers degraded, and the prognosis was bleak – even the nurses, who tried to remain upbeat, looked at him like he was a dead man walking.

When Cezar spoke again, his words sounded strangled. "I'm…I'm going to go to the bathroom and get some fresh air."

"Do it while you can, Major," Gavril said with a cadaverous grin, his gums receded sufficiently that his teeth looked too long for his face.

"Captain," Cezar corrected, painfully aware of the sour tang of dried perspiration wafting from his uniform.

He left the hospital room and made for the stairs, feeling for his pack of cigarettes as he walked. A familiar figure emerged from another patient room, and Cezar slowed and cleared his throat to get the man's attention.

"Doctor, do you have a minute?"

The physician checked his watch, obviously annoyed, and then his expression softened. "Certainly, Captain. But I can't be late for my rounds. We're shorthanded due to the flu."

"My brother…he's getting worse. His breathing is a rasp, and…he doesn't smell right."

The doctor nodded. "Yes. It's not easy to watch, I know. But there's not much we can do about it."

"Have you checked on the transplant list again?"

"Daily. There are no matches, and frankly, I think that hoping he hangs on until… Well, I'm not sure it's productive to invest energy in that direction. It's unlikely to happen." The doctor paused. "I'm sorry."

"Any idea how long he has?"

The doctor looked away. "It's difficult to say. If an infection hits, it could be…over quickly."

"What about liver dialysis? I read about that being a possible way of extending his life."

"Jury's out, but we don't have that equipment, so it's a moot point."

Cezar absorbed the man's matter-of-fact tone and fought to control his temper. This was his big brother they were discussing, and the doctor sounded as detached as though they were talking about a flat tire. Cezar knew intellectually he was just doing a tough job as best he could, but it didn't make the experience any easier. He took a deep breath and nodded his gratitude.

"Well, if you can think of anything else, I'm all ears."

"It's none of my business, but if I were you, I'd make my peace and prepare for the worst. I'm sorry. I wish it were different." The doctor checked the time again. "Now I really must get back to my rounds."

"Thank you. I understand."

Cezar walked to the stairs in a daze, his stomach churning, bile threatening to rise in his throat. He descended to the ground level and pushed out of the door to the brick area where he'd spent many hours smoking while watching his brother die. He tapped out a cigarette, lit it, and inhaled the acrid smoke, eyes closed against the morning glare.

Another smoker exited the door and walked toward him with a cigarette in hand. "Got a light?" he asked Cezar.

Cezar nodded and flicked his disposable butane lighter to life. The other man, olive skinned and sporting three days' growth, puffed the tip of his smoke to an ember and cocked his head at Cezar in thanks.

"Appreciate it."

"Sure. No problem."

The pair stood smoking, and then the stranger leaned into Cezar. "I'm very sorry about your brother. My cousin told me. A shame."

"Your cousin?"

"One of the orderlies."

"Ah."

"He is not doing well?"

Cezar's countenance hardened. "I don't want to talk about it."

The man nodded. "I understand. The only reason I ask is because there may be a solution you haven't considered."

"If you know about my brother, you know there's nothing more that can be done."

"Not necessarily. There are ways to get anything one wants…if one knows the right people."

Cezar frowned. "He needs a new liver. Now. Are you saying you can help?"

The stranger dropped his cigarette into a metal pail that served as an ashtray. "Filthy habit."

"I asked you a question," Cezar pressed.

"I heard you. The answer is yes. I can help."

"How?"

"I know the people who can arrange it."

Cezar's eyes narrowed. "We're not a rich family."

"Yes. That is a problem. But there might be another way for you to…help me help you."

"Another way?"

The man looked around as if suddenly aware of his surroundings and stepped closer to Cezar, a business card in hand. "Take this. Call me later today. I will make some calls. See if you can get as much information as possible on what your brother needs – blood type, antigens, that sort of thing." He hesitated. "Now I must go. If you want your brother to live, call."

Cezar watched unbelievingly with the card in his hand as the man sauntered back to the exit and disappeared inside the hospital without looking back. He peered down at it and saw only a first name and a phone number. Cezar stubbed out his cigarette and lit another automatically, his movements wooden, and stared at the card. He was unsure what had just happened, but the knot of anxiety in his gut tightened with each passing moment.

CHAPTER 4

Tel Aviv, Israel

A tall, muscular man clad in a dress jacket and tan slacks escorted Jet down a windowless corridor in a partially built office building she'd never been to before. From the outside, the edifice appeared to be stalled construction – the site was fenced off and the underground parking dark as a crypt – but once inside she noted that the area they were walking through was completely finished. The AC hummed quietly, the temperature cool enough to raise goose bumps on her tanned, bare arms.

Her running shoes were silent on the ceramic tile floor, her guide's crepe-soled shoes nearly so, and the only sounds were the climate control and the rustle of their clothes as they approached double gray steel doors at the end of the hall. The man hesitated before rapping twice.

A gruff, muffled voice called out from the other side. "Yes, yes. Come in."

The escort, the bulge of his shoulder holster obvious to Jet, regarded her with dead eyes and twisted the handle, pushing the door open and standing aside. She brushed past him and entered a large office space with floor-to-ceiling windows, the blinds closed. The director and two men she didn't recognize were seated at an oval conference table surrounded by chairs in the otherwise empty room, the only other furniture an under-counter refrigerator in a corner and a utilitarian metal desk by the windows.

"Come. Sit," the director said, waving a smoldering cigarette at one of the chairs. Her nose wrinkled at the smell of stale smoke as she neared, and she took a seat where he indicated, the director and the two men facing her. "Water? Soda?" he asked.

She shook her head and eyed the strangers. The director sat back and gestured to them.

"This is Levi, and this is Moishe. They're here to brief you," he explained. "Thank you for coming so promptly."

Jet nodded to the men. "I didn't have much choice. You were kind enough to send two agents to ensure my life and family didn't interfere with your needs."

"We all make the sacrifices we must," the director said. "I have a job for you."

"I gathered."

"Moishe here works closely with our antidrug taskforce. Levi is one of our specialists for field ops," he said, ignoring her irritation at being pulled from playing with Hannah in a park near their new home. "Focused on Asia."

Jet shifted her attention to Levi. "Asia?"

"That's right," Levi responded. "China, for the last...for some time."

The director cleared his throat and stubbed out his cigarette in a full ashtray. "We have a domestic situation that's causing us considerable concern."

Jet frowned. "Since when does the Mossad deal with internal issues?"

Moishe tapped a pen on the tabletop. "It has an international component. Specifically, one that we've traced to the Chinese."

Jet's eyes narrowed. "Drugs, I gather."

Moishe nodded. "That's right. Heroin. Israel has seen a marked increase in its use over the last two years, and it's becoming a real problem."

"I've read about it blossoming in the U.S., but I didn't realize it was here, too," Jet said.

"Well, it is, in a big way. You would think that with Afghanistan so close, that would be the main source, and it was our thinking as well; but it turns out that isn't where the majority of the heroin we're seeing originates."

Jet's gaze moved back to Levi. "China," she said, her voice flat.

"Correct," Levi confirmed. "We've identified a criminal network that's smuggling it through Egypt, but the source is Chinese. One of the larger triads operating out of Beijing, as well as several of the ports. They're into everything – weapons smuggling, counterfeit goods, drugs, murder for hire, slavery, prostitution...if there's profit in it, nothing is off-limits."

The director lit another cigarette and blew a cloud of smoke at the ceiling before taking over from Levi. "These gangs go back hundreds of years, since the British began the opium trade. They were a natural ally to the Brit merchants and grew fabulously wealthy in the drug business. When that dried up, they branched out into other areas. We've never encountered them until now – at least, not operating in Israel. Apparently they've put together a trafficking system and are shipping tonnage into our country." He paused and took another deep drag on his cigarette. "Which can't continue. We have enough threats as it is without this rotting us from within."

Jet met his stare without blinking. "What do you need me for? I don't speak Chinese – which you know from my dossier."

"Yes, but you have other skills we require, and you can pass for a local in a pinch, at least in terms of appearance, which we can heighten with makeup."

"Anyone who speaks to me will know I'm not Chinese in an instant," she countered.

"That's fine," Levi said. "We'll have a cover story in place. Your Italian is fluent, is it not?"

She eyed him. "That's right."

"Then we'll create an ID package that has you from Milan – a journalist." Levi frowned. "We have a team in place, but we need an extraction pro – none of the group has anything like the sort of experience you do."

"Who are we kidnapping?"

"A fellow named Zhao Yaozu. One of the top dogs in the White Dragons – that's the street name of the triad."

The director interrupted the exchange. "It's a complicated

scenario. You'll need to get the target to a safe house and interrogate him. He's virtually untouchable, surrounded by protection all the time, but we've gotten word of a function he'll be attending in two days, and that's when we make our move." He looked her up and down. "Levi will brief you on the details."

The plan was more convoluted than she would have liked, and allowing for travel time, it would be close. She read through a thick folder Levi gave her, pausing to ask questions and clarify ambiguous points, and then stopped at a collection of blurry photographs obviously taken without the subject's knowledge. Jet studied the man's face – a cruel mouth, the corners downturned in every shot, a nose that looked flattened from fighting, pig eyes spaced too close together.

"Why did you wait so long to bring me in?" she asked.

The director grunted. "It took some effort to convince everyone to introduce a new face into the mix. Even a specialist with skills such as yours."

She nodded. She knew how protective a control officer running an op could be, especially with a team that hadn't worked together before. Jet could imagine that the director had lobbied hard for her involvement, or Levi would have nixed it – ultimately, it would be the officer responsible for the mission who would have the final call unless the director pulled him off and assigned someone new. An impossibility, given the short fuse.

She looked to Moishe and Levi. "When do I leave?"

The director sat back. "There's a flight to Istanbul that departs this evening. You'll be in Beijing by tomorrow. The snatch will take place in the early evening the next day, so you'll have time to get a feel for the members of the team."

"What are their backgrounds?"

Levi's eyes darted to the director, who nodded.

"You may speak freely," the director said. "As I advised you earlier, she has discretion to refuse the mission if she isn't comfortable with the details or the assets."

Levi filled Jet in on the people she would be working with. When he finished, Moishe took over and gave her the rundown on what they knew about the Egyptian end of things, which turned out to be precious little.

"How did you learn of the triad?" Jet asked.

"We had an informer. We're confident the information is solid."

"Was it volunteered, or did you have to drag it out of him?"

Moishe bristled. "I'm not sure what that has to do—"

The director waved away his objection. "It was coerced. Two days of intensive interrogation. Why?"

Jet exhaled forcefully. "We all know that sort of intel is iffy."

"We have a high degree of confidence," Moishe said. "We corroborated the detail. It's good. You can take that to the bank."

"Chinese side, or Egypt?" Jet pressed.

"Neither. Palestinian."

She rolled her eyes. "Seriously?"

"We've been working the case for almost a year. It doesn't get any better than this."

The director pushed back from the table. "I'm hoping you'll take this one on. Should be straightforward for you. Get in, grab him, interrogate him, and be back home by the weekend."

Jet wasn't convinced. "How did you learn of the wedding?"

"Through one of our moles." He coughed, the sound phlegmy, and took another drag of his cigarette before stabbing it into the pile of butts. "There's a limit to how much we can tell you. That I've brought you into this should indicate the importance of the mission." He tried a smile, the leathery skin around his eyes crinkling, no trace of good humor in them. "I would very much appreciate it if you'd agree to helping, so we can get this show on the road. We don't have anyone else as qualified as you who we can pull into this on short notice. We only got word of the wedding three days ago, so it's been a scramble since. But we've done our homework."

She sighed and flipped the folder open again.

"Give me the rundown on the pilot."

CHAPTER 5

Pyongyang, North Korea

Captain Hong Yun Sa waited in a long line of officers filed along the side of the military headquarters responsible for coastal and air defense. A morning chill lingered in the air in defiance of the rising sun. Hong's lot in life was a desk job ever since he'd mangled his leg in a car accident, and he was one of hundreds who labored in solitude, his tiny office a perk warranted by the sensitive information he routinely handled.

His country had been in a constant state of war for fifty years, the cease-fire with the South considered temporary by his government, more so because of the regular training exercises that featured South Korean and U.S. forces simulating an invasion of his homeland. North Korea had never forgotten the destruction wreaked on it by the American bombers, which after destroying every city proceeded to target vital infrastructure – a war crime by any measure – resulting in the death of more than twenty percent of the population from floods when the dams were bombed and the starvation that followed the complete loss of huge tracts of the country's crops. The military was a large employer in a land where GDP per person was barely a thousand dollars per year, and Hong considered himself fortunate to have work he found at least marginally stimulating in a centrally planned economy where boredom and hopelessness were the rule.

The column of men shuffled forward toward the security checkpoint, everyone thin to the point of emaciation due to the scarcity of staples – a regular feature of life in the communist paradise, largely due to sanctions imposed by the West for its glorious leader's pursuit of weapons with which to defend itself from further aggression, if the rhetoric were to be believed. Than didn't question it – he'd lost his grandfather's side of the family in the war and most of his grandmother's, so the wounds and threat of devastation were still vivid in his mind even though he hadn't been born yet when the shaky cease-fire had been put into place over sixty years earlier.

He arrived at the guard post and smiled at the soldiers manning it, who were primarily there to prevent files or data from leaving the building, rather than fear of sabotage. The rigor with which the sentries went through his satchel and patted him down was as muted as the hushed conversation in the line behind him; mainly griping over the limited options for food this week, the weather, or whether the threats of invasion or military action against the country were finally going to come to fruition. The griping was a pressure valve, complaining over things that were unchangeable, unaffected by individual effort.

A corporal swept a wand over the arriving men to check for any unauthorized devices, and after he had been processed, Hong retrieved his bag from the inspection table and made his way to his cubbyhole office in the depths of the labyrinthine building. At the fourth office from the end of the corridor, he opened a plywood door and nearly struck the edge of his metal desk. The room was just large enough to accommodate an uncomfortable chair, a desk that was older than he was, and a PC that dated from before the turn of the century.

He sniffed the stale air and moved to the frosted-glass window, which only opened two inches due to faulty tracks that would never be fixed. After sliding it up, he removed his jacket and tapped a few keys to bring his computer out of sleep mode. The monitor that occupied a third of his desk, easily the size of an oven, was a relic of Chinese manufacture whose patchwork of dead pixels he knew by heart. It blinked to life with an audible snap, and the computer's hard disk clicked and popped as the drive labored to spin up to speed. The menu that would demand his user ID and password materialized in the middle of the screen, and he was entering his security code when the door to his office swung open without a knock and an officer stepped inside. Behind him stood two soldiers, who remained in the hall due to the lack of space.

"Captain Hong?" the officer demanded. Than looked up at the man's epaulets and saw he was a major.

"That's right, sir," he said with a salute as he struggled to stand, surprised by the unexpected intrusion.

"I need to have a word with you."

Hong's blood froze in his veins at the expression on the major's acne-scarred face, his ebony eyes unreadable but offering no warmth.

"Of course, sir. I would offer you a seat, but as you can see—"

"Not here. You are to accompany me to my office."

"Certainly, sir." Than reached for his jacket, which he had draped across the back of his chair, and the major shook his head.

"One of my men will get that."

Than tried to focus, unsure what to make of the unusual demand. Nothing like this had ever happened to him in over twenty years of service. He swallowed hard and nodded. "Of course, sir. May I ask where we're going?"

"You will find out in due time."

"It's just that I need to report my whereabouts to my superior if I leave my station for more than a bathroom break, sir, as you probably know. Regulations."

"I've already spoken to Colonel Bak."

Hong's stomach twisted with tension. "Do I need anything from my office, sir?"

"No. You are to accompany me. Now," the major repeated, his voice hard.

"Yes, sir. Of course, sir."

The major stepped back out of the office, watching Hong like a hawk as he rounded his desk and approached. The closest soldier clasped a hand around one of Hong's arms, confirming his impression that, whatever this was, it couldn't be good. He'd always been a good soldier, and his disciplinary record was spotless, but he'd heard horror stories of men who had disappeared for no reason, their memory scrubbed from the collective consciousness as effectively as though they'd been erased from existence. He'd always assumed they had done something to deserve the treatment, but now he wasn't so sure, and his heart was hammering in his chest like it intended to explode through his sternum as he was escorted down the hall.

When they reached a stairwell halfway down the corridor's length, the major directed Hong to the steps, and the three followed him down.

"Keep going to the basement," the major ordered, and Hong's unease escalated into full-blown panic – the basement was the province of the most feared arm of the government: the Ministry of State Security, an Orwellian group about which little was known other than that it answered directly to the ultimate leader; they were in charge of prison camps, counterespionage, and government dirty tricks. Members of all branches of the military were members, their exact roles shrouded in secrecy, but the one thing that was common knowledge was that to be summoned to an interrogation by the MSS was often a death sentence.

At the basement level the landing was painted a drab olive and boasted a single steel blast door, nothing else. The major depressed the button of an intercom mounted beside it and spoke in a hushed voice, rattling off a series of meaningless numbers and letters Than supposed was the day's access code.

The door swung open. Hong found himself facing two more soldiers with submachine guns hanging from shoulder straps and a lone civilian in an ill-fitting black suit, greasy hair slicked straight back off his forehead. The man eyed Hong without expression and then looked past him at the major.

"Show the captain to holding cell B. I will be along shortly," he said, his tone as menacing as a snake's hiss.

"What is this about? There's been some mistake, sir," Hong blurted, his leg muscles suddenly watery.

"Yes, well, I'm sure we'll learn the truth in short order. Major? Time's wasting."

The soldiers led Hong to a cell with a single steel bench in the center and a table and two chairs in the far corner. One of the guards unceremoniously cuffed his hands behind his back without speaking, and the major motioned to the bench, where a metal eyelet was affixed every three feet. "Sit."

"I haven't done anything, sir. You have to believe me."

"Sit."

There being no other option, Hong took a seat at the end of the bench. The soldier pushed him to the side and snapped the handcuff chain to the eyelet with a single deft motion, and then the uniformed men left him to his rush of thoughts, his head spinning at the sudden turn of events. That morning he'd kissed his wife and two children goodbye before wheeling his bicycle to the main road and joining the phalanx of predawn commuters bound for the base, his cares mundane and unexceptional, and now he was locked down for no reason, facing God knew what.

By the time the door opened ten minutes later and admitted the suited man, Hong's shoulders were slumped, his wrists numb from the cuffs. The civilian regarded him for a long moment and then walked slowly toward him, removed a small digital recorder from his jacket pocket, and flipped it on. He placed it on the table and turned to Hong, his face grim.

"I have questions for you about the unauthorized access of your work files from a remote location."

Hong's eyes widened in incomprehension. "I...I don't understand."

"Two days ago, or nights, to be accurate, your system was accessed remotely for twenty-six minutes. There's no point denying it – we have the data records. I want to know what you accessed and why. As you know, doing so is a capital offense. However, if you cooperate, I am willing to recommend leniency."

"I… It wasn't me. I swear."

"Captain Hong, you have a family, do you not?"

Than nodded, the blood draining from his face.

"We are determined to get to the bottom of this, and that means we will stop at nothing to learn the truth. I too have a family – two daughters. I would hate to bring innocents into this and would prefer if it were unnecessary to do so. But I will. Make no mistake, I will."

"I have no ability to remotely access my computer. None. There's a firewall. Codes."

"It is connected to the network, is it not?"

"Of course. But it has several layers of security."

"It was accessed from a remote location. We know that much. Only your computer. Nothing else was touched." The man glanced at a cheap metal watch and shook his head. "This is your last chance to come clean, Captain. Your many years of loyal service will count in your favor, but only to a point. Continue to lie, and there is nothing anyone can do to help you – or your beautiful children. Do you understand?"

Hong looked around the room as though seeking help. When he faced his interrogator again, his eyes were wild, and he despised himself at the warmth that spread from the crotch of his trousers. "It wasn't me. I didn't do it. Please. You have to believe me."

The man sighed and nodded slowly. "Yes, I was afraid you would say that. Ah, well. Every now and again it would be nice to be surprised. Today isn't my lucky day, I see."

"Please–"

"No point in begging. We will learn the truth."

"No…"

The man switched off the recorder and made for the door. Hong was panting like a caged dog, the stink of urine pungent as he watched the interrogator rap on the steel slab twice. When it opened, the man looked back at Hong pityingly and shook his head. "I gave you a chance. Now it becomes unpleasant. You should have cooperated when you had the opportunity – if not for yourself, for your children."

"I didn't–"

The door slammed behind the interrogator with the finality of a rifle shot and the lights blinked out, leaving Hong to consider his abbreviated future in a darkness that was as heavy as lead.

CHAPTER 6

Islamabad, Pakistan

A battered Toyota van rocked along rutted pavement that paralleled the Korang River's muddy brown wash, headed out of the capital city toward the verdant hills, the Himalayas to the north thrusting into an azure sky. Discordant music whined from the cheap stereo, the singer's voice eerily reminiscent of a strangling cat howling in protest over a polyrhythmic clamor. The driver stared at the remains of the road with the intensity of a gambler who'd bet his last dollar on a losing horse, the engine straining as they bounced up a winding grade.

"It isn't much further," he said in rusty Arabic to the figure in the passenger seat – a heavily bearded man who hadn't spoken since he had gotten into the van near the airport, his only luggage a stained overnight bag stuffed to the breaking point.

The passenger grunted noncommittally, his scowling countenance divulging nothing. Abu Azim had endured far worse in his thirty-seven years on the planet, the squalor of Pakistan nothing compared to the rubble that was his native Palestine. Years of shortages of everything from building materials to basic necessities had inured him to discomfort, and he barely registered the poverty and misery that paraded past his window.

The van slowed as it neared a fork, and a scrawny brown dog leapt from the scrub by the river to bark and snap at the rear tires before giving up, the amusement value of the effort outweighed by the heat. The driver twisted the wheel, and the van lurched onto a gravel drive that led to a gate in a cinderblock wall, the second story of a large house visible beyond it. Azim gripped the seat to keep from being thrown against the window by a particularly violent jolt, and then the van was coasting to a stop, its brakes shrieking like a dying bird.

The driver honked twice, and a metal hatch swung open in the heavy iron slab. A face appeared in the gap, and the driver nodded to the man, who slammed the hatch shut without a word. The driver snuck a look at Azim, who could have been cast in bronze, his skin the color of boot leather, his brow heavy, and his prominent Adam's apple barely visible for his beard. The driver seemed about to say something, but reconsidered and returned his gaze to the gate, which slowly swung open, pulled by two guards while a third stood within the compound with an AK-47, his eyes trained on the van. The driver goosed the gas and the vehicle rolled through the opening and pulled to a stop in front of a massive whitewashed home. Blue tiled Moorish domes adorned the roof, and the arched entry door was easily ten feet tall and ornately hand carved.

Azim swung down from the van and allowed the two gunmen who approached from the house to search him and his belongings before they stood aside and allowed him inside. Azim entered the foyer and looked around. A small man in a white robe appeared from a doorway at the far end of the room and offered an abbreviated bow.

"Welcome. Please. Allow me to take your things." The man paused. "He is awaiting your arrival with great anticipation."

"Thank you. As am I."

Azim tendered his bag, and the little man took it with a nod. "Please. This way."

They walked through the seemingly endless chain of rooms until they arrived at an oversized chamber with a two-story ceiling and an ornate stained-glass window through which sunlight streamed in a dizzying kaleidoscope of colors across the white marble floor. In the center of the room sat a man on a faded oriental rug, watching the newcomer with hooded eyes.

The figure rose and held out his arms. "Welcome, Abu Azim. It is an honor to invite you into my humble abode. Praise Allah that you made it without incident."

"The honor is mine, Mullah Nasreddin," Azim replied, addressing the figure with his honorific as well as his assumed name.

The men embraced, and Nasreddin stood with Azim at arm's length, taking him in before nodding once and breaking the hold. "Let us sit." He glanced at the servant. "Tea," he ordered, and the man scuttled away.

They sat on the rug, and Nasreddin beamed benevolence at Azim as they waited for the servant to return.

"I had no problem getting here, for which I am thankful," Azim said.

"As am I. You look fit."

"I feel older than my years from the struggle. But it is my life, and there is no other for me – or my people."

"You did not choose it."

"No," Azim agreed.

"We are all fortunate to have men such as yourself. We owe you a tremendous debt."

"For doing Allah's work? Hardly. It is I who owe you thanks for your continued generosity in our battle."

Nasreddin shrugged and looked away. "What is money but a tool? It is the least I can do to help right a tremendous injustice." He paused as the servant arrived with a hammered metal teapot and a pair of cups. When the man had departed, Nasreddin continued. "You battle the devil himself and his familiars, for which the faithful are grateful. If I have been blessed with prosperity, I am merely a vessel through which it flows. Thankfully, Allah has afforded me the vision to know how it is best deployed."

The older man poured his guest tea, and they took appreciative sips of the scalding brew before setting their cups down and turning to the purpose of the meeting. Nasreddin had summoned Azim, and the terrorist had dropped everything to see his sponsor, there being no more important person in his universe than the one who paid the bills.

Nasreddin fixed Azim with a knowing look. "I saw the news of the truck in Jerusalem."

"Another martyr gone to paradise. It struck the beast in its heart."

"Perhaps, but I cannot help but think that these smaller blows will not kill it. Rather, they reinforce the excuse to further oppress your people."

It was Azim's turn to shrug. "There are limits to what we can accomplish, unfortunately. Their security is impressive."

"I understand. But I feel in my soul that we need something more. Something…decisive. You cut one head off the hydra, and three grow back in its place. I cannot see how this will ever change unless we win a significant victory."

Azim appeared confused. "I would welcome such a thing. But what sort of triumph did you have in mind? What is even possible, given the enemy's resources?"

"I have been thinking a great deal, and I believe I have come up with a way to achieve all our goals with a single strike. Much as a handful of freedom fighters were able to bring the Great Satan, America, to its knees, we need something as big – no, far, far bigger. Something that will end this assault on the people once and for all."

"Anything I can do, you know that I will. Please. Of what do you speak? How can I help? Consider me your sword."

Nasreddin nodded and took another sip of tea. He inhaled through his nose and shifted on the carpet. "Sometimes force is not the best way to achieve an objective. Cunning can, when judiciously employed, wreak havoc where a frontal attack will fail."

Azim nodded, unsure of where the discussion was going but enthralled by the confidence he was sure would follow. "I am like a student before the master."

"Our adversary uses the power and the army of their lapdog, America, to pursue their agenda, and the population is blind to what is happening. It is our role to change that – to remove the scales from their eyes once and for all." Nasreddin paused and offered a small smile. "To do this, we will use their energy, their momentum, against them. We have been going about this entirely wrong. Rather than meeting force with force, we will do something they do not expect and, by changing our approach, will defeat them in a way that will never be forgotten."

"My heart soars. What are you thinking?"

Another smile, and Nasreddin lowered his voice to a whisper. "I have already put the pieces into play."

Nasreddin spoke for five minutes. When he fell silent, Azim didn't have to pretend awe at the audaciousness – and simplicity – of the mullah's plan.

When he made his way back to the van, his head was spinning with the possibilities the meeting had created for him and his countrymen. It was brilliant, daring, and – given the mullah's funding and contacts – entirely possible to bring to fruition.

His pulse quickened as he stepped out the door. Finally, after years of oppression, justice would be served.

And when it came, especially in the manner Nasreddin had described, his people's long-delayed revenge would taste sweeter than honey.

CHAPTER 7

Indian Ocean

The U.S.S. *Sawyer*, an Arleigh Burke-class destroyer temporarily assigned to patrolling the Indian Ocean, picked up speed through eight-foot swells until it was speeding along at thirty knots, its sharp bow slicing through the water with ease. A diffuse mango and amber glow illuminated the horizon as the smoldering sun rose from the ocean's eastern edge like a fiery god.

"Estimated time of interception, six minutes," Ensign Douglas said, glancing up from the radar at where the captain stood on the bridge, binoculars glued to his eyes as he fixed on a bulk carrier cargo ship pounding through the tumultuous seas ahead.

"Chinese flagged," Captain Morris said, lowering the glasses. "This is it. All hands to their stations."

Douglas relayed the order, and a klaxon sounded along the decks as men scrambled to their assigned positions for a boarding expedition. The *Sawyer* was part of an international taskforce chartered with intercepting suspicious vessels and inspecting them to confirm they weren't carrying contraband to the increasing number of nations against which the West had imposed sanctions, and the shipping lane the destroyer was patrolling was one of the most notorious for violators.

The Chinese-flagged vessel hadn't responded to the *Sawyer*'s hailing on all frequencies, nor had it slowed its thirteen-knot pace. Now it would be subject to boarding, its documentation checked and its cargo verified as legitimate before being allowed on its way. The inspections were a regular occurrence in modern shipping for all but the ships of well-established companies and a regular annoyance near the Middle East, certain parts of the Indian and Atlantic Oceans, and the South China Sea.

The captain raised the spyglasses again and regarded the mystery vessel's length; its dented and scarred black hull, seams bleeding rust; and its smokestack belching a black trail. He estimated the ship to be six hundred or so feet long and at least thirty years old – ancient by seafaring standards but common enough along this route and the coast of Africa, where vessels plied their trade until they disappeared with their crews; also a regular occurrence in certain areas, where ships were often hijacked and sold for their scrap value by pirates.

The destroyer neared the tramp freighter, and the captain activated the hailing system, his voice projecting across the surface of the sea from high-powered speakers. He advised the ship to cut power; and when, after two minutes, it hadn't obeyed, he repeated his order. The freighter showed no sign of slowing, and he turned to the ensign and gave the instruction to fire a round across its bow.

One of the deck guns boomed, and a plume of water fountained into the air. The smoke belching from the stack stopped, and the Chinese ship began to slow. When it was dead in the water, rising and falling in the swell, the captain authorized the helm to close within a few hundred yards, and he announced over the speakers the boarding party's intention to come alongside. A spry Asian in shorts and a tank top appeared from the superstructure with a bullhorn and demanded in broken English to know why the destroyer had fired across its bow. The captain gave him a radio channel to tune to, and waited until confirmation came that the Chinese craft was monitoring it.

The captain spoke slowly and deliberately to the freighter, instructing her to remain in neutral and to lower a rope ladder so the boarding party could come aboard to conduct its search. The vessel didn't respond for several minutes, but when it did, it acceded to the inspection.

The boarding party descended to a pair of inflatable tenders, and once fully loaded, the craft plied her way to where a rope ladder had been dropped down the port side of the cargo ship's hull. The destroyer kept its machine guns trained on the Chinese vessel in case anything unexpected took place. When the Americans were on the cargo ship's deck, three Asians emerged from the superstructure and greeted the armed men, one of them the same sailor who had called to the destroyer on the bullhorn.

Searching a bulk carrier was an involved affair that would take the entire day, and the inspectors went about their work with long-suffering patience while six of them watched over the crew in the superstructure. Seven hours after they had begun the search, the radio on the destroyer's bridge squawked and one of the squad leaders offered a report.

"Got us a live one. There's at least a hundred kilos of a white powder hidden in a pair of drums in one of the equipment rooms. And some suspicious metal forms in a grain hold. We're going to have to dig to get at them, but if I had to guess, based on dimensions, we're looking at antitank ordnance."

The captain frowned. "Think they could be SAMs?"

"Maybe. It'll take us a while to uncover them. I presume we have permission to dump as much of the grain as we need to?"

The captain and helmsman exchanged a glance, and the captain nodded. "Aye, aye. Permission granted. Make sure the crew remains contained."

"Yes, sir."

The likelihood that anyone on board the Chinese vessel would put up a fight was low, but the captain wasn't going to take any chances. Of course, nobody would admit to knowing the drugs or arms were aboard, and it was entirely possible nobody did – possible, but unlikely. That would be up to a court to decide, not the captain, and his next act would be to transmit to the Australian authorities a report on their find and let the Aussies deal with the crew.

Night had fallen by the time the suspect cargo had been uncovered – eighteen NK38 SAMs capable of downing a plane and definitely not on the shipping manifest. A check of the ship, in the meantime, had revealed that the vessel's owners had chartered it without crew, fuel, or stores – what was known in the business as a demise charter. The *Sawyer*'s captain had no doubt that once the smoke cleared, the customer who'd leased the ship would turn out to be a shell company owned by another shell in a different jurisdiction, making tracing the perpetrators all but impossible. It was a common enough tactic and virtually guaranteed to be impenetrable in the short term. The loss of the cargo would be an operating expense, a cost of doing business, nothing more, the crew dispensable, in all probability hired on the waterfront in China with no questions asked, their payment in cash.

The game of cat and mouse was ongoing, although to find both contraband missiles and drugs was a rarity – usually the dope smugglers didn't mix with the arms merchants and vice versa. Whether this signaled an alarming new trend or a singularity was above the captain's pay grade – he would leave that to the big brains in D.C. to figure out. For now, he was to wait for the arrival of relief and then continue on his patrol, keeping the Chinese vessel under guard until the Australians arrived to take over.

CHAPTER 8

Tianjin, China

Jet coughed as she stepped from the rental car in which Jiayu, the Chinese Mossad operative who would be working as her adjunct, had picked her up at Beijing International Airport. Jet blinked, her eyes burning from pollution so dense that visibility was down to less than a half mile, and grimaced. The noxious haze had thinned once they'd cleared the capital city, where it hovered over the buildings like a beige fog, but it was still thick enough to cause her problems, her eyes more sensitive after the long flight in pressurized air. Now that they'd arrived at the seaport of Tianjin, it was tolerable, but Jet wasn't looking forward to her return trip to Beijing and marveled that so many could live in such toxic conditions. She resisted the urge to rub her eyes, which had been changed from green to dark hazel with brown contact lenses. Along with an auburn wig with retro bangs, they altered her appearance so it matched her new passport photograph.

Jiayu had limited her conversation to responding to questions, which Jet preferred. She was about Jet's age, native-born Chinese, according to her dossier, but spoke good English and passable Hebrew, so communication wasn't an issue. A full-time Mossad operative who had been recruited while attending university as an exchange student in Israel, her cover job in Beijing was as a tour guide, which gave her ample opportunity to travel in the company of foreigners without raising any suspicions.

Jet knew from her reading that the other three members of the team were male, two Chinese who had been vetted by the head of station in Beijing and had worked with the Mossad for several years, and an Israeli named Amit in his early thirties – ancient in Mossad field agent terms. Then again, a perusal of his record had told Jet that he was mainly a desk jockey, specializing in computers. She wondered again at the wisdom of taking a mission on short notice, working with what was, by her standards, a team of neophytes.

She perfectly understood why the director had wanted her on the ground – she was the only one with real wet-work experience, although Jiayu had assisted in two prior extractions. A closer read though had revealed that both had been nonviolent: one a female diplomat, the other an aged industrialist who had been keeping the wrong kind of company, which meant Jiayu too was largely untested under fire. Jet silently hoped that the following day's mission would be seamless, but she had executed too many to automatically believe that would be the case.

Jiayu led Jet to the front door of a towering apartment complex and stopped beside it to punch a series of digits into a keypad. The door buzzed and Jet pulled it open, her travel bag draped over her shoulder, and Jiayu followed her inside a musty-smelling lobby and crossed to a single elevator door.

The apartment was on the fourth floor, the trip up in the cramped lift wordless. Jiayu unbolted the door with a key hanging from a chain around her neck and signaled for Jet to enter.

"Everyone's waiting," Jiayu said. Jet nodded as she stepped across the threshold and made her way down a hall toward the living area.

Amit and the two Chinese looked up at Jet as she entered the modest room, and Amit stood and extended his hand.

"You made it," he said. "Welcome. I'm Amit."

"Kris," Jet said, using the name she'd been given for the mission.

"This is Jimmy and Lee," he said, indicating the pair of Asians. "Lee's our pilot."

Jet nodded a greeting and looked around. Amit pointed to a chair. "Have a seat. How was your flight? Want something to drink? We have water and some of the local sodas."

She shook her head and set her bag on the floor beside her as she sat. "No. I'm good. Thanks."

Jiayu joined the men while Amit regarded Jet curiously, openly assessing her. "So this is the team," he declared.

Jet eyed the men and sat forward. "I want to go over the plan in case we need additional resources before the day gets away from me. Tomorrow will be here before we know it, and getting dropped into an active op like this at the last minute…"

Jiayu cleared her throat. "Nobody's thrilled about that, but it shouldn't affect the outcome."

"I'm hoping it will – in a positive way. From what I gather, this isn't going to be easy. We can expect the target to have bodyguards, and there will be additional security for the wedding party," Jet observed.

Amit nodded. "Correct, but we're not going to make our move until after the ceremony and reception, so the guards should be thinking they're in the home stretch and won't be as alert as when they arrive. That will be our edge. That and Jiayu, here, who will be working the wedding reception."

Jiayu nodded. "I'll make sure his final drink has enough knockout juice in it to drop a horse."

"What if you can't get assigned to his table?" Jet asked.

"I wouldn't worry about that. I can be very persuasive," Jiayu said with a small smile. Jet hoped she was right – she was cute and petite and could probably sway whoever was managing the affair into assigning her to the gangster's table. If not, she would have to drug the drink before it was taken to him.

"If you don't get to him, what's the backup plan?" Jet asked.

"We'll muscle him the old-fashioned way," Amit said.

"That isn't much of a plan," Jet commented.

"We take out the bodyguards and hustle him into our helicopter. We'll be in the air before anyone figures out what's happened," Jiayu said.

"Have you been to the site?" Jet asked. "Reconnoitered it?"

Amit nodded. "Of course. It's remote, about a hundred miles north of us, near the Panjiakou Reservoir, which will work in our favor. Most of the VIPs will be flying in – the roads are terrible for the last few miles, so only the less fortunate guests will use them. The wealthy will have their own aircraft. Helicopters are one of the hottest new status symbols in China for the ultrarich; we know the target owns one. Preparations are already under way, and there's a clearing adjacent to where the main tent is being erected where they'll land. We expect at least ten helos, based on the size of the gathering and the guest list." Amit gestured to Lee. "Lee will commandeer the target's bird and be in the pilot's seat when the guards bring the target to the helicopter. All we have to do is take them down, pour him in, and get airborne. The clearing is far enough from the ceremony that nobody will hear suppressed pistol shots."

"How do we get there if it's so remote?" Jet asked.

Jiayu pursed her lips and glanced at Amit. "We have a four-wheel-drive vehicle you'll take in. There's a dirt road we've already scoped out that will get you within a half kilometer of the clearing. You'll hike to the location from there."

Amit inclined his head toward the Asians. "Jimmy will be in the trees with a sniper rifle. He can take out anyone we don't."

"I'll be using subsonic ammo and a suppressor. It will barely make a sound," Jimmy explained.

"How big will the guard contingent be?" Jet asked.

"At least twenty men for the function, but they'll be staying low-key, so we expect pistols. Maybe a few with submachine guns on the perimeter, but nobody will want to alarm the crowd with a bunch of gun-toting thugs prowling around, so they won't be obvious about it."

The back-and-forth continued for an hour, at the end of which Jet was shown to the room she'd be using for her stay. The team seemed to have the operation under control, but Jet didn't like all the unknowns, especially the lack of clarity on the actual number of guards. The weather report was for partial clouds with a twenty percent chance of precipitation, and she offered a silent prayer that by evening that would increase, as inclement weather would make the security contingent even less effective due to the reduced visibility rain would bring.

The plan was for all but Jiayu to drive to the site the following afternoon, hike in from where they ditched the SUV, and lie in wait as the guests arrived. Jiayu would be bussed in with the rest of the service staff at midday and would work with the others, to avoid arousing suspicion. The wedding was a twilight ceremony, so the team would have the cover of darkness going for it when they made their move. Amit had given Jet a breakdown of the weapons and night vision gear that would be in the SUV and it all sounded good, which made her uneasy. Amit and Jiayu didn't seem overconfident, which was good; but the amount of preparation time had been woefully short by her standards, and Jet knew from harsh experience that a plan hatched in haste was sometimes worse than no plan at all.

She could still abort the mission if she had cause, but other than the inadequate prep time there was none – and she couldn't very well pull the plug based on gut feel. Everyone appeared to be competent and understood their role in the exercise, and despite any misgivings she might have, the operation would go forward.

Which left her with no option but to get as much rest as she could, having been unable to sleep on the planes due to turbulence for most of the trip, and the next day to keep her eyes open and trust her operational instincts, which in spite of her retirement were as keen as ever. The mission appeared to be a straightforward extraction and interrogation – something she'd done at least a dozen times without incident – and as long as everyone kept their wits about them, would likely be unremarkable; except for the target, who, if all went well tomorrow, was scant hours away from having the longest night of his life.

CHAPTER 9

Panjiakou Reservoir, China

Jet shifted in the dark. Amit squatted beside her, and Lee was out of sight somewhere in the high grass that ringed a clearing where eight helicopters sat on the ground. Only a handful of guards were watching the field from beneath the shelter of a huge tent. It had begun drizzling late that afternoon, and while that helped their abduction cause on the whole, it would make Jimmy's job with his sniper rifle harder, the reduced visibility a double-edged sword.

Jiayu was communicating on a micro transmitter from inside a temporary structure that had been erected beside a centuries-old castle, where several hundred privileged elites were gathered now that the wedding ceremony was over, eating and drinking as though it were their last meal. Vintage wine from Bordeaux and rare champagne flowed like water, and an endless procession of gourmet dishes was being served with automated efficiency. Jiayu had reported that the gangster was sipping wine, but not in any great quantity, and his two bodyguards sat alert on the benches near the entry amongst scores of other security personnel.

The trucks that had delivered the last of the party supplies were parked on one side of the clearing, lined in a long row, all bearing the name and logo of the Triad's shipping company – one of the larger in the region, part of the criminal syndicate's tendrils in many legitimate Chinese businesses as a function of the amount of money it laundered each year. She'd seen the same in Russia and Mexico; the global flow of illicit profits was a perennial part of the underground economy that powered much of the economic expansion in many areas of the world.

Jet's plastic rain parka only partially shielded her from the drizzle, and after six hours in place she was restless, but too disciplined to give in to her urge to stretch her legs. Even though she knew where the helicopter guards were, she wouldn't take the chance of being spotted. The mission objective was now within easy reach as long as nobody made any mistakes.

They had watched the helicopters arrive in the gloaming, blades beating the air overhead, and had easily made out the White Dragon boss when he'd stepped from his aircraft in his obviously expensive black hand-tailored silk suit and flanked by his entourage, clearly armed and dangerous. The guards at the field had been deferential upon his landing, offering bows and directing him to the main event. One of them showed his pilot to the smaller shelter that had been earmarked for them once he'd powered down the turbine and completed his postflight check.

Now the helicopters were bathed in the reflected glow emanating from the party. The boom and trill of a band drifted through the rain and a passable jazz singer tackled Billie Holiday, lending a surreal air to the remote setting as the sound echoed off the castle that loomed over the proceedings like a stone sentry. Jet checked the time and was feeling for her water bottle when the comm line crackled and Jiayu's whispered voice sounded in her ear.

"One of the guards is going out to get the pilot. I slipped Zhao the drug ten minutes ago. He's starting to get sloppy and slur. It's showtime."

Lee's voice purred over the channel. "Roger that. I'm in position."

The triad guard appeared by the service tent, water coursing down his raincoat in a wet slick, and stuck his head inside. Moments later the gangster's pilot emerged, and the guard hurried back to the festivities while the pilot made his way to the helicopter, one hand shielding his eyes from the drizzle as he picked his way along the path that bisected the clearing. One of the event security men, holding an umbrella, stopped him to check his identity and then allowed him to proceed to the aircraft, uninterested in the man once he was past his station.

Jet watched through her night vision monocle as Lee clubbed the pilot from the shadows near the helo and then dragged his inert form to the tree line.

Amit rose from his hiding place and whispered to her, "Let's move."

Jet leapt to her feet and they closed the distance to the clearing so they would be near enough to make a break for the helicopter once the mobster and his guards arrived. Thirty yards from the chopper, they crouched in the grass and listened as Lee cranked the turbine to life. Jet nudged Amit when three figures appeared on the path, one visibly unsteady, framed by bodyguards who were helping him stagger toward the helicopters. Jet tapped her earbud.

"Okay, Jimmy. Something goes wrong, take them out," she said, and then glanced at Amit, whose suppressed JS 9mm bullpup machine gun was clutched in his gloved hand. "You ready?" she asked.

He nodded, his expression serious. She screwed the suppressor onto her 9mm pistol and checked the monocle to ensure the headband was snug, and waited for the action to begin, sweeping the area with her NV scope in case a sentry appeared from nowhere.

The bodyguards ducked their heads instinctively to avoid the helicopter blades as they half-dragged Zhao to the chopper, and when they were at the open cabin door, Jet and Amit made their move, bolting toward them from behind. One of the men must have sensed their approach and spun, a pistol materializing in his hand. Amit opened fire, and a burst of rounds pounded into the bodyguard's torso from point-blank range.

The man went down, but reflexively squeezed the trigger of his handgun as he did so, the un-suppressed shot shattering the night over the thrum of the helicopter engine. The second guard dropped Zhao and spun toward them, rapid-firing three times wildly. One of Jet's bullets tore his lower throat out, sending him reeling back against the helicopter. He collapsed in a heap by the door, a crimson smear marring the blue and white cabin exterior, and then Jet and Amit were running in a crouch toward the triad boss, who was sprawled on the ground, groaning.

"You've got a problem," Jimmy said over the comm line.

Jet glanced at the service tent, from which gunmen were running toward them.

"Buy us some time," Jet snapped, and grabbed Zhao's arms to haul him to the helicopter while Amit covered her with his machine gun. The gangster was heavier than he looked, and it required all her effort to slide his upper body into the cabin. Amit turned to help and had managed to heave the mobster's legs in when gunfire erupted behind him, the guards finally having figured out from the shooting that something had gone badly wrong.

Amit turned toward them, loosed several short bursts, and ducked when answering fire pocked the metal of the cabin around him. Jet yelled over the revving of the turbine as Lee gave the beast power. "Jump in."

Whether Amit heard her or not, he didn't stop shooting until he'd exhausted his magazine, at which point he twisted toward the cabin door and threw himself into the gap as the helicopter rose off the clearing, the grass around it flattening from the downdraft. Jet's free hand locked onto Amit's windbreaker while her other gripped the steel frame of the bench seat, her pistol in her belt.

"Are you okay?" she managed, teeth gritting from the strain of holding on as the aircraft yawed alarmingly.

"I–" Amit began, and then his eyes widened and a flood of blood gushed from his mouth and coursed down his chin. He coughed, struggling for breath, and then shuddered and lay still against the carpeted floor as the chopper climbed through the drizzle.

Jet scanned Amit's back and spotted the two entry wounds that had cut his life short, and then was wincing and hugging the floor as bullets thumped into the fuselage and cockpit.

"Hang on," Lee warned, and Jet wedged herself between the open door and the triad boss to keep him from sliding out. Amit's body rolled toward the opening as Lee fought to control the aircraft, and then his corpse disappeared into the night, leaving a trail of blood in its wake.

An alarm sounded in the cockpit and warning lights strobed, and then another klaxon howled.

"What is it?" Jet demanded.

"They must have hit the fuel tank or a hydraulic line." Another alarm joined the cacophony, and Lee battled to keep the helicopter in the air. He scanned the trees below, and then the chopper leaned at a sickening angle, wobbling dangerously.

Lee called out over his shoulder to Jet, his voice tight, the tendons in his neck bulging from fighting the controls. "We're going down."

CHAPTER 10

Jet gritted her teeth as the helicopter lurched, and then the floor dropped from beneath her as the rotor locked up. The longest seconds of her life passed as the helo plunged toward the treetops, and then it was crashing through the branches, slammed around by the trees like a child's toy in a hurricane. When it finally crashed to the ground, the impact was so brutal Jet felt like she had been hit by a car; the force knocked her breath from her and sent a bolt of pain through her spine.

Steam hissed from somewhere near the motor, the alarms now silent. Jet sniffed the air as she gathered her wits in the darkness and frowned at the strong smell of raw fuel. The gangster groaned beside her, and she looked at him, thankful her NV monocle was still in place. She was surprised to see that he was apparently unharmed – no doubt a function of being completely relaxed from the alcohol and knockout drug. She twisted toward Lee and called to him.

"You okay?"

There was no response; the only sound was the hissing from the engine area and the tapping of something cooling from the cowling. Jet moved her legs and, when she was confident the only damage she'd sustained were bruises, pulled herself to her feet and leaned toward the cockpit. She froze when she saw Lee's head lolling at an impossible angle, his body still strapped in the pilot seat and covered with shattered glass.

Jet felt for her earbud, which was still in place in spite of the jarring collision, and tapped it to life.

"Problem. We crashed. Jiayu? Jimmy?"

Jimmy's voice came over the channel a moment later. "I saw. What's your status?"

"Amit's dead. So is Lee. I'm okay. The target appears to be, too."

Jiayu's whispered words were a hiss. "You need to get out of there. The guards will be on you any second."

"That occurred to me. But I don't see a lot of options."

Jimmy responded. "Can you get him to the vehicle?"

"I can try. But he's out cold. Be better if I had some help. How far are you from where we went down?"

"You only made it maybe three hundred yards," Jimmy said. "Get clear of the helicopter. I'm already halfway there." He paused. "Crap. Three gunmen are headed in your direction. Looks like I have my work cut out for me."

"Neutralize them," Jet instructed. "That should kill anyone's enthusiasm to search for us, at least for a while."

"You read my mind. Can you see the lights from the tent?"

"Barely."

"Head away from them and let me deal with this. You'll hear it. Can you handle him?"

"I'll manage."

"Hurry."

Jiayu cut in. "I'm slipping out of the party. It's chaos here, so nobody will miss me. I'll be at the SUV."

Jet glanced at the triad boss. "Okay."

She moved to the man and dragged him by the arms to the open cabin door, the stench of fuel increasing outside the aircraft. The helicopter had settled at an angle, but she was able to pull herself from the opening, one of Zhao's sleeves clutched in her left hand. She wedged her torso to use the exterior of the cabin for support and then hauled the inert thug halfway through the gap. He groaned again, but other than that showed no sign of life, and she heaved again and tumbled backward onto the grass with the triad boss in tow.

Jet's ribs protested the rough landing and she winced, and then the distinctive muted popping of Lee's sniper rifle from nearby spurred her into action. She struggled to her feet, lifted Zhao by the arms, and dragged him across the grass. The drizzle-soaked ground was slick, which helped her with the task.

She'd made it twenty yards when flames licked from the ruined helicopter's turbine, and she renewed her efforts to get as far as possible from the aircraft before the fuel caught. Another five yards and the darkness was shattered by the helicopter's explosion, which blew a shock wave of searing heat at her as a blinding orange fireball shot into the night sky. Jet fell flat and rolled, shielding her face from the worst of the force that swept past, and then struggled to her feet and resumed dragging Zhao, certain the area would soon be swarming with security.

"I see you," Jimmy's voice purred in her ear. "Be right there."

Jet waited, and thirty seconds later heard him crashing through the brush. He slung the sniper rifle's strap over his shoulder when he drew near and, after glancing at the triad kingpin, whispered to her, "You in one piece?"

"Yes. But we need to get him out of here. The explosion could be a blessing – there's no quick way of knowing who died in the crash, and that can work to our advantage."

"You take one arm; I'll take the other. Can he walk?"

"He's out cold."

"That leg doesn't look good, either," Jimmy said, indicating the man's left foot. Jet hadn't noticed until he pointed it out, but now noted blood and the splintered end of a tibia jutting through his sock, which was soaked bright red. She moved to inspect it and, after surveying the damage, glanced up at Jimmy.

"Compound fracture, and he's losing a lot of blood. Must have happened when we crashed." She thought for a moment. "Hand me your belt."

Jimmy did as instructed, and she cinched a makeshift tourniquet tight at the man's knee. The seep of blood stopped, and she stood and scanned her surroundings in the amber glow of the burning helicopter.

"Okay. Between the two of us, we should be able to carry him. You take his shoulders, I'll take his legs. You know where the SUV is?" she asked.

He nodded. "I can find it. But we need to get moving."

"Did you take care of the guards?"

"Yes. But there will be more."

"I know."

Jimmy hoisted Zhao's upper body and Jet lifted his legs. They trotted with him for a few minutes, and then Jimmy stopped. "This is no good. We need to drag him the rest of the way."

Jet lowered his legs to the ground and then moved beside Jimmy and took one of Zhao's arms. "How far do you think we are?"

"Maybe a quarter mile. His foot's going to be mangled by the time we get there, but I don't see any way around it."

Cries from the crash site drifted toward them, and Jet and Jimmy shared a dark look. "We don't have any choice. They'll pick up the trail eventually, and we need to be long gone by the time they sound the alarm. Let's do this."

Jimmy adjusted his night vision monocle and gazed back toward the burning helicopter before looking back at Jet. "Ready?"

Jet clenched her jaw and nodded.

Fifteen minutes later they were in the SUV, bouncing along the muddy track toward the main road, Jiayu driving, Jimmy in the passenger seat, and Jet in the rear with Zhao propped up so he would appear to be a passenger to any passing vehicles. The man's bloody trousers and jaundiced pallor would immediately signal that he was badly wounded if they were stopped, but with the chaos back at the wedding and the lack of cell reception, their hope was that by the time anyone notified the police of the attack, they would be well out of danger.

Nobody spoke for several minutes, allowing Jiayu to keep her attention on the road. Eventually they jolted from the mud onto the pavement running east toward the coast. There were no other cars to be seen on the rural road, and Jiayu accelerated until they were speeding along as fast as the conditions would allow.

Jet leaned forward. "Where are we going?"

"To the port."

"That's it?"

"We have a safe house near the waterfront where we can question him." Jiayu paused. "It will be more difficult without Amit. He had more experience with interrogation than I do."

"That was one of the reasons I was sent," Jet said. "His file says he speaks good English. I can handle it."

Jiayu's face was hard in the light from the instrument panel, all angles and planes, her eyes black as they darted from the speedometer to the rearview mirror and then back to the road. "Is he stable?" she asked. "This will all have been for nothing if he dies."

Jet eyed Zhao. "He's in shock, and the drug is still working. But his pulse is strong and his breathing seems okay. He'll live, although by the time we're through with him, he'll wish he hadn't."

Jet felt in his pockets and retrieved a cell phone, and with deft fingers unsnapped the back and removed the battery. She replaced the cover and pocketed both, and Jiayu glanced at her in the mirror again, a quizzical expression in place.

"In case they can track his phone," Jet explained. "We can't depend on the triad believing he died in the crash. With his bodyguards dead, they're going to do everything they can to locate him. No reason to make it any easier for them."

Jiayu's eyes widened and she nodded. "With everything else that's happened, I didn't even think about his phone."

Jet allowed herself a small smile and then winced when she probed her sore ribs, her side throbbing as the adrenaline leached from her system. "Just keep your eyes on the road. Be a shame for this well-executed plan to go off the rails because of an accident."

Her comment drew a harsh laugh from Jimmy. "Amit and Lee are dead, and we're in the middle of nowhere with the target bleeding out. Pretty much everything that could go wrong already has."

Jet shrugged. "We're alive, and we have him. That makes it a success so far."

"Right," he shot back. "Assuming we live through the night."

Zhao stirred and let out a low moan, and Jet sat back. "Stay focused, and worry about yourself," she warned. "I've been through worse and I'm still here. We'll make it."

"I'm not sure I share your confidence," he said.

"Doesn't matter. Just keep your mind on the job. We took some casualties, but we got through it and we're still breathing, we've got wheels, and our mission's been successful in spite of the road bumps." She shot him an annoyed glance. "Now, no more griping. It's getting on my nerves."

The sniper looked like he was ready to say something else, but instead his lips tightened and he stared off through his window in silence. Jiayu pressed the accelerator, the winding highway straightening as they distanced themselves from the wedding. For now the only sound in the cabin was the monotonous thwacking of the wipers, the throbbing of the tires on the pavement, and the steady drone of the engine as they sped toward the coast.

CHAPTER 11

Jakarta, Indonesia

Thousands of stars glimmered in the night sky over Soekarno-Hatta International Airport as a contingent of athletes from North Korea filed toward the buses earmarked to transport them to the housing complex they would call home during the Asian Games, the region's equivalent of the Olympics, which also took place every four years. The airport was bustling with tourists arriving for the competition, and several stopped to snap photographs of the North Koreans. The athletes were decked out in colorful uniforms, a contrast to the entourage of coaches in the drab garb of the impoverished nation's civilian population and the distinctive green military uniforms of the retinue of security.

Ye-ji, a willowy young female athlete in her late teens, whispered to the older woman behind her in line, her voice hushed in wonder. "Everything is so modern, so clean."

The woman glanced around to ensure nobody had heard Ye-ji's words. "Yes. We are fortunate to see it. But keep quiet – you don't want to be accused of seditious thought."

Ye-ji nodded. The idea of committing a thought crime wasn't alien to anyone who lived in North Korea, where questioning any official statement was considered treasonous – including the insistence that the country was the best in the world and was only in dire straits due to a conspiracy by Western financial interests and the governments they controlled, the most malevolent of which was the United States, the arch nemesis of North Korea's glorious leader.

There was some basis for the contention, as well as the enormous presence the Americans maintained as uber-villains in the collective psyche. During the Korean War, the U.S. had been merciless in its bombing runs, adopting a scorched-earth policy that had resulted in every city in the country being destroyed. When there were no more targets, the American command had deliberately gone after critical infrastructure necessary for the civilian population's survival. Every student in North Korea learned about the period in school, and the war crimes that had characterized it. But since the U.S. and its banking supporters got to determine who was charged with crimes against humanity, they went unaddressed, just as had the war crimes of most of the Japanese command, who had conducted heinous medical experimentation on the Chinese citizenry during the Second World War, including biological weapons deployment that had killed millions of Chinese civilians.

All of which was basic knowledge for North Koreans, who lived with South Korea and the hated Americans conducting military drills on their border whenever they liked, and considered themselves to still be at war with their southern neighbor.

A tall, thin man in an ill-fitting suit checked names off a clipboard as each athlete stepped onto the bus. When it was Ye-ji's turn, the official barked a question at her, demanding her name while staring at the list like it had insulted him.

"Ye-ji An," she said hesitantly.

The man made a notation halfway down the list and motioned for her to board, and stopped when he saw the older woman behind her in the line.

"This transport is for competitors only," he said, his tone cold.

"Yes, I know. I have a special dispensation. I'm one of the coaches of the rowing team."

The man grimaced like he'd swallowed a mouthful of sewage. "Name?" he snapped.

"Sang-mi An."

His eyes narrowed to slits. "You related to her?" he demanded, indicating Ye-ji.

"That's right. I'm her mother."

The official didn't seem to know what to do with that information other than glare at Sang-mi. After another perusal of the list, he waved her along, his expression clearly indicating his displeasure at allowing a nonathlete on the team bus. That there was no legitimate reason for his attitude had no bearing on his anger – but arbitrary abuse of bureaucratic power was another regular occurrence in North Korea that the locals were accustomed to.

Sang-mi slid onto the bench seat beside her daughter and watched the rest of the team troop aboard, her heart pounding but her demeanor outwardly calm. When the door closed and the air brakes hissed in anticipation of their departure, she released a breath she only then realized she'd been holding and patted the younger woman's hand.

The trip to Jakarta was the first time either of them had been out of their home country. They watched the city blur past, the postmodern skyline gleaming with a thousand lights a stark contrast to home, where lightbulbs were impossible luxuries for many.

"There are so many cars! And motorcycles," Ye-ji exclaimed as the bus made its way through traffic. Motorbikes swarmed around the oversized vehicle like bees around a hive.

"Capitalist decadence," Sang-mi said, speaking the expected words loud enough so any of the security force would hear her sensible response to a vision of unimaginable prosperity in the form of privately owned conveyances – which by their abundance, if not their very existence, underscored the poverty that was endemic in the communist regime. Although scarcity and impoverishment were presented to the population as equality, Sang-mi was worldly enough to understand that even in an egalitarian utopia, some pigs were far more equal than others, and the closer to the center of power the swine, the greater fortune shined upon one.

An hour after rolling off the airport grounds, the buses came to a halt in front of a hotel that would serve as official housing for the athletes. North Korea was one of the few nations that had refused to allow their contestants to stay in the Games Village especially built for the event, fearing the effects of fraternization with athletes of other, more permissive societies. After much negotiation, the event organizers had relented and provided six floors of a run-down mid-level establishment three blocks from the aquatic center, where the North Koreans would have their own security force to ensure no corrupting influences would taint their teams.

Sang-mi caught a glimpse of a waiting cadre of guards in shabby civilian suits, their military bearing giving them away, and stiffened when she spotted the obvious leader – a man she'd dealt with before, back home, during the travel preparations. The bus door opened, and the man stepped aboard to survey the expectant faces looking up at him from the seats.

"Everyone, off the bus," he ordered. "You will submit your belongings for inspection before entering the hotel, where you are to remain on your assigned floor unless escorted by one of the security contingent our benevolent leader has sent for your protection."

Sang-mi leaned into her daughter and whispered, "Slip me the drive. Don't let anyone see you do it."

Ye-ji nodded almost imperceptibly and retrieved a USB drive from the pocket of her team windbreaker. She passed it to the older woman, who stood and walked to the small toilet compartment at the rear of the vehicle, pushing through the athletes who were waiting to disembark. A minute later she emerged, towel-drying her hands, and made her way to where her daughter was still seated, one of the last of the group on the bus.

When they descended to the parking lot, a pair of the guards escorted them to where dozens of athletes stood in the humid night air, resigned to another routine indignity at the hands of their minders. The young men and women suffered the impromptu search wordlessly, their faces blank, the pointless imposition just another display of power to remind them that even though they might be on foreign soil, they were not to get any rebellious ideas.

When it was Ye-ji's turn to submit, she offered her duffel bag and watched as a pair of security men rifled through it, and then stood aside and allowed a stern matron to frisk her, feeling in her pockets before instructing her to remove her running shoes. Sang-mi watched in silence, and then the pair motioned her forward with her travel bag and put her through the same paces.

Finding nothing, the matron seemed disappointed, and Sang-mi could feel the eyes of the unctuous security chief boring into her as she led her daughter into the hotel, where a rail-thin man with a high forehead and a wolfish face ordered them to wait by the rear lobby wall while the rest finished with their search. Ye-ji murmured to Sang-mi when the man stepped away to corral three new arrivals, her lips barely moving.

"What did you do with it?"

Sang-mi didn't answer, preferring a small wince in response. When her daughter's eyes widened, she looked away, watching without reaction as the guards treated the athletes as prisoners instead of honored representatives of the country's best, her expression outwardly as untroubled as a Buddha, but beneath her shift her stomach twisting in an acid knot.

CHAPTER 12

Donggang, China

A pall of fog blanketed the waterfront of the Chinese port. The streets lay empty at the late hour, and towering orange cranes lined the jetty thrust into the overcast like ghostly limbs. The air was heavy with the stench of marine rot and petroleum that coated the surface of the water in an oily film. Massive cargo ships strained at their dock lines like fighting dogs in the gloom, their hulls bumping the concrete pier with muffled booms as the surge from the incoming tide washed into the mouth of the nearby river, its briny brown sludge filled with detritus and waste from upstream. For decades, the border river at North Korea's northernmost edge had served as a spillway for industrial pollution from both countries.

The pound of metal on metal echoed from the commercial fishing shipyard to the west, where decrepit scows were repaired round the clock by crews of welders and mechanics, the high pitched keen of hand grinders like the nocturnal calls of predatory birds. Three figures in long overcoats stood in the darkness by one of the sprawling warehouses, smoking in silence. One of them occasionally paced toward the open gate before returning to his companions and shaking his head.

The roar of a truck engine from the main river road split the night, and the men turned to where an ancient diesel bobtail materialized out of the fog, its headlights bouncing giddily as it negotiated the rutted pavement. One of the men flicked on a pocket flashlight and signaled to the driver, and the big vehicle ground to a stop, brakes shrieking in protest. The driver leaned from the cabin window and called to the men, who responded with a gesture at the darkened warehouse and terse instructions.

Gears ground, and the truck belched black exhaust into the fog as it rolled toward the building. Two of the men followed it to the open loading dock, where another flashlight blinked from the shadows to direct the truck to its platform. The driver spun the wheel and braked again and, after performing a series of back and forth maneuvers, reversed toward the dock, the vehicle's backup alarm beeping steadily as it neared.

The driver killed the engine once the rear bumper was wedged against the dock, and the truck shuddered twice before falling silent. The door opened and he stepped from the cab, waiting as the pair of men from the gate approached. One of them offered him a cigarette, and he shook his head.

"No, thanks. Don't smoke." He eyed the men. "Probably best if you don't either while we're unloading."

The men exchanged a glance and dropped their smoldering cigarettes to the ground. "Right. Didn't think about that," one of them said.

"Probably fine, but I'd hate to find out different."

A light flickered to life inside the warehouse, and the driver followed the men up concrete steps to the dock. He scanned the interior of the building and then moved to the rear of the truck, twisted the handle, and hauled the door up, revealing three rows of tall metal cylinders in the hold, secured upright in padded racks by filthy blue nylon straps.

The men peered into the cargo area with troubled frowns. "What's that hooked to the top of the tanks?" one of them asked.

"Refrigeration. You have to keep them at a certain temperature."

"That come with the delivery?"

The driver nodded. "That's right. I leave here empty."

A third man approached at a rapid pace from within the warehouse, a cell phone glued to his ear. The driver eyed him with concern, which became fear when he lowered the phone and hissed a warning.

"The cops are on their way in."

The driver's eyes bulged like he'd been gut punched, and his two escorts spun toward the gate, where a trio of men in the distinctive uniforms of the port authority police were marching toward them with obvious purpose. The lead officer's hand was on his holstered pistol, and his backup team toted assault rifles at present arms. The officer stopped by the truck and swept a flashlight beam across its length, stopping when the beam caught the men on the loading dock.

"Cargo delivery at this hour?" he asked.

"Late shipment," the man with the cell phone said.

"That right?" The cop eyed the driver's grubby shirt and pants, and then returned his attention to the man with the phone. "Where from?"

"Shenyang."

"Why the middle of the night?" the cop pressed.

The driver started to speak, but the man with the phone cut him off and edged forward. "The truck broke down on the way here. What's this all about?"

The cop glanced at the vehicle with a scowl. "That's what I'm asking." He looked back at the man with the phone. "You have all the paperwork for the shipment?"

The driver's expression grew tenser, and he didn't answer.

"Officer, I have it somewhere in my office," the man with the phone said. "If you'd like to accompany me, I'm sure I can find it. Everything is in order, I assure you."

The cop's lips twitched with the beginnings of a smile, and he turned to his men. "Stay here and keep an eye on things."

The cops nodded, and the lead officer mounted the stairs, studiously avoiding looking into the truck as he walked past it. The driver's gaze followed the pair as they disappeared into the darkness of the cavernous hall and then flitted to the rifle-wielding police.

The group waited in tense silence as the minutes ticked by, the officers glancing around the area periodically as though they expected an imminent attack.

When the lead cop returned, there was a noticeable spring in his step and amusement in his eyes. He again avoided looking too closely into the reaches of the truck, preferring to concentrate on making his way to the stairs without tripping. When he rejoined his men, he grinned up at the group standing on the dock and adjusted his holstered gun.

"Everything checks out. Sorry to intrude. Just doing our job."

The man with the phone nodded, his face unreadable. "Perfectly understandable. We're all the safer for it."

The cops returned to the entry gate, and the driver frowned as they vanished into the gloom.

"That was it?" he asked. The man with the phone didn't answer, instead looking to his helpers.

"Get the truck unloaded so we can shut down," he said, and then spun on his heel and retraced his steps back into the warehouse.

The driver's worry lines deepened. "What was that all about?"

The nearest man shrugged. "Locals making a little money for the weekend. No big deal. It's like they have radar or something, but the boss knows how to take care of them."

The driver looked uncertain. "You sure we're in the clear?"

"Absolutely."

"I don't want to get pulled over on the way out of here."

"Relax. It's over." The man paused. "You going to help us with this or stand around and watch?"

"We have to do it by hand."

The man eyed the canisters and nodded. "Then let's get to it so it doesn't take all night."

CHAPTER 13

Tianjin, China

Jiayu pulled the SUV into an underground garage beneath a mixed-use building with retail outlets on the ground floor and two stories of apartments above. Jet leaned forward as Jiayu parked in an open space.

"This is the safe house?" Jet asked.

She nodded. "We have an office on the ground floor. A travel company. It's built like a fortress, and Amit had the back area soundproofed. There's a loft upstairs with a bed and bathroom. It'll do for our purposes."

"How are we supposed to get him in there without being noticed? He's bleeding like a stuck pig," Jimmy said.

Jet shook her head. "Not anymore. The belt did the trick. It's mostly dried. If we carry him in, it should be okay. Jiayu, are there cleaning supplies in the office?"

"I…I suppose so."

Jet addressed Jimmy. "After we get him into the store, you should come back and mop up any blood that drips onto the floor, and we should be good." She returned her attention to Jiayu. "You have the keys to the place?"

"Yes."

"How far is it?"

"Not very. That door is for a stairwell that goes to the ground floor. We're two stores over from where it lets out."

"Any security we need to worry about?"

"No. One of the reasons Amit chose it was for its privacy after hours."

"Okay. Go open it up and we'll get our friend here out of the car."

Jimmy looked less than thrilled at the prospect of hauling the half-dead mobster up a flight of stairs, but Jet ignored the dark look he shot her and swung her door open. Zhao was barely conscious, but the drug was wearing off, and she estimated he would be alert enough to be questioned within the hour, if not sooner. She rounded the back of the SUV and joined Jimmy on the passenger side, and together they manhandled the gangster out and laid him on the concrete floor. Zhao moaned and his eyes opened slightly, tearing with pain.

Jimmy regarded the mangled ankle and grimaced. "He's going to lose the leg, isn't he?"

Jet's expression was stony. "Not our problem. And there's nothing we can do about it, anyway." She jabbed the triad boss in the ribs with the toe of her boot. He rewarded her with a grunt, but lay motionless. Jet nodded at Jimmy, her jaw set. "You ready to do this?"

"If it's not too far, it shouldn't be that hard."

"Only one way to find out."

Jimmy lifted Zhao's torso, Jet took his legs, and they carried him to the stairwell and up the steps. Jet's arms were burning by the time they reached the ground floor, but she ignored the discomfort. Jiayu emerged from a doorway to their left and motioned to them. "This way."

The front office was modest in proportion, the rear section easily three times its size. They set the mobster down on the floor and Jet flexed her arms, willing the pain away. She indicated the drops of blood trailing from the front of the store and looked to Jimmy.

"Clean that up and lock the car."

"And then?"

"Come back and keep watch while we have a discussion with Mr. Zhao."

Jiayu led Jimmy to the utility room for a mop and bucket, and Jet surveyed the storage area: several boxes, a coil of yellow nylon rope, a tool box in a corner beside a propane welding torch and a disposable lighter, several rags and a roll of duct tape, and a metal chair with handcuffs resting on the seat Amit had thoughtfully set out for the interrogation. Jet glanced at Zhao and moved to the toolbox, taking her time inventorying the items inside, and when Jiayu returned, fixed the crime boss with a cold stare.

"You support him while I tie him up," Jet said, and retrieved the cuffs. She snapped them open and moved to Zhao. "Roll him onto his side so I can cuff him."

Jiayu did as instructed, and Jet locked the bracelets around his wrists. His eyes fluttered open again and Jet offered him an arctic smile. "So you're back in the land of the living? Good. That will make this easier," she said, and nodded to Jiayu. Together they hauled him to the chair and sat him upright. He struggled weakly against the cuffs when Jet released her hold and moved to the rope, and Jiayu backhanded him across the face.

"Cut it out," she snarled in Mandarin.

Jet was back with the cord in a flash and made short work of lashing it around him several times, securing him to the back of the chair. When she was satisfied he wasn't going to be going anywhere, she stepped back and studied his maimed leg.

"That's ugly. I suggest you answer my questions so we can get you some help."

Zhao's eyes appeared puzzled, and Jet shook her head. "I know you speak English, so there's no point in faking." She allowed her words to sink in before continuing. "If you cooperate, we'll get you medical attention. The alternative is I take that torch to you – and that's just for starters."

Zhao glared at her without speaking.

She took a measured breath. "Here's your first question: How is your gang getting heroin into Israel?"

Zhao's chin lolled against his chest at her last words. Jet stepped closer and grabbed a handful of hair, forcing him to look at her. She repeated the question, and Zhao mumbled something in Chinese.

Jiayu frowned. "He says he has no idea what you're talking about."

Jet nodded, her expression unchanged, and stared hard at the mobster. "Mr. Zhao, have you ever smelled human flesh burning? It's sickly sweet. Once you smell it, you never get the stink out of your nose." She walked to where the welder rested and picked it up along with the lighter. "The agony caused by a torch like this is indescribable, and in the hands of an expert it can go on for hours – but that's nothing compared to the pain afterwards. Most beg to be killed. And all talk. I've never had anyone hold out for long."

Jiayu looked to Jet with a troubled expression. Jet ignored her.

"The problem then becomes whether they lied or not," Jet explained. "So once the barbecue starts, it has to continue, just to be sure." Jet flicked the lighter idly as she spoke. "I can't imagine how excruciating it would be to have a torch taken to the edge of splintered bone. But if you don't cooperate, we'll find out. Is that really how you want to play this? Because once I light this, there's no going back."

Jet could tell by Zhao's expression that the message had hit home, and she didn't require the string of curses he spat at her for confirmation. She waited until he fell silent, and then stepped in closer to him. "How are you getting heroin into Israel?"

This time the question elicited a longer response, but in Chinese. Jiayu's voice was softer when she told Jet what the mobster had said.

"There is a group in Palestine he works with. Some of what he said doesn't make sense, though. I think he might still be half delirious from shock."

"Why?" Jet asked.

"He said the Palestinians don't use real names – but halfway through, he said it might be Israelis, not Palestinians, and then he said something about Egyptians in the same breath. Like I said, it doesn't make sense."

Jet ignored Jiayu and spoke directly to the mobster. "I know you understand. Again. This time in English."

When Zhao spoke, he was obviously struggling. His skin was pale, and his lips trembled with every word. "It's either Palestinians or Egyptians," he growled. "But it doesn't matter – drugs are the least of your problems." He paused. "That's right. I can guess who you are."

Jet eyed him. "What do you mean they're the least of our problems?"

Zhao coughed. "Soon you're going to get what's coming to you."

Jet held up the torch. "Not a great idea to be making threats, is it?"

Zhao hissed something in Chinese, and Jiayu's face drained of color. "He said he wasn't threatening. It's... He says that disaster is headed our way. To remember him when it hits."

"What does that mean?" Jet demanded.

Zhao laughed before his chin dropped to his chin again and his eyes closed. Jet slapped him, but he didn't respond, and she was stepping forward with the torch when Jimmy burst through the door, holding his rifle, his eyes wild.

"Three vanloads of gunmen are on the street and headed our way. We have to get out of here."

"What? How?" Jiayu demanded.

"They must have tracked us somehow..." Jet said, and then the entry door exploded in a shower of glass behind Jimmy and the building went dark.

CHAPTER 14

Jet ducked and closed her eyes, trying to present as small a target as possible, and waited for her eyes to adjust. She whipped her pistol from her waistband and flipped off the safety, and then whispered to Jimmy and Jiayu.

"Is there a back way out of here?"

"A delivery door. But no way to find it in the dark," Jiayu said.

"Where does it let out?"

"A back alley."

Flashlight beams played across the storefront, and they all heard the crunch of glass beneath shoes from the street. Jet shifted, gun in hand.

"Jiayu, you have a weapon?"

"No. But if I can get to the cabinet by the rear exit, there's a pistol in there."

Jet flicked the lighter to life and handed it to Jiayu. "Where do those stairs at the side of the room lead?"

"The loft."

Their discussion was cut off as a glow of light brightened in the front office. Jet squinted to avoid being blinded by it. Jiayu moved quickly toward the rear of the space with the lighter in hand, and Jimmy raised his rifle and pointed it at Zhao.

"They're here for him. Our only leverage is to threaten to kill him."

"I doubt that will work," Jet said, and then the bouncing lamp beams stopped and flashed across the connecting doorway. As she edged toward the stairs, Jet heard the door of the cabinet open, and then the barrel of an assault rifle appeared in the doorway.

Jimmy called out in Chinese, his voice unsure. "I have a gun pointed at your boss's head. Come any closer and I'll blow him away."

There was a long pause, and Jet continued inching toward the stairs, gun trained on the doorway. Jimmy was so focused that he didn't notice, and then Jet heard the distinctive sound of Jiayu chambering a round in the pistol from near the cabinet.

Gunfire shattered the silence, deafening in the confined space, and ricochets whined off the concrete floor. A round caught Jimmy in the chest and he tumbled backward, the shot he fired at Zhao catching the mobster in the shoulder. Jet squeezed off three shots at the doorway and threw herself at the stairs, seeing no way to make it to the back door without being cut down. Jiayu emptied half her pistol's magazine and then bolted toward the rear exit. She had almost made it when a burst of fire from the front office stitched across her back, sending her flying forward and face-planting onto the floor.

Jet rolled closer to the steps and fired again and again to buy herself a few seconds, and then leapt to her feet and ran up the stairs two at a time, the light from the attackers' flashlights barely sufficient for her to make out the steps. More gunfire barked from behind her, but the shots missed her by inches, gouging divots out of the cinderblock wall by her head, and then she turned the corner and was out of sight from the gunmen, the loft only a few feet ahead.

Zhao's voice called out to his men in Chinese, and Jet didn't require a translator to understand what he was saying: the Mandarin equivalent of *get her*.

Jet made it to the loft and spotted a rectangle of light above the dark shape of a single bed. She ran to it and felt for the window latch. When it wouldn't open, she broke it with her pistol butt and knocked the shards free with her elbow. The sound of running boots below told her she was out of time, and she slid the pistol in her waistband, gripped the window base, and hauled herself through it, aware that there could be a dozen gunmen waiting in the alley but with no other options.

Jet looked left and right, scanning the narrow strip of pavement, and then hoisted herself the rest of the way out, the windowsill thankfully deep enough for her to grip while she lowered her body into empty space. Any impulse to hesitate evaporated when a man appeared in the stairwell, holding an AK-47, and she released the sill and dropped to the street below.

She tucked and rolled when her feet hit the ground, absorbing the worst of the shock with the movement, and ignored the spike of pain from her left ankle as she tumbled twice. She was already in motion when she completed the maneuver and forced herself up. The chatter of the AK from the window provided all the motivation she needed. Bullets peppered the alley where she'd been only moments before, and she zigzagged like a maniac, putting distance between herself and the shooter that was the difference between life and death. She knew from experience that a gunman with a weapon like a Chinese Kalashnikov firing at a moving target, eyes unadjusted to the darkness thanks to using the flashlight to see up the stairs, would have a hard time hitting her for a few precious seconds, at least, and she had to leverage that to full advantage if she was going to stay alive.

More shooting echoed from the window, but the shots went wild. She turned the corner and bolted at top speed away from the alley. With any luck, the triad gunmen would delay for critical seconds while they freed Zhao, buying her the necessary time to make her escape. She pushed herself to the limit of her endurance, the pain from her ankle now a numb ache that radiated up her leg with each jolting footfall, and then the sound of a distant siren reverberated off the buildings around her, signaling that the attackers had outstayed their welcome and would have to clear the area if they expected to get away.

Jet drove herself harder, her chances of escaping increasingly realistic with every yard, and when she reached the end of the block, she continued across the intersection at flat-out speed, her legs pumping like pistons as she raced into the inky Tianjin night.

CHAPTER 15

Seoul, South Korea

Jet sat in a small room in the Israeli embassy, waiting for a secure line to Israel to be set up so she could speak with the director. Her escape from the triad had been a narrow one, but she'd managed it after running for a good mile and flagging down a taxi in Tianjin. It had taken her to the safe house, where she'd collected her things and placed a call to Levi to let him know about the disastrous outcome of the mission. He'd listened in silence as she delivered her coded report, and asked her to call back in an hour when he could conference in Moishe.

She'd done as requested, and Moishe had asked a series of questions related to her impressions of the interrogation's effectiveness – whether the mobster had been telling the truth.

"I think so," she'd said. "But I didn't get a chance to confirm. The uninvited guests showed up right when I was going to move into phase two."

"What about the threat?"

"It wasn't so much a threat as gloating. He seemed genuinely convinced that, as he put it, disaster was heading our way."

"But he didn't elaborate?"

"No. Just that we would soon be getting what we deserve, and the bit about disaster. Our discussion was cut short at that point."

They'd authorized her to fly to South Korea, a short hop across the Bohai Sea. She'd paid cash at the airport and been on the first flight out. When she reached the embassy, the Mossad station chief, a tall man in his forties with olive skin and wiry, curly hair threaded with silver, had debriefed her, and she'd given him the gangster's cell phone to search for any meaningful data. An hour had passed after she'd done so, and then another, and then she'd been advised that she needed to speak with the director and they were arranging for a secure line.

That had been forty-five minutes ago. She was getting stir-crazy in the small space, although the food and drink they'd brought her had rejuvenated her somewhat. She was annoyed that the station chief hadn't told her why the director needed to speak with her, but she presumed it was for an admonishment or a grilling.

The door opened and Rami, the station chief, entered with a somber expression, his body language stiffer than when he'd greeted her earlier. He met her curious stare with a flat one of his own, revealing nothing. "Follow me down to the basement. Everything's ready."

Jet rose, and he indicated her bag. "You can leave that here. No one will touch it."

She accompanied him to the elevator to the ground level of the twenty-story building, where he led her across the gray granite floor to an unmarked door, which he unlocked and held open for her while eyeing the empty lobby. Jet pushed past him and found herself on the landing of a stairwell painted a white so bright it made her eyes hurt. He bolted the door behind him and escorted her down three flights of stairs, and then keyed in a series of numbers into a keypad and stood directly in front of a small scanner that verified his retina for identification.

The communication room was even smaller than the one she'd been waiting in. Rami indicated one of the two simple wooden chairs and took the other himself. On the table were a file folder, a speakerphone, and two glasses of water.

He flipped open the folder and slid a photograph to Jet. She eyed the picture of a middle-aged Asian woman and sat back.

"Do you know who this is?" he asked.

"I have no idea. Why?"

"This was one of the items we lifted off Zhao's phone."

"Should I know her?"

The station chief shook his head and sighed. "No. You wouldn't have any reason to."

"Then what's the significance?"

"There is a limit to what I can tell you; however, she is…the subject of a current op."

"Related to drugs?"

"Negative. It's a complicated scenario, made worse by the fact that our operation is top secret, even within our ranks. Only the director and I are privy to all the details, and I, only because of my proximity to the location." He reached forward and stabbed the speakerphone to life. "Director, are you there?"

The director's gravelly voice answered. "I am. I trust you have our prodigal daughter with you?"

Jet's eyes narrowed. "I'm here."

"Good. Rami filled me in on your report. We've been monitoring the Chinese news, and there were only two mentions of the incident, both saying it was a gangland slaying in which four lost their lives. Nothing else. The target was not one of those identified as a casualty." He sighed. "The operation was almost a total loss except for the photo, which opened an entirely new can of worms. Has Rami told you the significance?"

"Only cursory."

The director paused to light a cigarette – Jet could tell from the snicking of his lighter and the subsequent deep inhalation, followed by an unhealthy-sounding cough. "We were approached by this woman several months ago. She claimed to have information vital to our national interests. In exchange for passing it to us, she wants money and for us to fake a kidnapping so it appears that she and her daughter were taken against their will."

Jet waited for him to continue.

"The reason Rami is involved is that she and her daughter are North Korean. We've accepted her deal and have assembled an extraction team in Jakarta."

Jet's eyebrows rose and she exchanged a glance with Rami. "I didn't realize North Korea had a Jakarta."

The director laughed. "They don't. The woman and her daughter are currently in Indonesia for the Asian Games, where the daughter is competing. She's on the rowing team." Another long pause. "I don't suppose you know why a triad boss would have this woman's image on his cell, do you?"

"I have no idea," Jet stated flatly.

"Neither do we. Which is troubling in the extreme. We are well down the road with this operation, and unknowns popping up at this point aren't welcome."

"Were there any notes or files that seem relevant to the photo?"

"We're still working through the encrypted section, and the tech people assure me we'll have it cracked shortly; but at this point, no. Nothing. Which brings me to the purpose of this call." He took another long drag on the cigarette, and they could hear him exhaling heavily before continuing.

"I'm going to ask you to go to Jakarta and help the team there. You have the experience, and you're in the neighborhood."

"If I remember correctly, Jakarta's over four thousand five hundred kilometers away."

"Compared to where any other competent agents I have who could blend in are, that's rock-throwing distance."

Jet frowned. "What's the situation on the ground?"

"The team lead is experienced and thorough. He's got three assets he's working with."

"Locals or field agents?"

"Two agents, one local."

"Another small team," Jet said. "That didn't go so well in China."

"We're thin in the region," the director acknowledged. "No question. I'm sure they would welcome the help. Rami? Fill her in on the high notes of the operation."

Rami spoke for five minutes. When he was finished, Jet's frown had deepened. She sat forward and locked eyes with the station chief.

"If I do this, I need to have autonomy and discretionary veto power over anything that looks iffy to me. So I'd have to be co-lead, with the authority to override the current lead. Otherwise, I'm not interested."

Rami bristled. "We've spent a great deal of time on this extraction…"

"Maybe. But I'm not going into another situation cold, without the power to change whatever I think needs to be changed. If I'd had that ability in China, the team might still be above ground."

"Then we'll have to do without you," Rami snapped.

The director cleared his throat. "I'm going to pull rank here and say yes to her demand. Sorry, Rami. See to it that our young friend is supplied anything she requests, and let's get her on a plane to Jakarta."

"But, sir–"

"We're on a short fuse here – there's no time for debates. My decision is final. If you'd like to discuss it further, call me back in two hours when I have time to explain, but rest assured I won't be open to arguments. Alert the team and make it very clear that the lead is to defer to our new co-lead." The director paused. "Is there anything else?"

"Not from my end," Jet said.

Rami scowled at Jet and then hunched over the speakerphone. "I'll call back."

After a moment's hesitation, the director grunted. "Feel free. In the meantime, make the necessary arrangements and give her the file so she can familiarize herself with the players on the way there."

The line went dead. Rami gave Jet a look that made clear how he felt about what he'd been ordered to do. Jet looked down at the photo of the North Korean woman a final time and then returned her attention to the station chief.

"Look, Rami. I understand you aren't happy with me butting into your op. But we're going to have to make the best of it, so how about we declare a truce, and you take up any misgivings you have with the director? I won't make any changes to the current plan unless it appears to me that it won't work, okay? I'm not pulling a power play here – I just don't want another situation like what happened in China."

Rami nodded and his face relaxed. "You must walk on water for the director to make you the top dog on the team, so I'll assume that in spite of your recent performance, we're lucky to have you involved."

Jet ignored the irony in his tone, the memory of everyone on the Tianjin team now dead fresh in her mind.

Her brow furrowed. "Rami, let's be clear about one thing: I didn't ask for this assignment. If you can talk the director out of it, I'd just as soon get on a plane to anywhere but Jakarta, and I'd wish you the best of luck with your mission. I've been shot at enough for one week, and I'm not looking for another opportunity to put my life on the line."

Rami rose and shook his head. "I think we both know the chances of him changing his mind."

She pushed her chair back and stood. "I'm afraid so."

CHAPTER 16

Beijing, China

Zhao Yaozu sat in a wheelchair in a room in his mansion that had been converted into a medical suite, his wife and two children gathered around him. The stump where his left foot and ankle had been was elevated and wrapped in gauze, and an IV pole had been erected beside the wheelchair, supporting a half-empty bag of clear fluid that dripped steadily into the cannula embedded in his right arm. A five-hundred-dollar hand-painted silk shirt was draped over his bandaged torso.

After being spirited away from the torture chamber by his men, a top surgical team had been summoned to a discreet clinic that catered to an exclusive clientele. But there had been no saving his foot; the damage from the injury and the tourniquet was too extensive for even the most skilled surgeons in China. They'd been forced to amputate mid-tibia, and even though sixteen hours had passed since the operation, Zhao could swear he could still feel his foot, the pain only somewhat moderated by the morphine cocktail coursing through his veins.

The slug that had caught him in the shoulder hadn't done severe damage. It had fortunately passed clean through at an angle, missing both his upper lung and his shoulder blade when it exited; but between blood loss and shock, he'd been touch and go until the doctors had gotten him stabilized. When he'd regained consciousness, a physician and nurse had stayed by his side through the night and half the next day, but he'd banished them to another room once he'd felt human, and summoned his business associates.

He was waiting for them to arrive as he reassured his wife that he would be fine and that, per the physicians, with a prosthetic limb his infirmity would be hardly noticeable. She nodded agreement, her face a mask of fake optimism, and the children dutifully followed suit, unsure how to respond to this sudden reversal of their father's good fortune. His wife knew of his involvement in organized crime but never inquired too closely about his affairs, and the children believed him to be a businessman, both of them too young to inquire exactly what sort – for now, import/export was sufficient explanation and would likely continue to be for the foreseeable future.

The kidnapping hadn't been reported to the police, and the triad had left two of their own dead at the scene along with two of the kidnappers in their rush to evade the law. Because of the secrecy imposed on the clinic and the gunmen involved in the attack, nobody outside of those who had participated in the gunfight knew that Zhao had come perilously close to losing his life. Which was the way he wanted it – any suggestion that he might be compromised would invite rivals or competitors to exploit his incapacitation for their own ends, making his already difficult situation far worse.

He tried a wan smile for his children and turned his head toward his wife. "It is unfortunate. I should have had more bodyguards for the wedding. There are many unsavory players who will stop at nothing to gain an advantage these days."

"At least you're alive and well. We're all thankful for that," she said.

"I'll be fine. A couple of days and I'll be on the road to recovery. Don't worry about a thing."

His wife looked unsure. "But if they try again…"

"They won't. I've hired the best security money can buy. They won't have another chance to harm me. I'll see to that."

After a decade and a half with Zhao, his wife knew better than to question him too deeply about the incident. A former beauty queen, she enjoyed the life of a socialite, part of the Chinese elite who vacationed in Hong Kong and Macau and had properties in New York and Vancouver and Sydney, and she wasn't about to risk that lifestyle by rocking the boat with her husband. She'd supplied the obligatory offspring, glad of her husband's connections that enabled them to have a second child at a time when it was neither encouraged nor legal, and she was a dutiful mother, albeit with a domestic staff that would have rivaled a royal court of old to assist her. She saw Zhao himself only rarely, which was fine by them both.

She offered him a reassuring smile. "Well, let me know if you need anything. I've canceled my trip to Tokyo. I can go shopping with the girls some other time."

"There's always next week. I should be...better...by then." A knock at the door interrupted them, and Zhao called out, "Yes?"

"Sir, your visitor has arrived. He's downstairs in the great room," one of his guards said through the door.

"Good. Show him up in two minutes. I'm just finishing up," Zhao said, and then returned his attention to his family. "Thank you for being here for me. Now, I need to attend to some business, so..."

His wife nodded and herded the children to the door. When they were gone, Zhao's placid expression changed to a furious scowl, his eyes blazing as he stared at the stump where his foot had been. That anyone would dare to abduct him and subject him to such misery was not only unconscionable but an unforgivable loss of face for the triad, for whom Zhao was a figurehead as well as the ranking member of its centuries-old inner circle. The other bosses had already been advised of the events and had been unanimous in their reaction: the attack would be avenged, no matter what the cost or how untouchable the perpetrators believed themselves to be. They would take a scorched-earth approach, and the responsible parties would pay a price that was multiples of the one Zhao had – there could be no other way, or their organization was effectively finished.

Zhao hadn't shared with them that he knew who was behind it – the Israelis, in retaliation for the side deal he'd set up ferrying drugs into their country. His fellow triad bosses hadn't been cut in on the profit, believing that the heroin was being wholesaled to a trafficker in the Middle East, nothing more. That Zhao had negotiated a substantial chunk of the take from the distribution in Israel wasn't their affair, and now he couldn't come clean or they would turn on him for bringing dishonor to the triad. They would have agreed that he'd been reckless to take on a nation-state and risk reprisals of the sort he'd fallen prey to, and would have arranged for him to disappear, his judgment having proved inadequate for his position within the criminal enterprise, even if he was its effective leader.

If they'd known about the other matter…he wouldn't have lived till morning.

He was jarred from his musings by the arrival of Ali Malouf, the representative of a gentleman with whom Zhao had secret dealings. Malouf entered the room and the guard closed the door behind him, leaving Zhao and the Arab to converse in private. Malouf took in Zhao's wounded leg and IV without comment, and took a seat where Zhao indicated he should.

"I'm sorry to intrude at a time like this. Your man told me you'd been in an accident…" Malouf began, speaking English.

"Yes. Most unfortunate, but the roads are never completely safe no matter who you are," Zhao said in kind. "Still, I am honored that you have flown all this way to meet in person, so I couldn't cancel your visit."

"It was very gracious of you." Malouf paused. "I have confirmation that the shipment arrived, so I have been authorized to make the second payment."

"Of course it arrived. You should never have had any doubt."

"Yes, I know. But in these uncertain times, nothing is guaranteed."

"My word is your guarantee."

"As I completely understand. Do you have an account number and wire instructions you would like the funds transferred to?"

Zhao nodded and pointed to a small envelope on the table beside the Arab's chair. "There are the details. A reliable conduit account in the UAE, which will then bounce it around the globe in order to avoid any difficult questions." The latter was a lie – Zhao had a money manager in the United Arab Emirates who would sanitize the funds through a variety of vehicles, mostly in the derivatives markets, which were completely unregulated and were the preferred mechanism for money laundering of large sums. In this manner, hundreds of billions in illegal drug and arms trading profits moved around the globe before entering the banking system clean as a whistle. No country would move to regulate the industry lest their clandestine intelligence agencies be prevented from using the same systems to transfer their own illicit funds.

"You have no problem with unwanted scrutiny?" Malouf asked.

"There are ways around everything. The tight banking regulations do not affect our organization. They're intended to clamp down on individual financial privacy, not to stop any serious movements. Without the liquidity of groups like ours, the entire international system would freeze up in no time."

"Indeed. May I?" Malouf asked, reaching for the envelope.

"Of course."

The Arab opened it, removed a card, and tapped the information into his smartphone. Six minutes later, the telephone on the nightstand beside Zhao's wheelchair rang, and he wordlessly raised the handset to his ear. When he set it back down in the cradle, he smiled at Malouf.

"It is verified as accepted. Many thanks."

"Likewise. I will touch base on the other matter in a few days."

"When do you return home?"

"I'm headed for the airport from here."

"Very well. Please let us know if you have anything more you require."

"Just updates as matters proceed."

"It shall be so."

Malouf stood. "Then I shall leave you to your recovery, which I hope will be speedy."

"As do I. Again, many thanks. I will stay in regular contact."

The Arab left, and Zhao's security chief appeared ten minutes later.

"Your next visitors are here."

"Bring them up."

His lieutenants entered a few moments later, along with an unfamiliar woman holding an oversized sketchpad. Chen, his right-hand man, introduced her as a police sketch artist who had agreed to assist them for a reasonable sum. She sat across from Zhao, while the lieutenants stood on the far side of the room as though fearful of getting too near their boss, and began questioning Zhao about the young woman she was there to draw.

She worked quickly, modifying eyes and noses until Zhao was satisfied that the image she'd drawn looked like the woman who had been in charge of the interrogation – the one who'd gotten away. He nodded approval when she was done, and Chen escorted her to the door, where he handed her a fat wad of yuan in exchange for the pad. When she was gone, Chen took a seat in the chair Malouf had occupied, while the other two lieutenants remained standing.

Zhao gave a bitter laugh. "That woman…she's working with the Israelis. Possibly Mossad. In fact, probably. I want you to circulate the drawing far and wide. I want her found."

"If she's Mossad, she's probably long gone."

"Maybe. Maybe not. Either way, do as I say. And send it to our contacts in Israel and Palestine. It's a small place. Eventually she will surface, and when she does, we will be waiting for her."

"We can circulate it to immigration and to the police. They'll send it to Interpol."

Zhao nodded, deep frown lines etched into his face. "Make it so. She cost me my leg. I want her taken alive, and I want to personally peel her skin off. I don't care how long it takes to find her. Every day when I look down and see only one foot, I'll be reminded that she's still out there. You're to make this your top priority. Understood?"

Chen signaled his assent and rose. "I'll spread the word. Is there anything else?"

"I want any information the police discover about the identities of the two that were killed. There might be a clue there that can lead us to the woman."

"I'll arrange lunch with the usual suspects. We'll know whatever they do before the report is filed."

Zhao exhaled heavily and eyed the IV bag. "Good. Now let me get some rest."

CHAPTER 17

Jakarta, Indonesia

Jet adjusted her seatbelt as the Airbus A330-300 banked on final descent to Soekarno-Hatta International Airport. The pilot had warned the cabin a few minutes earlier of a bumpy approach due to a summer storm brooding over the island, and the plane shuddered and bucked like a frightened animal as it shed altitude, the brilliant azure of the sky outside Jet's window replaced by anthracite as the plane cut through the clouds.

The aircraft hit a particularly ugly spot of turbulence and lurched to the side like it had been smacked by an invisible hand. A child three rows behind Jet screamed in fright, and the pit of her stomach rose in her throat when the plane dropped as though in free fall before slamming so hard Jet's neck twinged from the jolting.

Then they were through the cloud cover and slicing through a torrential rain, and water streamed from the wings in horsetails as the flaps rose to slow the plane's descent. It banked again over the sea, and Jet could make out the city and the runway lights to the north. Another loss of altitude and the wheels touched down, and then the cabin was filled with the roar of reverse thrust, signaling they'd arrived unharmed, if frazzled.

Customs and immigration barely glanced at her passport and travel bag, and she wended her way through the crowded terminal to the exit doors. When she stepped outside, the chill of the air-conditioned building was replaced by a stifling blanket of heat and humidity, the air redolent with the tropical decay of jungle, and her clothes were almost instantly heavy with moisture. She moved to the taxi line beneath the shelter of the terminal overhang and waited patiently for her turn at one of the small cars idling in an endless column.

The ride to the address she'd been given was a careening slog through flooded streets, the rain and the taxi's minimal tire tread conspiring to make the trip as eventful as possible short of a collision. Incessant honking accompanied revving motors and suicidal lane changes, all of which left the driver apparently as untroubled as a newborn lamb. The rain had abated by the time they pulled to a stop outside of an apartment complex, and a sliver of blue sky peeked through silver clouds as she paid the driver and climbed from the backseat, bag in hand.

Once the cab had disappeared around the corner, she backtracked two blocks to a low-slung bungalow surrounded by banyan trees. After checking her surroundings and seeing nothing suspicious, she opened the rusting iron gate and walked up a stone path to the front door. Her knock was answered by a man with deeply tanned skin, dark hair clipped close to his skull, and intelligent eyes the color of espresso. He regarded her for a long beat and then stood aside so she could enter.

"Welcome. I'm Jerry," he said, not extending his hand to shake or offering to help with her bag.

"Kris," Jet said. She'd kept her identity from the Chinese mission, there being no time to create a new cover for her or issue another passport.

"The others are waiting," he said, pulling the door closed and brushing past to lead her down a long hall to a large living area. Three men sat on a pair of sofas facing a set of French doors, beyond which were lush green tropical grounds with a fountain on the far perimeter wall. Jerry indicated an overstuffed love seat and took a seat on one of the couches beside a small ferret of a man with darting eyes and rodent-like features.

"I'm Ben," the man said. "And this is Saul," he said, indicating the other Caucasian, "and Wally," he finished, motioning to a young

Asian man with skin the color of tobacco.

Jet nodded to the men. "Kris. Nice to meet everyone."

"Kris will be co-lead on this operation," Jerry said, his tone flat.

Jet offered a friendly smile. "That's right. I've been briefed on a big-picture level, but I'm anxious to hear everyone's impressions here on the ground and to see where we'll be running the op firsthand." She studied each man, and then her gaze settled on Jerry. "Why don't you walk me through your plan of action so I'm up to speed?"

If Jerry could appear less enthusiastic, she didn't see how. He gave a dry recitation of the operation, which was to be a defection with the cooperation of the mother and daughter, designed to appear to be a kidnapping to the North Korean security force, which would be actively trying to stop them.

"It was part of the mother's terms that it not look like they went willingly," he finished.

"Why not?" Jet asked.

"She doesn't want her actions to cause any blowback for her friends or family back home. If it appears that this was a voluntary defection, the government will take its revenge on them, so it has to look like a snatch."

Ben nodded. "I'm to meet the mother tomorrow morning to complete the first part of the transaction. She wanted the advance payment in bitcoin, in return for which she'll provide half the documents she's holding. We get the other half once we've gotten the two of them safely away from the security team."

"I don't like that part – if anything goes wrong, we're left holding only half what we paid for," Jet said.

Jerry frowned. "That was the deal we made. It wasn't negotiable."

"What's the source of these documents? Any idea?"

"She stole them from the military facility where she works. She said that she has copies with her. The originals are still in North Korea." Jerry paused. "HQ made the decision that we would meet her terms. It wasn't my call – I had no choice in the matter. For what it's worth, I voiced the same objection you did, but I was overridden."

Jet nodded. "Has she articulated what they plan to do once they've defected?"

"That's not our problem."

"It's liable to become our problem once she thinks it through. Have any of you met her?" Jet asked.

Ben shifted. "I have. Once."

"Impressions?"

"A lot of anxiety, which is understandable. And she's…shifty. Suspicious."

Jet nodded again. "Also understandable. Have you met the daughter?"

"Negative. But the mother assured us she'll play along."

"How confident are we that the North Koreans won't be armed?"

"Reasonably," Jerry said. "Still, we'll be carrying, and if they are, we've been authorized to take them out."

"You aren't worried about the reaction of the locals to all this? Won't there be armed security for the Games?"

"Yes, but the way we've planned it, we'll be grabbing them in a location where there's unlikely to be much. Between the pandemonium from the smoke grenades and the flash bangs, we should be able to get in and out before anyone realizes what's happened."

Jet's expression was neutral. "I want to scout out the area where this will go down. We have two more days before we move?"

"Affirmative," Jerry said.

"Have you been monitoring the North Koreans to see how much attention they're paying?"

"I've gone to several of the events, and Wally here knows some of the people working the Games. We shouldn't have any problem. They seem to be treating this like a vacation."

Jet frowned. "That doesn't sound right."

Saul shrugged. "First time they've been outside their country, and all the forbidden fruits they can't get their hands on in North Korea are here for the taking. It doesn't surprise me that the security detail would be more relaxed than they might be at home – they're probably staying up half the night getting drunk and hitting the whorehouses. Remember that after the Games are over, it's back home for them, with food shortages and all the rest to look forward to."

"Makes sense," Jet agreed, but doubt still colored her words. "I wouldn't depend on them being inept, though."

"You asked whether we've been keeping them under surveillance. You've got your answer." Jerry hesitated. "This isn't our first operation."

Jet returned his stare without blinking. "I read everyone's files. I'm not being patronizing. Just saying that complacency can get us all killed. That's all."

"Nobody's being complacent."

"Okay. Do you have any photos of the daughter? Any background that isn't in what you sent to headquarters?"

Jerry tapped a folder on the coffee table. "It's all in there. Maybe you can look it over in your room? We've got work to do."

"This is your work," she fired back.

"Yes, I know," Jerry said. "But much as I enjoy going over the minutiae of the plan with someone about whom I know nothing, there are preparations that need to be handled, and we're short on time."

Jet stared daggers at him. "You know I was sent by HQ, which should tell you something. That they made me co-lead should fill in any blanks. We're going to have to work together, so can the attitude, all right, Jerry? If you can't, I'm going to have to ask HQ to pull you off the operation." Jet stood. "I don't want to butt heads. This will go easier if we cooperate with each other."

Jerry nodded, albeit reluctantly, and Jet relaxed slightly. It didn't take a lot to imagine the resentment he was feeling, but she needed to assert authority and put him in his place right up front or risk jeopardizing the mission — and there was no way she was going to allow that to happen. When Jerry didn't say anything, Jet rose and glanced down at her carry-on. "Where do I park my gear?"

"I'll show you your room," Ben said.

Jet scooped up the file and her bag and followed Ben down the hall, leaving Jerry to stew over the unfairness of the world on his own. If his attitude didn't improve by that evening, she would make a call that would kill his career – something she didn't want to do, but would in a heartbeat if she felt like he wasn't playing ball. They had a tall enough order with the faux kidnapping without having a personality conflict thrown into the mix, and she wasn't about to allow him to continue with the hostility; to do so would be correctly interpreted as weakness, and like it or not, she, not he, was now the boss.

CHAPTER 18

Islamabad, Pakistan

Mullah Nasreddin sat in his usual place on the centuries-old carpet in his meeting room, sipping tea as a dark-complexioned man in modern Western dress sat at a small collapsible table, typing into a laptop computer, his brow creased in concentration. A strong scent of incense hung heavy in the air; a cone smoldering by an open window perfumed the room. Outside, a dog's insistent barking intermingled with the laughs and peals of joy of children playing somewhere not too far down the road, from which drifted the occasional growl of a poorly muffled vehicle limping along the rutted way.

Nasreddin's manservant entered on silent feet with a fresh pot of tea and set it before the mullah, who was studying a handful of paperwork with quiet intensity, eyes hooded beneath his heavy brow. When he had departed, the mullah glanced up at the man working at the laptop and set the papers down.

"The accounts are swelling. The year has been good to us so far, no?" he asked.

"Yes, praise Allah. But as you can see, we have lost eight of our most promising prospective customers."

Nasreddin shrugged. "It is unavoidable, I suppose."

The man nodded. "The nature of the business."

"We can only help so many."

"It is true. We do what we can."

Nasreddin nodded as though his accountant had spoken a great truth. The traffic in human organs, which the mullah had the foresight to set up when he'd toured several of the Syrian refugee camps in Iraq and Turkey, was robust, but unfortunately insufficient to accommodate all of those seeking replacements for their failing parts. His customers were funneled to him by agents all over the world, but the lion's share of his business was with rich Chinese and Russians looking for a new lease on life. Matching those in need of a kidney, liver, heart, or lung with a willing donor had turned out to be a simple way to fund his war against Israel and its allies in the West, and his keen mind had immediately seen the possibilities. Now, five years after starting the brokerage, he was richer than he'd ever dreamed, with an endless income stream as the reputation of his black-market service had spread.

He was careful to accept as donors only those his Salafi faith allowed him to view as expendable, such as unfortunates from the camps full of Christian and Shi'a refugees, which in his view were a boon from his maker to help him fund the ongoing war of resistance against the Israelis. The head of an ultraconservative brand of Wahhabism, Nasreddin was convinced that nonbelievers were less than human, savages whose lack of enlightenment made them disposable. That his view was nearly identical to the one held about his people by those against whom he battled was lost on him. His beliefs were the true ones; all others were idiocy that ensnared fools and those with evil at their core.

"I see we still have six prime candidates for livers," Nasreddin observed. "It is a blessing that we can get over a million dollars for one, is it not?"

"A miracle of sorts."

"Praise Allah."

"Praise him indeed."

The usual customer for a liver was one of two types: a debauched alcoholic who had destroyed his own organ from a lifetime of excessive drinking, or someone whose liver was afflicted with hepatitis. Fortunately for the mullah's trade, both varieties of customers filled the ranks of the rich. The alcoholics were largely European and Russian, and those with hepatitis Chinese, the virus endemic in China, where hundreds of millions suffered from it. Nasreddin's prices were at the high end of the scale, but then again, he guaranteed satisfaction, whereas his lower-priced competitors were largely criminals and scammers who didn't have the infrastructure of laboratories, surgical suites, physicians, and transportation that he did. Too, his clientele wasn't price sensitive, which he perfectly understood: if you only had months to live and were worth hundreds of millions of dollars, you weren't looking for a bargain, you were literally buying more life with your money, and cost wasn't an issue.

By cultivating the right contacts among his former schoolmates with whom he'd studied at Oxford before adopting his monkish life as a cleric, he had developed a network of the elites across the continent, and there was no demand he couldn't fulfill. As a natural sideline to the organ trade, he also trafficked in humans, usually young boys or girls sold into sex slavery, or used for sacrifices by wealthy Satanists who dominated the world's governments. He saw no moral dilemma in this – they were all animals, doing what animals do, and his only involvement was in supplying a demand. His life was chaste and pure, and he could go to his grave with a clear conscience. What others did was of no concern to him, any more than the rutting of wild goats was of interest; the death of one of them gave him no more pause than the wringing of a chicken's neck.

Nasreddin scowled at the printout beside him and tapped it with a finger. "I see we have a match in the camps for one of our Russians. Have you dispatched a harvesting team?"

"Yes. They're on their way even now."

"When will they collect the donor?"

"Within a day. Two, at most."

"Have you spoken to the buyer's agent?"

"We have. We've confirmed the blood type and the cytotoxic-crossmatch assay results, and it looks good. The buyer has indicated that he is ready for the organ and offered us a sweetener for prompt performance."

Nasreddin's eyebrows rose. "How much?"

"He's offered to double our price if we can deliver within forty-eight hours."

Nasreddin nodded. "Then that is what we shall do. Charter a jet for the courier. Spare no expense."

"I have already put it into motion."

"Very good. And what about the children for our other project?"

"We're working on it. We're still trying to locate a sufficient number of matches. But do not worry. We'll have them in time. You have my word."

"You understand the importance – what is in the balance."

"Yes, Mullah. Of course. I will not fail you."

"I never doubted it." Nasreddin paused. "How much do we have accumulated in precious metals now?"

"Eleven million. The artificially low price set in the paper futures markets by the manipulators has been a blessing, although locating sufficient physical is increasingly a problem in any quantities." It was an open secret that the Western banks kept the price of gold and silver depressed by selling many years' worth of production in the futures markets, the contracts never expected to have any metal delivered – the exchanges had altered their rules, allowing the sellers of option contracts to settle them in paper money instead of the underlying commodity, effectively destroying any price discovery. Central banks could, through intermediaries, depress the market value to whatever they liked by printing unlimited numbers of contracts to influence the price; contracts that would be settled in dollars they printed at will instead of gold, which distorted the principle of supply and demand out of existence. The issue they faced was when the physical price of a metal disconnected from the phony paper price of the futures contract, which was typically only in times of political tension or crisis.

"It is good. And in dollars?"

"Nearly twice that."

"Then we are ready to deliver the final blow to the Zionists," the mullah said. "The final payment is ten million dollars. Praise Allah. He has seen his way clear to make that available to us."

The accountant nodded, a small smile in place beneath his mustache and beard. Praise Allah, indeed. He was getting rich with what he managed to skim from the mullah's transactions – only a few percentage points here and there, an inflated broker's fee the usual mechanism he used. Nasreddin was not one to dwell on details. With annual revenues in the fifty to a hundred million range, he would never miss a million here or there, and the accountant had also been the recipient of his maker's beneficence.

"Yes. Praise Allah," the accountant intoned. "God is good."

Nasreddin shifted on the carpet and gestured at the teapot. "Some tea?"

The accountant rose and walked to the carpet to sit before his master. "Thank you, Mullah. It would be an honor."

CHAPTER 19

Jakarta, Indonesia

A housekeeper pushed a cart loaded high with snow-white towels past two North Korean plainclothes security men at the end of the hotel hall and turned the corner to the final stretch of rooms, a row of doors on either side. He stopped at the first and rapped softly. A young woman answered and he pointed at the towels with raised eyebrows. She frowned and shook her head, and he repeated the act at the opposite door, continuing down the corridor until he was near the end.

When he reached Sang-mi's room, he glanced over his shoulder to confirm the security men hadn't followed him into the hall, and then knocked three times. The door opened and Ye-ji peered out at him and then stepped aside so he could enter, pulling the cart after him.

Sang-mi was sitting at a small circular table with two chairs, looking out the window at the city lights. She turned to the housekeeper and motioned at the chair.

"Please. Sit," she said in Mandarin.

"Thank you," Ben replied in passable kind. "We need to make this fast. Two minutes, no more, or security might get suspicious."

"Fine. You have the bitcoin?"

"Yes. A hundred thousand dollars' worth, as agreed." He retrieved a cell phone from his pocket and held it up. "I can transfer it as soon as I see the documents."

She held out four sheets of paper. "I was able to sneak into the business center and print them."

Ben squinted at the documents and photographed each with his phone, the Korean characters meaningless to him. When he was done, he forwarded them to a blind address for processing, and nodded to the older woman. "I should get an okay shortly."

"You can take those," she said. "They're the only copies of that information outside North Korea. They're now yours. You'll get the rest after we're free."

"We've arranged that." Ben told her the plan, and she nodded when he was finished. His phone pinged, indicating a message. He thumbed to the inbox, read the single word it contained, and then pulled up a bitcoin wallet and made the transfer. When it was confirmed, he held up the screen so she could see it. "The bitcoin is now in your account."

"Very well."

Ben stood, and Sang-mi reached out and grabbed his arm. "There's one more thing."

He checked the time, worried. "What is it?"

"Another request."

Ben frowned. "We already have a deal."

"Yes, well, I need something else."

"What?"

"Your people need to get us out of the country. Somewhere safe."

He snorted. "We're not magicians."

"Do what you need to do. I know you have the ability to get us papers so we can leave. Our North Korean passports will be flagged. I don't want to risk it."

"So now you want passports, too?"

"That's right. And air fare to a country of my choosing."

Ben digested the information. "I'll have to check."

"There's no time. Either it's a yes, or we have a problem."

"Nice of you to mention this after the transfer."

"I have to ensure my daughter is safe. I do what I must."

Ben sighed. He was sure that Jerry wouldn't say no. "Fine. But that's it. Two passports, and one-way tickets. Now I need to get out of here before your security goons get suspicious."

"How long will it take to get the passports?"

"I'll check. Maybe a week. We'll keep you at a safe house in the meantime."

She held his stare. "We're trusting you."

Ben nodded. "I know. And I you. We're partners now, like it or not."

"Don't let us down. Our lives are in your hands."

"We'll honor our promise." He looked over at the daughter, who obviously hadn't understood a word of the discussion. "You'll explain everything to her? There can be no mistakes."

"I have told her. But I will go over it again."

He nodded. "Do so."

Ben walked to the cart and pushed it to the door. He brushed past it and opened the door, and then pulled it into the hall and retraced his steps back to the service elevator, where the guards were sitting, obviously bored, reading forbidden Korean magazines easily purchased at a bookstore around the block. Ben trudged along, the cart now half empty, and stood waiting in front of the elevator with the downtrodden expression of the hopeless everywhere in the world. Makeup had accentuated his vaguely Asian features, a genetic endowment from a Filipino grandmother, and he could easily pass for one of the locals with his skin darkened with cosmetics and his hair dyed jet black.

The elevator pinged its arrival. He pushed the cart inside and stepped in after it, the basement button already stabbed as the doors closed. The guards barely registered his passage, the cart too small to smuggle anyone in and their interest in the housekeeper nonexistent. One of them tapped a cigarette from a worn pack and lit it; the rare Western delicacy was another forbidden fruit to be enjoyed while they had the chance. Their options would be few after the Games, when they would return home to a nation where food was a scarcity and frills like Marlboros and entertainment magazines impossible to come by.

CHAPTER 20

Jet watched through binoculars as the North Korean maintenance squad prepared a boat for the lightweight double sculls rowing competition event. Both sides of the waterway were packed with spectators in spite of the broiling afternoon sun. The glare was relentless, and many in the throng were using umbrellas to shield themselves from the harsh rays. Jerry was in the crowd in his predetermined position, awaiting the all clear signal from Saul, who was on the same side of the waterway in a second-story apartment window a hundred and fifty meters from the staging grounds with an unrestricted view of the area, a radio and automatic rifle in hand.

The plan was for Jet to grab Ye-ji before the young athlete could make it to the boat with the rest of her team, and for Ben to simultaneously remove Sang-mi from her minders in the chaos that would accompany Jerry and Wally detonating smoke grenades and flash bangs, simulating a terror attack that would ideally have the local security force scrambling for cover while trying to identify the threat. The unknown was how the North Korean goons would react, but the bet was they would follow the lead of the Indonesians, enabling Jet and Ben to flee the scene before anyone could react coherently.

Originally Ben had been chartered with handling Ye-ji, due to his innocuous appearance; but Jet, dressed as a local, would be all but invisible among the hundreds of other young women there to see the competition. Jet had a black nylon backpack with a dark windbreaker in it for Ye-ji, who would be sporting the team's bright colors. She would change at the first opportunity, and then they would make their way to the van two blocks away, where Wally would spirit them to safety, leaving the police to chase their tails.

Jet had spent the prior day at the waterway for the men's competition, her pass purchased from a compliant bureaucrat who handled matters relating to the press. Her cover as an Italian journalist allowed her free access to most areas, which would be critical to getting near enough to the team to abscond with Ye-ji. The original plan had Wally handling the mother, but Jet's arrival had presented the team with an improved opportunity. Wally therefore replaced Saul at the wheel of the van, freeing up Jerry to handle the grenades while Saul kept watch and reported the security men's movements.

Jerry had stopped being adversarial once he'd accepted his new role in the mission and had even been willing to accept the modifications Jet had proposed based on her reconnoitering of the area, without any pushback. Her suggestions made sense and improved their chances of success, and he'd gone as far as congratulating her at the end of the day when she'd spelled out exactly how they would execute the new plan.

Nothing would change from the Korean woman's perspective – she and her daughter would appear to any bystanders to have been taken against their will. Jet and Ben both had handguns they would wave around and would ensure were noted by as many of the spectators as possible, so in the post-operation questioning by the authorities, it would be clear that the women had been kidnapped by an armed group.

Jet's wig, black hair straight down to the middle of her back, her bangs blunt cut across her forehead, altered her appearance sufficiently that with the makeup, she appeared five years younger. Nobody was checking the press passes particularly closely, so she wasn't worried about the fact that she looked markedly different than her hastily snapped photo on it – the intended idea being for any description circulated after the kidnapping to bear little resemblance to the Italian journalist she was pretending to be.

The comm bud in her left ear was covered by her hair, and when it crackled to life and Saul's voice warned them of the arrival of the bus with the North Korean athletes, Jet stiffened slightly. "The target is in the house," he said, and she immediately slipped the binoculars into a pocket of her backpack and walked briskly toward the barriers that held back the crowd. She flashed her press pass, and an Indonesian security man with a bovine expression nodded indifferently and allowed her to the restricted side of the fencing, where various officials from the competing teams milled with local bureaucrats and judges, sweating plastic water bottles in hand. She'd tested the pass earlier in the day to confirm she'd have no issues, and by now the Indonesians had seen her enough that they paid no attention to her coming and going.

"I'm twenty meters from the target," Ben whispered over the channel, and Jet resisted the urge to crane her neck to see where he was standing by a vendor, sipping a soft drink. He sported a new goatee that had been glued into place, and a black baseball cap with the distinctive checkmark logo of one of the game's main sponsors completed his disguise. "There are two obvious NK security nearby, but no weapons I can see."

Saul cut back in. "They're off the bus and moving toward you. Four NK security goons with them, also no guns in evidence."

Jerry's voice came over the channel. "Let me know when to hit with the flash bangs."

"On my count. Five…four…three…two…one…go!"

Jet steeled herself for the explosions she knew were coming and kept focused on Ye-ji as she approached. The young woman was only twenty feet away when two detonations followed each other almost instantly, drawing panicked cries from the crowd. The Indonesian guards spun toward the blasts, submachine guns at the ready, and shouted orders. Jet held her breath as several metal canisters sailed through the air toward her position, and the athletes froze when they struck the ground behind them and began belching thick white smoke in massive clouds.

The light breeze carried the smoke toward the team as another smoke grenade hit only a few feet from Jet, instantly engulfing the surroundings with haze. Eyes locked on the daughter, she whipped her pistol from the backpack and ran for her, filtering out the screams and more explosions as Jerry continued to rain havoc on the proceedings.

Any question about whether the North Korean security men were armed was answered when she neared Ye-ji and spotted a semiautomatic in one of the suited men's hands. Jet didn't hesitate and fired point-blank at him from only a few yards away – an impossible shot to miss. The crack of her pistol panicked the athletes, who bolted away into the smoke, leaving Jet to grab Ye-ji's arm and pull her along to where she knew the far edge of the barrier fence was.

Saul called out a warning in her ear. "You've got a shooter on your tail," he said. "I'm taking him out."

The bark of his suppressed rifle was barely audible over the screams of the throng, and Jet didn't slow to verify he'd been successful with the shot. Her eyes were streaming tears from the smoke as she held her breath and pulled the daughter along, and then the barriers materialized out of the cloud ahead, several of them knocked down against the pavement by running athletes.

Ben's voice cried out in the earbud. "Damn. The target ran toward me, but one of the guards saw me and took a shot. They hit her. She's down."

The sound of more shooting came from where Ben was, and Jerry's voice sounded in Jet's ear. "Ben? Are you okay?"

Static was the only answer, and after a pause, Jerry continued. "Saul?"

"You've got three soldiers converging on you, J. Get out now."

"Can you see Ben?"

"Negative. Move. They've got your position."

"Give me some covering fire," Jerry ordered, and the rattle of Saul's rifle confirmed he'd heard. The screaming from bystanders intensified at the gunfire and another flash bang Jerry tossed behind him as he ran; and then the louder, distinctive blast of a burst from an unsuppressed rifle from where Jerry had been lobbing the ordnance further panicked the crowd.

His voice cried out and gurgled in Jet's earbud and fell silent. Jet half-dragged Ye-ji across the nearest fallen barricade, and the girl yelped when she misstepped and wrenched her ankle, almost going down. Jet muscled her forward, and then they were in the midst of the spectators. Jet waved her pistol at several of them and yelled incoherently as she pulled Ye-ji forward, and was rewarded by terrified expressions and a stampede away from her.

Satisfied that she had made an indelible impression, Jet paused and slipped the gun back into the pack and withdrew a baseball hat and the windbreaker. She passed them to the girl, who shrugged into the jacket and donned the hat. Jet glanced around, and when she was sure there was no imminent threat, grabbed the daughter's arm again and directed her away from the scene of the battle, her imperative now to make it to the van.

She heard more suppressed rifle shots from Saul's direction but didn't slow. Whatever was happening with him and Jerry or Ben, she couldn't help. With the operation in flux, all she could do was perform her role the best she could and get Ye-ji to safety. There would be time to evaluate their losses later, but for now she had one objective, and she would have to overcome anything that jeopardized it.

A woman yelled something in the native tongue and pointed at Jet and the girl, her eyes wide with fright, and Jet realized she must have been one of the bystanders who'd seen her with the gun. Another took up the cry, and a whistle blew from their left – the direction they needed to take to get to the van. Male voices shouted through the lingering haze of smoke, and Jet made a snap decision to veer right. She urged the girl to a limping run before cutting across a grassy area and disappearing with her down a narrow street. The screech of police whistles followed them like banshee howls.

They turned a corner, and Jet tapped her earbud as she ran. "Status check. Report."

Ben's voice came onto the channel, sounding strained. "Took a bullet, but it's not fatal."

Jet listened for any word from Jerry or Saul, but heard nothing.

"Can you manage the wound?" she asked.

"For now. Got me in the shoulder. I'm losing blood and still have hostiles on my tail."

"Good luck. We're almost to the van."

"Don't wait for me. Get out of here. Jerry's history – I saw him go down."

"Saul, too?"

"Unknown, but he's not on the channel, so assume the worst."

Jet slowed as they neared the intersection where Wally was waiting. "Good luck."

"You too. Over and out."

Ye-ji looked to her with wide eyes, waiting for Jet's direction. Jet stopped and peered around the corner and scanned the street and, after a long moment, looked back at the girl, her expression grim.

There was no sign of the van.

CHAPTER 21

Jet tapped her earbud and spoke slowly, covering her mouth with her hand to block any background noise.

"Ben, did Wally say anything about an alternate pickup spot?"

After thirty seconds with no response, she tried one final time, her hopes sinking as she spoke. "Ben, come in. Do you read?"

Nothing.

Jet looked around the corner again to confirm that Wally wasn't circling the block for some reason, her mind racing over possible explanations for his absence at the most critical time – none of them good. All she could come up with were a loss of nerve, an act of betrayal, or discovery by hostiles that had forced him to abandon his post.

She cursed silently as she mulled over her next move. She was in a strange country whose language she didn't speak, with a captive with whom she couldn't communicate, her support network wiped out or so badly incapacitated as to be useless, and the mission another unmitigated disaster, only slightly better at this point than the Tianjin fiasco – the thought that none of this was her fault bringing her no comfort.

So what were her options? The mother had been shot, per Ben, and was either dead or wounded, creating a scenario where Jet could expect little cooperation from the daughter once she learned the truth. With Wally a question mark, she couldn't make any predictions about what she was up against – if he'd chickened out or been scared off, then the safe house was probably still secure, but if he'd sold them out for some reason or been caught, then Jet couldn't use it to hide the daughter, which left her few choices. And worst of all, with the mother off the table, Jet had no way of securing the other half of the documentation – by far the most troubling for her, given the importance the director had ascribed to it.

Jet removed her scrambled cell phone from her pocket and dialed a number from memory. A metallic machine voice answered and prompted her for a password, which she keyed in. A tone sounded and Jet left a brief message with the low points of the operation's outcome and then hung up, secure that she'd receive a call back shortly.

Ye-ji eyed Jet with a frown and held out her hands in obvious question of what they were going to do now. Jet checked the time and motioned to the far side of the street – they would keep moving until she received guidance from her masters. The Korean girl dutifully followed Jet, who stopped in a doorway to pull off her wig once they'd made it another hundred yards and turned her light windbreaker inside out, which was gray instead of black on the reverse side. Jet removed a baseball cap from her backpack, dropped the wig inside, and handed Ye-ji a pair of cheap wraparound sunglasses to further alter her appearance.

She studied the young woman for a moment and hesitated as her phone vibrated in her pocket. "Yes?" she answered.

"This is most troubling. Do you have any color on the mother?" Rami demanded.

"Negative. The agent in charge of her took a bullet, and now he's not responding."

"The news is already reporting the strike as a terrorist attack. There's nothing about a kidnapping, so you may be in the clear for now."

"We both know that won't last. The North Koreans saw the whole thing."

"It will buy you some breathing room."

"What happened with the driver?" Jet pressed.

"We don't know. We're working on it." Rami paused. "Find someplace, like a restaurant, where you and the girl can lie low until we come up with a new plan."

"This fell apart from the get-go. Someone leaked," Jet stated flatly. "Probably the driver."

"We've considered the possibility," Rami replied, matching her detached tone. "Are you being pursued?"

"We lost the police tail. But I have to believe they'll put out a bulletin sooner or later. We're living on borrowed time."

Rami grunted. "Maybe the girl knows where her mother kept the USB drive she smuggled out."

Jet sighed in frustration. "I don't speak Korean."

"Find someone who does and have them translate. Can't be that hard. There are thousands of immigrants there."

"Translate what question, exactly?" Jet asked, beginning to lose faith in her control officer.

"Figure it out. We need that information." He paused again. "In the meantime, go someplace where you won't stand out. There are a million tourists in town for the games. Shouldn't be too hard."

"There's going to be a city-wide manhunt for her sooner than later. We both know that."

"Maybe. Maybe not. So far, nothing. I'll get back to you when I have more. Right now we're scrambling – we can't get the girl out until we've got more assets in place to run interference. We need time."

"We don't have any."

"Make some."

The call terminated, leaving Jet to stare at the phone. She fought to control the anger rising in her gorge and tapped a query into her cell's search engine. Nine restaurants popped up, and after a quick perusal of the map, she located the nearest one to the tourist area of the waterfront and plotted a course using her street navigator. A voice told her in English to make a left at the next intersection and continue straight for two hundred yards. Jet nodded to herself and gestured to Ye-ji to accompany her.

They arrived at the restaurant fifteen minutes later, both sweating through their clothes, the light cotton windbreakers ill-suited for tropical hikes. Jet led the girl to a table at the rear of the restaurant and removed her phone from her pocket, sighing in relief at the blast of arctic air from the air conditioner. She typed in a question and waited for the translator to process it, and then held the message up for Ye-ji to read in Korean – an idea the navigation program had given her as they'd trekked to their destination.

Ye-ji frowned as she read, her expression puzzled, and then shook her head.

Jet nodded. She didn't know the whereabouts of the USB drive. Or at least, she claimed not to. Had her mother worked out a contingency plan with her in case things went wrong?

That drew a different response – one of dawning awareness. Ye-ji practically snatched the phone from Jet, fiddled with it, and typed in a message in Korean. She held the device out to Jet, who took it and translated it into English.

Where is my mother? Is she okay?

Jet debated how to answer the question and then entered her reply.

I don't know. Our communication system failed. That's why I was hoping you'd discussed a contingency in the event something went wrong.

Ye-ji read the text and then slid her hand beneath her top and retrieved a sweat-soaked piece of paper folded in half. She unfolded it carefully, and Jet spotted the logo of the hotel across the top. Ye-ji handed her the sopping note, and Jet studied the intersecting lines of a hand-drawn map.

Jet typed a message. *What is this?*

The response was short. *My mother gave it to me.*

What is the address?

I think it was where your people were going to take us. A safe house, she called it.

Jet's face gave away nothing, but inwardly she swore. Jerry had held out critical information from her – she'd been under the impression they were to bring the mother to the same safe house as Jet had been instructed to bring the daughter to; but that was nowhere near the spot on the map. Why he'd done so was a troubling question – passive-aggressive payback? Double cross? Or…was there more going on than there appeared to be?

And if so, was Rami aware of the divergence in information? Was she being played, a pawn in a larger game she wasn't even aware of?

She didn't like the possibilities, all of which were ugly. At the very least her co-lead had left out a key piece of information. At worst, he might have been the one who'd betrayed the mission, giving different instructions to Ben than to her, with the intent of…

What?

That made no sense. More likely it was natural secretiveness and need-to-know. He, for all of his orders to cooperate, had probably decided Jet didn't need to have the address of the mother's safe house, just the one the daughter was to be taken to. If the mission had gone as planned, he would have simply explained that the two were being kept separate until the mother honored her part of the bargain and produced the second half of the information. Withholding the daughter's whereabouts would have served as insurance the mother performed.

That fit far better, in Jet's mind. She just hated that she had to guess. Guessing could get you killed on an active op, and right now she was in hostile territory, guilty in Indonesian eyes of a purported terrorist attack as well as a kidnapping, her support network obliterated, and her control officer obviously at a loss for what to do next.

The map might or might not help. If the North Koreans or the Indonesian security force had learned about the map – which, given Wally's disappearance and Jet's suspicion that the spectacular failure of the mission hadn't been a matter of bad luck seemed a reasonable possibility – either or both might be awaiting their arrival. Which left Jet exposed, with few good avenues she could see, a fugitive on an island with no ready way to get off.

Jet tapped in a final question. *Is there another copy of the material your mother was exchanging for our help?*

Ye-ji's frown deepened when she read it. *Why? What happened?*

I'm just asking. My superior needs to know.

Ye-ji typed furiously. *Just the original back home. It's hidden in our apartment.*

Where?

Ask my mother.

Ye-ji's face now radiated distrust, and Jet's instinct was to stop probing lest she spook the girl completely. They were already in a tough enough position without her becoming adversarial. Jet did her best to adopt a calm demeanor, but the anxiety in her stomach burned like battery acid.

If it could get any worse, she didn't see how, and Jet tried to quell her misgivings so she didn't alarm Ye-ji any more than she already had. The last thing she needed was the Korean girl to do something foolish that would give them away, and if she thought that Jet had lost control of the situation, that was a good possibility.

What Jet would do when the inevitable photograph of Ye-ji was broadcast on the news was another story altogether – one she would have to develop a plan for quickly, because it appeared that her assumption that the daughter would be ensconced at the safe house by the time her image went viral had been wildly optimistic, and she was now facing a worst-case scenario with no backup…and no way out.

CHAPTER 22

Mafraq, Jordan

A thirty-year-old war surplus truck rattled down a dirt track toward the Zaatari refugee camp. The sun was already high in the sky and beat down on the beige desert with a vengeance. As the conveyance neared the huge settlement, the occupants of the cab could make out the white temporary shelters that served as homes for many of the refugees – those fortunate enough not to be spending their years in the camp in a ragtag collection of tents.

The driver, a heavy man with four days of salt-and-pepper growth adorning three chins, grunted and downshifted as his two companions on the bench seat squinted through the hazy windshield at the camp gates. Just in front of them, a dust devil was twisting its way across the road. Chain-link fencing encircled the enclave, the razor-wire coils that topped the barrier gleaming in the sun, and they could make out six members of the Jordanian army lounging near the entry in the meager shade provided by a tarp slung from the fence to a pair of poles by their troop carrier.

The soldiers looked up as the truck rolled to an unsteady stop in front of the gate, and one of the guards approached the driver's window, his rifle hanging from a shoulder strap. His steps were slow, as though the pervasive heat had sapped his energy. When he pulled even with the open window, he grinned at the driver; the truck was one of the regular visitors to the beleaguered camp.

"Back so soon?" the sentry asked, his smile revealing yellowed teeth with several gaps from those surrendered to decay.

"Idle hands, right?" the driver said with a knowing chuckle. A rivulet of sweat rolled down his grimy cheek, and a fly buzzed through the window and landed on his crown of greasy hair. He swatted at the insect with a hand the size of a Ping-Pong paddle, and the bluebottle took to the air again in search of more hospitable climes.

"Where you headed?"

"Making the rounds."

"Anything in the back?" the guard asked, glancing at the olive canvas that covered the metal framework over the bed.

"Bunch of dancing girls and a Lear jet," the driver said, and both men laughed.

"All right, then," the guard said, brushing the driver's hand as he leaned against the door, the passing of bills imperceptible to anyone not watching for it. "Stay out of trouble."

"Always."

The guard murmured into a two-way radio as he returned to his station, and the gate creaked open. The driver ground the gears until he found a favorable one and the truck lumbered forward through the gap, trailing a cloud of diesel exhaust and road dust. Several reed-thin men watched it enter from near one of the temporary buildings, showing no reaction, their eyes as vacant as those of prisoners on a chain gang.

The man beside the driver checked his watch – an expensive model on an alligator strap – and scowled at the dashboard air vents.

"We're earning our money today, aren't we? Must be a hundred and twenty out," he said.

"Why, Doctor, since when would you allow nature to keep you from your duties?" the other man said, wiping perspiration from his brow.

"It would be nice if they bought something with air. With what the mullah is making…" the doctor replied, and then thought better of continuing, preferring discretion even though it was only the three of them.

"You've already done the deal with the parents?" the driver asked.

"Of course. This is just a formality."

"An important one, obviously."

Both the passenger and the doctor nodded in unison. "If her bloodwork and physical checks out, they'll be free of this hellhole for good," the doctor agreed.

The driver turned off the main road, which was paved, onto one of the dirt tributaries that branched through the camp. Bars covered the windows of all the structures, signaling that even among kindred unfortunates with nowhere to go, thievery and worse were constant threats. Haunted faces regarded them from inside the shelters as they passed, the heat outside too much for any but the hardiest or most desperate.

"This is it," the driver said, and the truck eased to a stop in front of a string of shabby tents, each large enough to house ten people. Flaps in the sides were open for ventilation, and the stench of decay hit all three men when they stepped from the truck. The doctor's nose wrinkled even though the odor wasn't unexpected.

A man with a nose like a hawk stepped from the nearest dwelling and bowed his head at the new arrivals. The driver returned the gesture, the doctor and his companion nodding once.

"Welcome. Please, come in," the refugee said in Arabic.

"Very kind of you, but I'm afraid we can't take advantage of your hospitality today. We're on a schedule," he said, and offered a small bundle of bills to the man. "As agreed, here is half. I will deliver the rest when she checks out."

"And passage for my family?"

"Already arranged. To Germany, as you requested. The asylum documents have already been processed."

A woman's face appeared in the dark tent entry, her haggard face sagging, her eyes as sad as a basset hound. The man seemed to sense her presence and, without turning, waved her away with a curt gesture. She retreated back into the gloom like a specter, and the man unbound the bundle and eyed the wad of low-denomination euros.

The doctor glanced around. "Three thousand, as agreed. Now where is she?"

"She...she went to clean up. Should be back anytime."

"The agreement was you would have her waiting," the companion snarled, his tone hard as stone.

The refugee looked over the doctor's shoulder at a figure approaching along a road that ran from one of the larger buildings, the heat waves that rose from the earth distorting the structures in the background. When the figure drew near, it became clear it was a young woman, her face horribly scarred from shrapnel or a fire, one eye milky in its socket, the other vacant but friendly. The puckered tissue twisted into a mockery of a smile, and the refugee forced a grin to his lips that never reached his moistening eyes.

"Ah, Rima, there you are," he said, a slight catch in his voice.

"Hello, Papa. It's fierce hot, isn't it?" Rima said, her tone musical, almost childlike.

"That it is, Rima. Did you get good and clean?"

"I did, Papa. Just like you and Mama said."

The refugee nodded and motioned to the men. "Rima, the doctor is here to take you to get some medicine. Like we talked about yesterday."

"I don't feel sick," she said, her voice doubtful in the way of a toddler.

"If you're good and behave, after they give you the medicine, they promised a treat," the refugee finished, his final words strangled.

The doctor nodded. "That's right. Ice lollies and candy. Whatever flavors you want." He paused. "And dates."

"Mmm. I like dates," Rima said, her good eye still uncertain but warming at the prospect of unimaginable rewards to come. She looked to her father, who nodded mutely and then studied his sandaled feet.

"Everyone loves dates," the driver agreed. "Ready to get your treats, Rima?"

"If Papa says it's okay. I'm not supposed to go anywhere without asking Papa, right?"

"That's right," the doctor agreed. "You're a very good girl indeed, Rima."

The scar tissue twisted into another smile, and Rima clapped her hands. "Oh, goody. Where are we going? Can Papa and Mama come?"

The doctor shook his head. "No, sweetheart. It's just for you."

"Can I bring some treats back for them, and for my brother and sisters? They get awfully hungry."

The doctor and driver exchanged a glance, and the doctor nodded solemnly. "Of course you can, Rima. Now, up into the back of the truck you go."

The driver escorted her to the rear of the big vehicle and helped her into the bed while the doctor's companion had the refugee sign a document in triplicate, his scrawl barely legible. When the refugee finished and looked up at the doctor, his expression was tortured. "She's simple, always has been. And with the scar, at sixteen...she has no future to look forward to. No man would..." he said, and his voice trailed off as though he'd run out of breath.

"You're doing the right thing. Bought yourself and your family a new start, and saved someone's life in the bargain. It's for the best," the doctor said, the reassurance polished from years of delivering it to the parents of organ donors, the words chosen carefully to avoid any last minute changes of heart.

"She... There won't be any pain, right?"

"Like I said before, she'll never feel a thing. I promise you that."

The refugee swallowed hard and nodded weakly. "When will you...?"

"I'll send someone tonight with the money," the companion assured him. "Then you can put this behind you. Your other children will have a different future because of your sacrifice. I know it must be hard, but you've done what you must in difficult circumstances, and they'll be better for it."

Rima's father didn't answer and instead turned and retraced his steps to the tent. His shoulders trembled as he walked away without looking back. The truck engine started, and after a hiss from the brakes it rolled away, the rumble of the engine almost drowning out the anguished wail that followed it down the track from inside the tent, where a mother bemoaned an impossible choice that would haunt the family's nightmares until their final days.

CHAPTER 23

An hour and a half crawled by, and Jet's phone remained silent as she and Ye-ji finished a late lunch of local fish and steamed vegetables. Ye-ji had attempted to communicate more using the translation engine, but Jet couldn't answer most of her questions, the answers as much of a mystery to her as they were to the girl, who was growing increasingly agitated as time dragged on over Jet's inability to give her any information about where her mother was.

Jet was watching a television mounted on one wall, where an Indonesian soap opera was droning with abundant violin music as frowning actresses clutched their blouses at dramatic high points involving angry male counterparts. The scene changed to a news bulletin, and Jet almost choked when footage from the scene at the waterway popped onto the screen, with soldiers holding back the press, who were filming from wherever they could, the area in obvious chaos.

The broadcast continued, and while Jet couldn't understand what the newscaster was saying, the film was self-explanatory, the live feed interrupted by interviews with obviously distraught spectators, which then cut to bodies covered with sheets, and several women being escorted to ambulances with bleeding head wounds presumably caused by trampling when the crowd had panicked.

The scene changed again to a reporter standing in front of a collection of emergency vehicles. Stern-faced soldiers behind her held machine guns like they intended to use them at the slightest provocation. Jet began to relax when the report continued without any variation, but her breath caught in her throat when a still photograph of Ye-ji flashed onto the screen with her name across the bottom. It was a terrible likeness, her face serious, staring into the camera for a passport shot or official ID, but good enough to give Jet problems if anyone was paying attention.

She had paid the bill several minutes earlier, and tapped in a quick message on her cell, translated it to Korean, and held the screen up for the daughter to read.

Your photo is on TV. We must get different clothes. Something local.

Jet had seen numerous women wearing hijabs, the headdresses Muslim women favored, paired with colorful long-sleeved tunics that came to mid-thigh, worn with pants underneath. If they could find a store where they could buy outfits in that style, they would blend in far better, and nobody would recognize the girl, especially with the sunglasses and a bit of judiciously applied makeup. Right now, with her red athletic team pants, even with the baseball cap and glasses there was too much of a chance that someone would make the connection. Jet's sense of urgency mounted and she stood and guided Ye-ji to the exit, wary of any eyes following them out. Ye-ji glanced over her shoulder at the TV, but Jet tightened her grip on her arm and steered her forward, past the smiling cashier and back out into the muggy swelter.

The sidewalk was swarming with the beginning of rush hour, and Jet followed the crowd away from the waterfront, figuring that it would be only a matter of a few blocks before they found some sort of store or market selling the garb she wanted. Ye-ji seemed preoccupied, the image on the television hammering home the reality of her plight, believed to be a kidnapping victim due to the charade her mother had insisted upon rather than the customary, and far simpler, strategy of a political defector seeking asylum from a persecutory regime. If she was having second thoughts, she didn't show it, but Jet could read her body language well enough to see that she was still in shock from the day's events, even if she was managing it well.

Three blocks further inland, Jet spied an open-air market teeming with humanity, with tarps over the stalls to block the sun. The aisles stretched at least a hundred yards to the next street. A wizened man with a Fu Manchu mustache at the entrance of the market was coaxing a monkey to perform tricks with its hat and several props to the delight of a throng of children, their smiles radiant white in pecan-hued complexions. Jet led Ye-ji along the stalls, past a pair of speakers blasting rap music to demonstrate the fidelity of the car stereos for sale, and another with a dizzying collection of counterfeit purses and fragrances. They arrived at another aisle, where she spotted a clothing bazaar with at least ten women's apparel stalls grouped together, the area crowded with shoppers admiring the offerings.

Jet walked with the girl past a T-shirt vendor selling bootleg concert shirts to a double-wide boutique that had at least a hundred hijabs and tunics in every color of the rainbow. They entered the clothing market and looked through the headdresses, surrounded by other women conversing in the local tongue, and Jet selected two hijabs and a pair of muted blue tops. She eyed the garments, approached one of the vendors, and pantomimed asking the price. The woman jabbered something Jet didn't catch, and the vendor shook her head and motioned for her to accompany her to a small counter at the back, beside a row of changing rooms fabricated from sheets hung from a steel frame. Jet gave Ye-ji an outfit and pointed to one of the dressing slots. The girl took it from her and sulked into the farthest one while Jet haggled with the vendor, who seemed hell-bent on making the transaction as difficult as possible.

After a minute of using her fingers to go back and forth on a price, Jet fished out a wad of rupiah and counted off the appropriate number of bills, her patience worn thin. The woman inspected each as though suspicious that Jet had printed them that morning, and finally nodded and handed her a scrawled receipt with a Hello Kitty logo in the upper corner. Jet pocketed it and turned to the changing rooms, emerald eyes roving over the modesty coverings, and walked to the one the girl had disappeared into.

"Ye-ji?" she called softly. When there was no answer, she pushed the sheet covering the stall aside. The inside was empty, the clothes gone. One corner of the sheet at the rear had been torn free from the plastic tie wrap that had secured it to the mounting base, and the edge flapped in the light breeze. Jet's blood froze in her veins and she cursed and then moved to the back and stepped into the next stall, where a sea of faces swiveled toward her from where they had been watching a presentation of a vegetable-slicing gizmo being demonstrated by a young man with an elaborately lacquered hairstyle.

Jet pushed past him and through the gathering to another artery lined with vendors, and scanned both directions. Hundreds of women, a third of them clad in the traditional hijab, moved along the displays, some ambling aimlessly, others walking hurriedly, their shopping done. Jet tried to pick out the daughter, but saw nothing that looked familiar. Her lips tightened and she made for the street where they'd entered the market, the view blocked by hanging purses and cages with brightly plumed birds, the odor of cooking oil and roasting meat carried along the crowded way as she fought through the current of humanity moving in the opposite direction, her heart rate climbing in the stifling heat.

When she finally spilled onto the sidewalk, her eyes roamed over the countless pedestrians hurrying along, seeking any glimpse of the girl's red pants. After a minute of fruitless effort, she exhaled and stepped out of the sun, cell phone in hand, resigned to making the call she'd been dreading since seeing the empty stall.

The line hummed with static and rang three times. When Rami answered on the fourth ring, Jet's voice was hushed, tight with worry.

"The girl bolted. I lost her."

"What? Tell me you're joking," he sputtered.

Jet blinked away frustration and stared down the street, the subtropical heat oppressive even as dusk approached.

"I'm not. She's gone."

CHAPTER 24

Donggang, China

A lavender sky had faded to black as the sun dropped like a smoldering ember into the polluted haze over the western hills and the lights of the port town had blinked to life, a thousand electric fireflies defying the darkness with their glow. In the wharf area, the buildings loomed large in the gloom. The day laborers had gone home to heaping portions of fish and rice, leaving the deserted shells of the waterfront warehouses for the night birds to claim.

A man on a bicycle rode along the frontage road, a cap pulled low over his eyes, the bulky seaman's coat he wore to fend off the evening chill flapping with each squeaky pump of the pedals. He slowed as he neared the front gate of one of the larger structures and braked to a stop before he swung off the seat and leaned the bike against the perimeter wall, took a few steps toward the gate, and relieved himself.

When he'd finished his business, he stood outside the gate, staring through the bars at the darkened building. The surrounding grounds were empty save a few rusting containers and several barrels lying on their sides. After a glance in either direction along the road, he tapped an earbud concealed by the flaps of the cap and spoke in a whisper, his words almost inaudible as he looked around casually for any movement on the periphery of his vision.

"It's quiet. Doesn't look like anyone's around."

The response was immediate. "We're moving in. Stay in position."

"Roger that."

The rider moved back to his bicycle and crouched down,

pretending to fiddle with the chain in case anyone was watching from a hidden position or there were surveillance cameras an earlier reconnaissance hadn't picked up. The element of surprise was one of his group's key assumptions in taking the warehouse without casualties, so he would maintain the pretension of being an innocent rider as long as possible.

Two men materialized out of the shadows, walking at a leisurely pace, carrying rucksacks, outwardly seamen making their way to one of the vessels lining the pier, or perhaps workers late for the night shift at the nearby shipyard. The ruse wouldn't work for long, but they were disciplined, and if it enabled them to gain a slim advantage, they would keep up the act until shots were fired.

When they reached the rider, one of them glanced at the gate and then tapped a cigarette from a pack, pausing to offer smokes to the others before pocketing it and pretending to search for a light. When his putative search came up empty, he shrugged off the shoulder strap of the rucksack and dug into it while the others watched the road and the compound grounds.

He straightened after a moment, a pair of bolt cutters in hand, and swiftly moved to the gate's padlock while the rider straightened and pulled a bullpup submachine gun from beneath his jacket and screwed a sound suppressor into place with practiced hands. A sharp snap from the gate announced that the lock had been cut, and the second man retrieved the submachine gun's twin from his bag and tossed it to the lock cutter before freeing another identical weapon from the rucksack and looking to the rider.

"The others are coming in the back side," the rider said, unnecessarily, as every man knew the operation cold. Seven hardened IDF commandos who didn't officially exist were scaling the back wall, and four more approached the gate at a run from across the road, heavy packs strapped to their backs, their faces blacked out to reduce any glare, night vision goggles in place. When they arrived, the three Mossad agents who had been posing as locals donned NV goggles as well, and together they pushed past the open gate and made for the loading docks, the only sounds the distant whine of a drill working through steel from the shipyard and the pounding of their boots.

At the first loading dock, the men fanned out and the rider looked to one of the pedestrians, who now appeared to be anything but an innocent sailor out for a stroll; the NV gear lent him the appearance of a cyborg. The man nodded and set his rucksack down by his side before moving to a single steel door beside the dock and inspecting the lock. The others remained crouched out of sight behind the shelter of the concrete platform, studying the roofline with their scopes for any signs of CCTV cameras they might have missed from afar.

The man at the door extracted a length of thermite rope from the pocket of his peacoat, stripped the backing from the adhesive section of the cord and molded it into place, and affixed a small charge just powerful enough to ignite it with a trigger attached. He tapped his earbud and murmured a few words.

"We're in position. The charge is in place. Signal when you're ready on your end."

Ten seconds later a voice answered, "Trigger in five."

He counted off the requisite seconds, flipped two micro toggle switches on the integrated timer, and tore back to the shelter of the dock, flipping the goggles out of his field of vision as he ran.

Ten seconds later a pop barely louder than a champagne cork echoed from the door, and a loud hiss, like steam escaping under high pressure, emanated from a blinding flare of neon yellow where the lock had been moments before. Before the sound had died away, all the men were in motion, running toward the dock. The leader kicked the door once and it flew open, the entire locking mechanism dropping away from where the thermite had cut through the metal like a hot knife through butter, and then they were inside the warehouse, spreading out as their counterparts performed the identical maneuver at the rear of the building.

Two minutes of hurried searching passed, and the leader walked back to the door he'd demolished and closed it with a sigh. He tapped his earbud and spoke in a low voice.

"There's nothing here. It's a wash."

A pause ensued, and then the voice of their mission commander boomed in his ear. "Repeat."

"You heard me. There's nothing in the warehouse but garbage and a few pallets."

"Are you sure?"

"Positive. Thing's a goose egg. It's empty. This was a bust."

One of the men called out from a far corner. "Jacob, over here."

The leader spun in his direction and trotted to him. "What is it?"

The man pointed at a half dozen discarded aerosol cans scattered across the floor. Jacob frowned behind his NV goggles. "Paint?"

The man shook his head. "No."

Jacob exhaled impatiently. "Then what?"

"Those Chinese characters? They say Freon."

The two men were silent for a long beat, and then Jacob tapped his earbud again. "There are six Freon cans in here." Jacob knelt and examined one. "Used. You can see the thread marks on the tops. And they're not dusty, so they're relatively recent."

The booming voice replied, "They were keeping something cold."

"Looks that way."

"Damn. We're too late." A pause. "Get footage of everything. The cans. The interior of the building. The works. Then return to base. We're getting out of here as soon as you're aboard."

Jacob hefted the can, which weighed almost nothing, and nodded again. "Roger that. We'll be on our way back in a few minutes."

Jacob turned to his men and issued instructions over the common channel they were all connected to, the commander's feed audible only to him but silent now that the bad news had been delivered. The mission had been painstakingly mounted, no expense spared, personnel flown in to meet the ship in Japan before it had steamed to China…all for nothing. Their quarry had eluded them; but worse than that, the presence of the Freon confirmed the worst-case scenario – terrorists had obtained something that required constant refrigeration, and the list of possible items was exceedingly short. The rumors of a bio-attack being readied against Israel that had been circulating for the last month had just taken on undeniable substance, and the country's worst fears had suddenly become real: parties unknown intended to launch the unspeakable, and the Israelis had no idea what agent was going to be used, how it would be deployed, or where.

CHAPTER 25

Beijing, China

Zhao Yaozu rolled his wheelchair to the window of his expansive study. The near-constant pain from the amputation had finally dulled to a throb that required only a third of the morphine he'd been initially prescribed. His chest still hurt when he strained it, but if he was careful, he could make it through an entire day with only a few agonizing reminders of his brush with death.

The doctor had told him that he would be ready for a prosthesis in a few more weeks, but that there was no rush and to take his time. A conscientious young woman had come from the manufacturer to take measurements the prior day, and the humiliation of a twentysomething he would have cheerfully pursued before his incident doing her best to keep pity and revulsion out of her eyes still stung like a lash across his pride. Everyone had put on a brave front to pretend that they hadn't noticed the elephant in the room, and their efforts only further reinforced his shame at being crippled, with no hope of ever being whole again.

All because of the woman and her masters.

Not an hour went by when he didn't curse her memory, and his spare hours had taken on a life of their own. His imagination conjured up countless ways he could torture her before she finally succumbed in the most horrible manner possible: gang raping, burning, dismembering, acid, electric shock, disemboweling all played through his mind whenever he thought of her and the role she'd played in his affliction.

And that was what it was – an affliction. Even though the physical therapist and physician had reassured him that in time he would hardly notice his foot's absence, he suspected that was a lie designed to comfort him and prevent him from falling into the depression that threatened to engulf him; the only thing keeping him from succumbing to it were the flames of a hate so intense it could power a small city.

A musical chime sounded from the intercom he'd had installed in his study, and he wheeled himself to the box, gritting his teeth at the twinge from his shoulder.

"What is it?" he growled.

"Mo and Ken are here to see you."

The pair of his top lieutenants had called earlier, and he'd told them to come over whenever they received the news they'd been awaiting. Now, after a week, they'd gotten their first lead on the woman's whereabouts – far sooner than he'd dared to hope.

"Send them up."

He waited impatiently, tamping down a thrill of anger that rose in his throat and threatened to choke him. He would remain calm, as was his customary state. There was every chance this was a false alarm, a dead end that would lead nowhere. And yet…

A rap at the door interrupted his dark mood, and he took a deep breath before speaking. "Come in."

The two men entered, and he directed them to an Italian leather sofa that had cost as much as a car. They sat, Mo with a manila folder in his hand, their expressions neutral. Zhao wheeled himself closer and fixed them with a withering stare.

"Well?"

"You'll have to be the judge. Our man in Indonesia contacted us, and it looks…it's difficult to say." The triad had sent the sketch of the mystery woman to its network, with a reward of a king's ransom for any information that led to her apprehension. The White Dragons did business all over the world and had eyes and ears throughout Asia, most of Europe, and the United States. What might have seemed like a long shot could have hit pay dirt, which Zhao would know soon enough.

He held out his hand. "Just give me the picture."

"We have several," Ken said. "From traffic cameras in Jakarta. I took the liberty of having the most promising blown up so you can better make out her face."

Mo stood and approached Zhao with the folder. Zhao snatched it from him and set it on his lap, a nearly imperceptible tremor in his hand. He opened it and removed a grainy photograph of two women crossing a street, both wearing sunglasses, one clutching the other's arm.

Zhao flipped to the next in the series, which was a close-up of one of the women's faces. He blinked to be sure he wasn't imagining things, and stared at the image so hard a vein in the side of his temple began to throb. He shifted in the chair and eyed the third image, another close-up, and then the final picture, which was a digital rendition of the sketch, for comparison.

Mo sat down heavily and watched his boss. Ken leaned forward. "The hair is different, and the glasses make it hard to be sure…"

Zhao glanced up at him. "It's her. I'd know her even if she had a mustache and a fake nose. It's her."

"Are you positive?"

"Of course I am. You think I wouldn't recognize her after what she did to me? I'd know her from miles away. When was this taken?"

"The time stamp is from six hours ago. There was an attack on the North Korean rowing team at the Asian games, and–"

"I read all about it. She's involved, obviously." He paused to slow his breathing and compose himself. "I want her found. We know she's in Jakarta. Mobilize whoever you need to. Pay whatever it costs. If she's taken into custody, I want her. If she is wounded and goes to a hospital, I want to know. Find her, and take her alive if you can. If not, kill her as painfully as possible." He stopped himself, recognizing that his speech was increasing in speed and his tone was becoming angrier – two losses of control he wouldn't permit himself. "Put our best people on it. She must not escape."

"The police are hunting her as well."

"Of course they are. But they can be bought." Zhao looked out his picture window at a mockingbird on the terrace railing beyond the glass. The bird's head bobbed, and it turned as though watching him, its black eye moving from Zhao to his men before settling where Zhao's foot would have been. Zhao blinked away the illusion, an artifact of the morphine, he was sure, and steadied himself before returning his attention to the two gangsters. "You have your work cut out for you. Now go."

"We'll report back with any news."

"Yes. Do so."

Mo and Ken exchanged a glance. "Do you want to keep the photos?"

Zhao shook his head and gathered the snapshots into the folder. "There's no need. It's her. Distribute the images as you see fit. But do not allow her to escape."

"There are no guarantees, sir. We'll do our best, but with Jakarta in a state of emergency…"

"Do what you must. But I want her head. I will not tolerate failure."

Mo nodded, and Ken followed suit. They both stood and made their way to the door. Zhao did a slow pirouette with the wheelchair and faced the window, a headache forming behind his eyes, his vision darkening as though he were in a tunnel. He scanned the railing, but the bird was gone.

The tremor in his hand was intensifying. He waited for his men to leave and then rolled to his desk, where a bottle of tablets waited like a lover, nestled in the recesses of the top drawer. Zhao fumbled with the top and mumbled a curse when he dropped the bottle, sending the pills skittering across the hardwood floor. He swore again and rolled to the intercom, hating his condition and lack of mobility every inch of the way, his pride battling with his need for narcotic relief. In the end, his hunger for the drug won the contest.

"Kim? Come to the study. I've had an accident."

CHAPTER 26

16 miles south of Bucharest, Romania

A column of NATO personnel carriers rolled down a secondary road, a large split-axle equipment truck positioned in the middle of the procession. All moved at a rapid clip on their daylight run to the Bulgarian border, where they would be met by two more military vehicles to escort them through that country. The Romanian soldiers in the carriers were bored; the trip was one they'd made numerous times, and escorting the truck was as uneventful a duty as any.

The driver of the lead vehicle eyed the speedometer as he approached a bend. The unending farmland on either side stretched to the horizon, the Transylvanian Alps so far to the north he could barely discern their peaks against the blue of the afternoon sky. His wingman whistled along with music playing from his cell phone – a violation of the rules, but one neither man felt applied when operating on friendly terrain. The convoy had hit the road that morning at daybreak, departing a supply depot in Belgrade to ferry a load of surface-to-air missiles to Ankara. The plan was to drive straight through the night and be in Turkey the following day, after which the men would take a few days' leave before returning to their permanent base in Romania.

The driver yawned and gave his companion a sidelong glance; the four men behind him in the vehicle were either dozing or texting, both also against the rules while on duty but understandable, there being nothing else to occupy their time on the long trip south.

"Do you have to do that?" he asked, lips pursed.

His companion stopped whistling. "What?"

"That. It's annoying as hell."

The other man smirked. "Someone have a bad night last night? Little too much to drink?"

"No, I just don't want to spend an entire day listening to it."

"Sorry. Excuse me for trying to enjoy myself." He shifted and frowned. "They aren't making these seats any more comfortable, are they?"

The driver didn't respond, his attention drawn to two emergency vehicles parked on the road ahead with roof lights flashing. A large flatbed truck overloaded with bales of hay was blocking the lane. A policeman waved a flag to caution the column and the driver obliged, taking his foot off the accelerator and allowing the heavy carrier to slow, an expression of disgust on his face. "Just our luck."

"Wonder how long it will take to clear?"

"That truck looks older than your mother."

"What have you got against trucks?"

Both men laughed as the driver braked to a halt. The cop approached, his uniform jacket stretched tight across a powerful chest. The driver rolled down the window and peered out at him.

"What's the problem?" the driver asked.

"Thing dropped its tranny in the middle of the road," the cop replied. "Where you headed?"

"To the border."

The cop's eyes roamed down the line of vehicles. "This all of you?"

"That's right. Why?"

"Ground's pretty firm, depending on how heavy you are. If you go slow, you can make it around on the shoulder."

"These things can climb over cliffs. German ingenuity."

"Okay. Give it a try, one at a time. But be careful not to get too far from the road. We don't need you guys bogged down, too. Follow me. I'll walk you along the best bit."

"Appreciate it."

The cop strode away from the lead vehicle and, when he was five yards ahead, motioned for the driver to put it in gear. The driver radioed the rest of the column and gave them a two-sentence report, and then inched forward. Six other police stood by their cars, watching the vehicles as they passed. The personnel carrier lurched as its oversized wheels scrunched onto the soggy ground, occasionally churning the muddy dirt as they fought for traction.

"Boy, he wasn't kidding, was he?" the driver said as they drove by the truck, its bulk blocking both lanes, its hood up.

The cop signaled the driver to slow further as the equipment truck drew parallel to the stalled vehicle, and then motioned for the driver to stop. He approached the window again.

"What is it?" the driver asked.

"I don't think you're going to make it past here. The ground's too wet. You should take a look before you try."

The driver nodded and swung his door open. The cop adjusted the H&K MP7A1 hanging from a shoulder strap and pointed to an area in front of the carrier. The driver squinted at it and turned to the officer. "Looks okay to me."

The first burst from the machine pistol cut the driver in half, and the grenade the cop tossed into the carrier before slamming the door closed and moving away detonated seconds later. The ensuing blast blew the glass from the windows along with disembodied pieces of flesh and bone. Multiple antitank rockets streaked from behind the hay bales on the back of the stalled truck. All found their targets at the close range, and the three remaining troop carriers exploded in flames.

Three of the other police officers jogged to the flaming wrecks and tossed grenades through the ruined windshields for good measure, while the lead cop ran to the equipment truck and emptied his weapon into the cab. When he pulled the driver's door open, the man's body tumbled out onto the muddy ground, his torso riddled with wounds and a look of shocked incomprehension on his face as the light faded from his eyes.

Five minutes later the truck was barreling down the road toward a pair of pickup trucks waiting at the shoulder. The lead cop slowed to a stop in the middle of the road and signaled for the men by the pickups to approach.

"We need to make this fast. Get the guidance systems. Nothing else matters," he said in Arabic.

The men nodded and moved to the back of the truck. The cop stepped down from the cab, blood smeared on his uniform, and quickly stripped off the jacket and pants, his jeans and T-shirt beneath them unspoiled. The police vehicles pulled up behind them, and the other cops got out and did the same, tossing their uniforms into the cars before gathering at the cargo bed to watch their compatriots work.

"Four guidance systems in all. Just as we expected," one of the men called out from inside the bay, where heavy rockets lay in racks.

"Excellent. You know what to do. How long?"

"No more than ten minutes."

When the technicians had removed the parts they needed and transferred them to the two pickups, the others piled into the beds of the trucks, now to all appearances agricultural workers on their way home from a shift that had started at dawn. The lead cop walked to the police cruisers and lobbed grenades into their cabs, the machine guns and uniforms piled inside. He was halfway back to the pickups when the first fireball soared into the sky. The whump of the detonation made his ears pop.

He grinned as he climbed into the bed of the closest truck, and one of the men gave him a high five. He yelled to the driver in Arabic and the truck rolled onto the road, spraying gravel behind it, and continued south toward Bulgaria, leaving spires of black smoke reaching into the sky in their wake.

CHAPTER 27

Jakarta, Indonesia

Jet hurried from the market, acting on Rami's instructions to get clear in case the girl sounded the alarm or was apprehended by the police. He'd told her to stay on the move and had assured her that he would contact her as soon as he had clarity on the situation in Jakarta, which was still in a state of turmoil from the earlier attack. He had deployed two lower-level agents to seek information about casualties from their contacts in the police department, and hoped to know more about the team and Sang-mi shortly.

She didn't fight him on his order, the question of Wally's whereabouts more troubling by the minute. If he hadn't checked in with his control officer, it was looking increasingly like he'd either been caught or turned on them, which might explain the mission blowing up. Jet slowed at the corner and ducked into a doorway, donned her tunic and hijab, and studied herself in the reflection of her cell phone screen. She looked nothing like the woman who'd kidnapped the Korean girl – different hair and clothes had worked miracles, and she no longer felt like she was a moving target for the first sharpshooter who laid eyes on her.

Now the question in her mind was, with the girl lost and the mother wounded or dead, what had they accomplished by raining hell down on the games? True, they'd obtained the first half of the mother's info, but had that been worth it? There was no way for Jet to know, but she suspected not – between Saul, Jerry, and Ben, they'd lost three seasoned agents, a high price for even the most valuable intelligence. Contrary to popular fiction, agents were not expendable. The Mossad had a tremendous investment in each one, and they were only put in harm's way when there was no other option.

The other issue was the safe house where Jet had left her things –
her passport being the most critical item. If it was compromised
because of Wally, she had no way of getting out of Indonesia until a
replacement could be sent, by which time even the slowest
bureaucracy would have anyone matching her general description
being given additional scrutiny that could trip her up. Cover stories
were put in place based on the assumption that they would be
discarded with identities once a mission was complete; they weren't
designed to withstand in-depth verification. Her vocation might pass
a cursory sniff test, even as far as having her identity inserted into a
company computer so it checked, but if a skeptical investigator took
the extra step to call and see whether anyone had ever worked with
Jet or seen her, it would all come apart. And she had to believe that
given the circumstances, she should expect the worst.

She walked along the busy street, the traffic gridlocked, and
considered her paltry options. Without a passport she was stuck, and
with only the wad in her pocket and the pistol in her waistband, she
wouldn't last long in a country where she didn't speak the language
and had no contacts. Would it be worth the risk to make a move on
the house? Absent a call that a boat was waiting at the wharf for her,
she couldn't see any other way to proceed. The problem being that if
the safe house was being watched, she was as good as dead.

Unless…

Her phone vibrated in her hand, and she stabbed the call to life.
"Yes?"

"You're to get to the airport as soon as possible. First flight to
Korea you can get on. There are a number each day."

"Why Korea?"

"I'll explain in person."

She hesitated. "There's a hitch." She told him about the passport
and her concerns about Wally. When she finished, there was a long
pause.

"I'll have to see what I can do."

"Time's not my friend."

"I know. Let me put out some feelers. I'll get back to you."

"Any word on the mother or the others?"

"Casualties are still coming in, but I haven't heard from anyone on the team. I expect the worst."

"Don't leave me hanging out to dry."

"That won't happen."

The line went dead. Jet stared at the phone for a long beat and then slipped it beneath her robe, her mind churning. She had slim faith that Rami would do anything meaningful in time – she wasn't his asset, rather an unknown foisted off on him by the director; a liability if caught who'd been involved in back-to-back disastrous operations in the span of a few days.

Jet resumed walking, allowing herself to be carried along by the crowd, considering how to proceed. She slowed as she passed a beggar, the woman's blackened gums and grubby outstretched hand giving her pause, and fished a coin from her pocket to drop in the cup at her bare feet. The woman nodded a thanks to Jet, but she didn't notice, otherwise preoccupied as the last of the light went out of the sky.

CHAPTER 28

A mangy street dog barked at a skinny brown Doberman chained to a post in the front yard of a clapboard house that faced a street enshrouded with shadows, the few illuminated porch lights inadequate to counter the pervasive gloom. An occasional tuk-tuk putted along the way, dodging puddles of inky fluid in potholes that dotted the pavement still slick from an evening cloudburst. A heavyset figure waddled down what passed for a sidewalk, her steps labored and obviously painful, toting an overstuffed plastic bag in each hand. The beggar, hijab wrapped tight around her head, continued to the end of the residential block and turned the corner, her hacking cough audible as she disappeared from view.

Jet picked up her pace once she was out of sight of the safe house, her spidey senses tingling. There had been a number of suspicious vehicles parked within surveillance range, but none that had occupants, and no obvious tells, such as cigarette butts accumulated below windows or glass lowered for ventilation in the heat. Still, she was uneasy and hesitant to try her luck with a frontal approach.

Which left her only two possibilities: forget about trying to get in, or attempt to enter through the rear, scaling the wall of the home whose yard backed onto that of the safe house and going in through the kitchen door – the problems being numerous, including dogs and being detected by the occupants of the other homes.

And of course, being fully exposed once she was in the backyard in the event she'd missed any watchers.

Faced with no other option, however, she trod to the next street and made a right, shuffling along as she had before, scouting for any signs of irregularity. In her experience the regular police in most countries were easy to spot, their technique amateurish, but given that the attack was being treated as a terror event, and further given Wally's questionable disposition, she had to expect that the Indonesian intelligence service would be involved – and they would undoubtedly have a more refined touch than the cops.

She passed the home directly behind the darkened safe house and noted that none of the lights were on. The hour was late for working families and the occupants likely asleep. Jet slowed further as she pretended to catch her breath, eyeing the garbage can as a homeless person might. There were fewer vehicles on this street, which made it easy for her to verify as she rested that none held watchers, and she made her decision to try for the back door by traversing the adjacent home's yard.

Jet moved to the garbage can and lifted the lid, glancing around a final time, and then her deliberately laborious steps quickened and she darted for the side gate. When she neared, Jet could make out a bolt that was padlocked, but instead of slowing, she increased her pace and threw herself upward, arms extended over her head.

Her fingers clamped onto the bar at the top of the gate, and she hauled herself up and over in a single smooth motion, landing in a crouch on the other side. She remained immobile for several seconds, listening, and when she heard nothing, picked her way along the side of the house, past three partially open windows – bedrooms, she was sure.

The wall that separated the safe house yard from where she stood was eight feet high and mortar over brick, with no obvious handholds. She stopped at the base and cocked her head, listening again for any sound from the other side of the wall. After thirty seconds of silence, she retraced her steps and bolted toward where the side and rear walls joined, running two steps up the side wall before pushing off as hard as she could and hurtling toward the rear edge.

She gripped the top of the wall and used the momentum from her vault to complete the maneuver, swinging her legs over the edge and dropping to the ground below, rolling when she landed. Back on her feet in moments, she moved toward the rear door while scanning the darkened windows. The night was silent save for the soft squishing of her soles on the spongy lawn. Jet was about to step up onto the back porch when she froze at the sight of a nearly invisible thread of monofilament strung twelve inches above the surface. It shimmered in the faint moonlight, the ends disappearing behind the support posts on either side.

Jerry hadn't mentioned anything about rigging the house with tripwires, but that didn't mean he hadn't when he'd left on the mission. The question was whether it was more likely that Indonesian intelligence had set a trap for her – which she had no way of answering.

She looked around the yard, and her eyes locked on a small box on the far side of the yard: a motion detector.

The Doberman tied to the pole on the other street, which had fallen silent, suddenly began barking again, its yapping urgent in a way it hadn't been when it had challenged the other mutt. The sound eliminated any hesitation for Jet, and she spun and sprinted for the rear wall again as fast as her legs would carry her. She was up and over it in a heartbeat and tore toward the gate, any concerns about waking those inside gone at the prospect of being caught.

She repeated her vaulting maneuver over the iron barrier and took off down the street, a blur in the darkness, her plastic bags abandoned by the garbage. If she was right and the Indonesian intelligence service had laid a trap, they would be on her in moments; the only elements working in her favor were her tradecraft and the overall lack of illumination.

Jet would have loved to believe that because there was nobody in the yard now, anyone checking would assume it had been a false alarm – a cat or other animal that had triggered the motion detector – but because of the damp ground she was sure she'd left footprints a blind man could follow. The thought drove her to greater speed, and she ducked around the corner at the next intersection as the sound of tires squealing on the street behind her confirmed her worst suspicions.

Jet ran like the devil was on her tail, covering the long block in under thirty seconds. The faint glow of headlights blinked off the windows of the houses in front of her as she reached the far street, and she veered hard right. Another block, and then another, and she slowed, unable to keep up the pace. At the next intersection the neighborhood transitioned into a commercial district, with markets and restaurants and a scattering of pedestrians ambling along the sidewalks, and she resumed her decrepit beggar stride, keeping her head down, hands clenched into fists by her sides like she was mentally unbalanced. If anyone took notice of the filth on the cheap clothes she'd bought at an outdoor vendor earlier, deliberately selecting the least expensive and darkest of the oversized tops and pants, they didn't show it, and she focused on quieting her trip-hammering heart and heavy breathing, confident she'd eluded her pursuers – for now.

The phone in her pocket vibrated, and she felt for it as she turned down an alley with a strong odor from the garbage overflowing the dumpsters. When she answered, Rami's voice sounded tense, his words clipped.

"Get to Halim Perdanakusuma airport, south of town. There's a prop plane waiting for a night flight to Singapore. Someone from the embassy will meet you when you land with a fresh passport."

"I went by the safe house. It was compromised. Either a leak, or someone talked after being captured."

"Damn." He paused, considering the information. "Doesn't change anything. You'll be off the island as soon as you can get to the airport."

"They'll have my passport. With a photo."

"Which is why we took it in the wig and makeup. Just wear your hair differently and you'll be fine."

"It may not be so easy if they circulate it outside the country."

"We can't worry about that now. Get moving."

Rami hung up, and Jet nodded to herself. She had enough money to pay for a taxi, but not much more. Which hopefully was all she would need. She looked around the alley and pocketed the phone, and then pulled off the oversized pants, keeping the potato sack of a shirt on. Jet tossed the pants into a garbage can and went in search of a cab, relieved that Rami had come through for her in the clinch, even if he sounded morose at doing so.

An hour later she was strapped into the seat of a single-engine Cessna 172 Skyhawk that was rolling toward the runway, piloted by a local who hadn't said a word since her arrival. The engine revved and the plane began its run, pressing her back in the seat, and within ten minutes of hitting cruising altitude, she was asleep, her energy depleted by the long day's ordeals.

CHAPTER 29

Jet sat in an apartment on the outskirts of Singapore, waiting for Rami's arrival. A runner had met her at the private charter terminal and given her a new passport when she'd landed, and she'd cleared immigration without any problem. The clerk had barely given her new ID a glance, the photo one of the rejects she'd taken for the Italian one, which Israel had sent via email to Singapore for printing and processing. In this French document, which appeared genuine to her, she'd been fitted with a different wig, lighter in color, and appeared more Asian, her makeup adjusted to make her look younger. Her birthdate in the passport put her at twenty-five, which was believable given her fitness if she wore no makeup.

The runner had dropped her off at the building with a key and a scrap of paper with the apartment number scribbled on it. Upon her arrival she had found the refrigerator well stocked and made herself a sandwich. The fruit juice in a plastic bottle was fresh, and the cold water she'd washed it down with as quenching as any she could remember. She'd dozed off after eating, and had started awake five hours later with barely enough time to shower before Rami was due – and he was now late.

She sighed and blinked away her fatigue, the last week weighing heavy on her. Then she rose and made her way to the living room window to pace. The city's gleaming steel and glass skyline in the distance was blinding in the morning sun, and beyond the cluster of towering buildings the Singapore Strait glowed a deep cobalt blue.

The sound of a key in the door stopped her. It swung open and Rami entered, carrying a messenger bag and a briefcase. He looked her up and down and then nodded a greeting. The dusting of beard on his face and dark circles beneath his eyes spoke to a sleepless night.

"Got here in one piece, I see," he commented, taking a seat across the coffee table from the sofa. She sat facing him and met his gaze.

"You too."

"We got the casualty information from a contact in the police department. Jerry was killed, Ben is in intensive care and likely won't make it, and Saul is in stable condition."

"And the mother?"

"Also dead."

"So bad all around."

"No question."

"You track down Wally?"

"Negative. But your instinct is probably correct. He sold us out." Rami paused. "I want you to know I'm not holding you responsible for this op. The failure is mine."

"What about the daughter?"

"Hasn't surfaced yet. But she will, I'm sure. If she's smart, she'll demand political asylum. She'll be put in a prison camp, or worse, if the North Koreans get their hands on her."

"Was the information you got out of her of any value?"

He exhaled and sat forward. "Yes. But we need it all. There's a lot at stake here."

"I gathered."

"You don't know the half of it."

She shrugged. "I'm used to that."

"I'm here to brief you on what's happening and ask you to help us finish this operation."

"Finish it? I'd say it's pretty finished now, wouldn't you?"

"We raided a warehouse in China yesterday. We'd gotten word that a terrorist in Pakistan has purchased a weapon of mass destruction and is preparing to use it against Israel." He let that sink in. It was the worst-case scenario anyone could think of. "The Korean woman's information enabled us to track it to the warehouse, but we got there too late. However, there was evidence of what we're dealing with, and it confirms that it's bad. A bioweapon. Probably a virus or a nerve agent. North Korean."

"How do you know it's a bioweapon? From the document she gave you?"

"That, and refrigeration. They had to keep it cold. There are a number of scenarios our people have run with what we got from the Korean document, and none of them are good. If a biological weapon gets deployed within our borders, it would be catastrophic – the end of Israel. Our enemies would be emboldened, and the Palestinians would seize the opportunity to create pandemonium." He paused. "We can't allow that to happen. We need to understand what we're dealing with, as well as find out when it's going to be deployed, and where."

"I have a feeling I'm not going to like this part," she said.

"Probably not. The only way we're going to be able to stop the attack is to get our hands on the other half of the information. Which is in North Korea. In the mother's apartment."

Jet's eyes narrowed. "You want me to go to North Korea?"

Rami nodded. "The director asked. He wants you to call him if you have any doubts."

"Doubts? Let's start with how do I get into the most paranoid and cloistered country on the planet?"

"There's a tour group going there tomorrow morning. You can be part of it. We can handle the paperwork. Once you're in Pyongyang, you can sneak into her apartment and canvas it."

"That's it? That's the plan? Sneak in?"

"The attack is going to take place within the next week, tops, based on what we've picked up. We're out of time. For an operative like you, breaking into an apartment and finding a CD or USB drive should be a piece of cake."

"You don't even know what I'm looking for?"

"It won't be hard copy. If she has a computer, we'll give you equipment to scan it, but that's a long shot. What's likely to happen is that you check all the usual places, and when you run across something promising, take it."

"How do I get into the apartment?"

"We'll supply everything you need. Comm gear, lock picks, anything else you require."

"And how do I get out once I have it?"

"You'll get sick. You're a tourist, and once you're ill, you'll demand to go back to South Korea. They have no reason to keep you."

"What do you know about North Korea?"

He opened his briefcase and pulled out a thick binder. "Everything. Here's a primer. Light reading."

"I haven't said I'll go."

Rami frowned. "You have to. We don't have a plan B. You're it."

"That's not encouraging."

"You should call the director." Rami removed a scrambled cell phone and placed it beside the binder.

She powered the phone on and Rami instructed her to press redial. She did, and the director's voice came on the line on the second ring, sounding even crustier than usual.

"You made it," he said.

"Barely."

"Rami's filled you in?"

"On the flying-by-the-seat-of-your-pants excuse for an operation? Yes."

"Did he make it clear that we have no alternatives?"

"He did."

The director must have been able to intuit from her tone that she wasn't especially receptive to the idea, because he went straight for the jugular, demonstrating why he was the head of the Mossad. "I want you to take a second and think about your daughter, as well as your mate. If a bioweapon is released, they'll be among the probable casualties. We both know that. Tel Aviv will be a key target, as will Jerusalem. So if you won't do this for me, do it for them."

"You understand my reluctance? Getting myself killed in a harebrained scheme won't help them either, or anyone. And this fits that description, if anything does."

145

"Your odds of success are far higher than if you were operating with a team. You work best solo, anyway. This gives you a chance to take whatever action you like, as long as it's effective. There's never been a more critical mission. We both know that."

Jet frowned and closed her eyes, thinking. The director pressed his hand.

"Your daughter. Hannah, isn't it? A beautiful name. Finally safe, in her homeland. You have to want that to continue, don't you?"

Jet's eyes snapped open. "Is that a threat?"

"Of course not. We're far beyond threats, aren't we? I wouldn't ask you to do this if there were any choice in the matter. But there isn't, and there is no way I can accept a no. I don't want to, but I'll do whatever I have to in order to see that Israel isn't decimated by these animals. Including your daughter. Make no mistake: her life, and those of millions of others – that's what's hanging in the balance."

Jet took a calming breath. "You really have no soul, do you?" she whispered. Rami's eyes widened at her words, but she ignored him.

"I sold it long ago," he agreed.

"After this, I've done enough."

"I agree. I won't call you again unless it is a matter of national survival."

She closed her eyes again and exhaled loudly. "You win," she whispered. "I'll do it."

There was no victory in the director's tone, no chortling or satisfaction, just the sound of a very tired old man who'd outstayed his time on the planet and had seen all the misery and malfeasance of the ages. When he spoke, his voice was uncharacteristically soft. "Nietzsche warned those who fight monsters to be careful that they don't themselves become monsters in the process. Sometimes the abyss is too close. I hope you never have to fully appreciate what I'm saying."

"You're too late."

"Perhaps. But not for Hannah. Do this for her."

"That's the only reason."

There was a long pause, and she could hear the snapping of his lighter as he lit another in the endless stream of cigarettes that would be the death of him – something he had to be aware of, yet was powerless to control.

"I know."

CHAPTER 30

Pyongyang, North Korea

Jet stood in a queue at Pyongyang Sunan International Airport, a Soviet-era building as depressing as any she'd been in. Her fellow tour members were a hodgepodge of French and Italians, most older pensioners, with a few younger couples. Jet was the only young woman, which aroused considerable attention from the four male immigration clerks as the line slowly made its way toward them.

Jet had spent most of the prior day preparing for her new assignment, checking her specialized gear to ensure it was acceptable and couldn't be detected in the carry-on bag Rami had obtained – the equipment designed by the Mossad technicians to appear to be part of the collapsible handle and roller system.

When it was her turn, she approached the open station and presented her passport and visa, the latter freshly minted and showing in the North Korean system as genuine – a tribute to the Mossad hackers who had access to most government networks in the world, as did the major intelligence services in the U.S., Russia, China, and the EU.

The clerk scrutinized her passport page by page to check her travel history and then studied her visa like she was wearing a jacket with an American flag emblazoned across the back. Green-uniformed soldiers with machine guns stood at every doorway, all eyes on her as she waited for the clerk to finish his screening. Eventually he nodded and reluctantly stamped her passport, as though disappointed he couldn't find anything unusual, and motioned to the next in line – a German couple in their sixties from Frankfurt.

Jet proceeded to the customs area, where her things were

subjected to a rigorous search by two serious men wearing latex gloves. She'd been assured that the airport's X-ray scanners were nonfunctional, so her gear wouldn't show up on a screen, but she was still nervous about the in-depth check the men performed with practiced hands. The inspection seemed to take longer than she'd noted for the other members of the tour; every item of clothing and her hygiene kit were removed and rummaged through before being returned to the bag, again with seeming regret at not discovering a grenade or kilo of cocaine.

Once out of the airport, the group was met by their tour guide and six minders – North Korean security force in plainclothes, it was obvious to all. They were escorted to a bus and loaded aboard, followed by their escorts, who displayed all the warmth of death row guards. The bus rolled from the terminal, and they were advised not to take photographs by their guide, who pointed out that the nation was under martial rule due to the state of war that had existed for over sixty years – and that any violation of the guidelines would be met with a harsh response.

Jet had heard about the Stalinesque attitude of the regime, but was too young to have encountered it firsthand in Russia on her missions there. The unfriendly attitude of all concerned matched the descriptions she had read about the former U.S.S.R., where there was no incentive to be nice or to deliver any better performance than the absolute minimum standard necessary for a job.

That was brought home when they crossed a bridge spanning a river and arrived at the hotel, one of the tallest buildings in North Korea, where the reception area staff's attitudes mirrored the guide and their escorts, their grudging demeanors clearly conveying they were not happy with their lots in life. The woman who checked Jet in never cracked a smile and, when she demanded that Jet turn her passport over, was actively unfriendly, holding out her hand impatiently. Jet presented the document with misgivings, even though she'd expected the request – without it, she wouldn't be able to leave the country, which limited her options once she found the data in the mother's apartment. She'd brought that up to Rami, but he'd dismissed the concern, assuring her that there was no reason for the North Koreans to have the apartment under surveillance or to suspect anyone would break in, so if Jet were careful, she'd have no issue.

Which had sounded great to a control officer in Singapore, but not so much to Jet now that she was knee-deep in the mission. That impression strengthened when a bellboy escorted her to the elevator and she was followed in by a man in a suit who had no name tag or other identification. He got off on her floor — the third, which she'd requested ostensibly due to her fear of heights — and then had a murmured discussion with another suited man seated by the elevator while Jet was shown to her room.

As soon as the room door was closed, she did a visual sweep of the interior, looking for obvious hiding places for a hidden camera. She didn't spot anything, but couldn't rule out the possibility and would have to assume she was being filmed. She dutifully removed her clothes and hung them in the closet, and then rolled her suitcase to the bathroom to unpack her hygiene bag.

Once out of sight of the main room, she studied the vent fan and the mirror, and when she was satisfied that she wasn't being observed, quickly dismantled the bag and recovered her gear: a miniature sat phone with a USB port and shockproof screen, a set of lock picks, a carbon-fiber knife, ten Chinese one-ounce gold coins, a penlight LED flashlight with a single tiny battery in its handle, a waterproof pack for it all, and a tiny composite semiautomatic pistol, the only metal parts the three-inch barrel, sound suppressor, and ten subsonic 9mm rounds — all integrated into the bag's handle mechanism. She stowed it all into the waterproof pack and fit the kit into a cavity beneath the sink, reassembled the suitcase, and returned to the main room before padding to the window to take in the view across the river.

Jet's true interest was not the city with its distinctive glass pyramid jutting skyward into a haze of pollution but rather the window latching mechanism and the exterior of the hotel, which she'd studied in the satellite photos Rami had obtained for her. After confirming that the photos of the hotel had accurately portrayed the construction, she turned to the bed and, with a yawn, threw herself down on it. She had four hours before she was expected at a welcome dinner in the hotel restaurant, where the guide would go over the itinerary with the group for the next week's activities as well as more do's and don'ts for their stay, which Jet suspected consisted primarily of don'ts.

She slept for three hours. Upon waking, she luxuriated in a hot shower before dressing in a loose blouse and baggy cargo pants, her equipment pack strapped out of sight around her waist in case an opportunity to lose the security personnel presented itself at the dinner. Jet was keenly aware that she was working on a compressed timeline and planned to make her move that night. Her interest in remaining in North Korea was nil, and she would present with all the symptoms of food poisoning by daybreak and insist on being ferried home early regardless of what assurances the local physicians gave. Given that medicine was in short supply due to the embargos, Rami hadn't viewed it as likely that the North Koreans would insist on her remaining, and if all went according to plan, by midday she would be winging her way to Seoul and from there back to Singapore, none the worse for her forty-eight-hour detour.

The restaurant at the penthouse level was surprisingly modern, the fare a combination of local cuisine and the tasteless chicken and pork dishes that passed for continental on the menu. Jet picked at her food, opting for the local seafood in a mild ginger and soy sauce, and made small talk with the German couples on either side of her, noting that there appeared to be one security man for every six tourists – a ratio that was anything but reassuring. The guide waited until everyone had finished their main course before standing and launching into another cautionary speech, praising the government for the happiness of its people and for doing as well as it had in the face of Western imperialist oppression that had gone on for longer than most of them had been alive.

When he was done extolling the virtues of the leadership, he then recited a long list of off-limits actions, including unauthorized photography, the taking or defacing of any signs, political agitation – which could easily include any critical comments about the government or leadership or the conditions in any of the areas they traveled – and on and on.

No opportunity to lose the security guards manifested during the speech, by the end of which Jet wasn't alone in appearing to want to be finished with the experience. The group broke up, a few lingering over strong local beer, and Jet took her leave. Her security guard shadow accompanied her to the elevator and down to her floor, and watched until she had disappeared into her room before returning to the restaurant, his obligation to monitor her now passed to the seated man.

CHAPTER 31

Jet took her time undressing and preparing for bed. The room was dark, only faint light seeping from the sides of thick blackout curtains, which hopefully rendered any camera in the room a nonissue. She would have been wary of infrared or night-vision-equipped technology anywhere else in the world, but from what she had seen of the general repair of the systems in her short time in North Korea, that wouldn't be an issue for routine surveillance of tourist rooms.

After two and a half hours of pretend slumber, she crept from the bed and crawled to the bathroom, where she donned her black top and pants in the dark, stepped into her running shoes, and strapped her equipment pack in place. She debated removing the pistol and slipping it into her waistband, but would wait until after she'd gotten free of the hotel grounds – for now, she needed everything secured tightly to her body so she could move with unfettered mobility. Jet had eight hours of expected sleep time in which to make it to the apartment, locate the goods, and return to the hotel without being detected. With dawn coming at 6:40, she really had only five hours if she allowed a reasonable margin of error, so she'd need to work as fast as she'd ever done in her life.

She crawled around the foot of the bed to the curtains and passed beneath them, taking care not to jar them and allow more light to enter the room. Jet used a coin to unscrew the locking mechanism that kept the sliding window from opening, and after working the threaded bolt free, eased the glass to the side, grateful that there was so little traffic noise; cars and trucks were a rarity with a destitute population that walked or rode bicycles everywhere.

Jet surveyed the deserted area around the base of the hotel as well as the lobby, where any activity would be concentrated at the late hour on the other side of the building. She watched for ten minutes, immobile as a statue, and when she didn't see anyone patrolling the grounds, turned to face the room and lowered her body down the structure's side. When her legs were hanging below her, she extended her arms until her feet were twenty feet above the grass, and then swung her legs left, pumping with her arms to gain momentum. When they swung back like a pendulum she repeated the maneuver, and her legs moved as though of their own accord. At the high point of the swing she released her hold on the window and reached for a metal beam four feet away, one of hundreds that were a design feature of the exterior of the thirty-story hotel.

Her hands locked onto it and she clamped her knees against the steel. After a beat, she inched down until she was only ten feet from the ground and pushed herself away from the building. She landed on the grass and rolled and was up and running for the gloomy area at the periphery of the parking lot in a blink, which contained a handful of official vehicles parked beneath the tall lamps that struggled to illuminate the expanse. When she reached the hedgerow at the edge of the lot, she glanced back at the hotel, a blackened monolith rising into the night sky. Only a few rooms glowed with lights behind heavily tinted glass.

The bridge she would have to cross stretched over the twisting current of the Taedong River, and she jogged toward it. The island was devoid of traffic at this hour, and her racing figure the only one on the approach to the four-lane span. She slowed as she neared and then ducked behind a tree at the sight of two soldiers with rifles sitting at the bridge entrance, near a shelter that hadn't been visible on the satellite images – which Rami had admitted were dated when he'd presented her with them.

"Great," she muttered to herself. With the men there, she wasn't going to be able to cross on the pavement, which left either trying to swim the river or finding another way. She peered into the shadows at the base of the bridge and saw rungs leading up a piling from the water's edge. After a moment's hesitation, she skirted the bridge on-ramp and made her way down the bank of the river, and then crept along the rocky soil toward the bridge, hoping that the guards were watching the bridge and not the rush of the river.

Her foot slipped as she neared the piling and she nearly splashed into the water, saving herself at the last minute but straining her ankle – which had been reminding her of her earlier sprain, which wasn't fully healed. She choked down the pain and righted herself and continued to the piling. The rusting rungs led up to a maintenance walkway that disappeared among a tangle of pipes and cables.

Jet pulled herself up to the catwalk, which while rickety, seemed stable enough to support her, and crept forward, ducking when snarls of cables hung across her way; the mountings that held them in place had long since been eroded by the elements. Near the halfway point, she felt the catwalk wobble beneath her and grabbed one of the pipes just as a section collapsed beneath her and dropped into the froth fifty feet below. She swallowed hard and pulled herself along the pipe hand over hand, her feet dangling in open air before reaching the other side of the gap. Jet made a mental note to remember the approximate location for her return trip and tested her weight on the platform. When it held, she proceeded to the far side, beads of sweat dotting her brow as she felt her way forward.

At the far bank, Jet lowered herself down an identical set of pilings. Once on the shore, she skirted the water until she was far enough from the bridge that she wouldn't be seen if there were another guard outpost on this side of the bridge. She scrambled up the bank and, at the crest of the natural terrain where the slope met the road, peeked over the strip of asphalt but saw no soldiers, which confirmed for her that the guards were to keep the foreigners on their hotel island, not intruders out. When she was sure that the approach was deserted, she brushed the rust and grime from her pants and climbed the rest of the way up the bank, increasing her speed once she was on the road that led north.

Jet came to a darkened building and stopped in the doorway, loosened her pack, and extracted the little pistol and the sound suppressor. She threaded the silencer onto the end of the barrel, hefted the weapon, and slid it into her waistband. Her fingers felt in the pack for the carbon-fiber knife in its leather sheath and slipped it into her back pocket, the handle barely protruding above the edge. After another check of her surroundings to confirm she was unobserved, she removed the sat phone and powered it on. As it was acquiring a signal, she thumbed the map of the city she'd uploaded in Singapore onto the screen, the woman's building clearly marked.

A moment later, a blue dot identified her present position. After verifying the most direct route to the mother's building, she powered the phone off and dropped it into one of her side cargo pockets and cinched the pack back into place. She threw a final glance up the street to ensure she was still alone and took off at a moderate pace.

The apartment was only a mile and a half away, and if her luck held, she would arrive at her destination in less than a half hour, with plenty of time to search the apartment and make it back to the hotel before daybreak.

But given that nothing had gone as planned in any part of the ongoing debacle so far, her hopes weren't high that things would suddenly turn positive, and she steeled herself for the worst as she worked her way up the block, leaving the hotel and the bridge in the distance, the weight of the pistol slim comfort as she crept through the muggy night toward a complete unknown.

CHAPTER 32

Jet was only a few blocks from the apartment when she turned a corner and nearly ran headfirst into a policeman, startling him almost as much as herself with the near miss. She mumbled and stepped out of his way, but he barked something in Korean that needed no translation – he was demanding either her papers or to know what she was doing on the street at that hour.

Her lack of familiarity with the language would be a giveaway that she was a foreigner who was forbidden to be out after the curfew time, so she did the only thing she could think of, which was to moan a nonresponse and point to her ears and mouth, signaling through pantomime that she was deaf and mute. The cop's eyes narrowed and he spoke slowly, holding out his hand in obvious demand, pointing with the other.

Jet nodded as though understanding, reached into her back pocket while adopting a puzzled expression, and then whipped the knife free of its sheath and drove it into the man's neck, catching him by surprise. Jet stepped away as he clawed at the handle and pulled the blade free, having anticipated the geyser of blood that accompanied the removal, the carotid artery severed exactly as she'd intended. The cop's knees buckled and he slumped to the sidewalk in a pool of blood, and Jet waited to retrieve her blade until the pulsing had ceased. She pried it from his fingers and wiped it clean on his jacket, and then confiscated the pistol in his belt and his spare magazines, reasoning that it couldn't hurt to have more firepower in the event of a problem.

A quick scan of the surrounding buildings revealed no lights on, so for the moment, at least, she was in the clear. The problem being that once the cop's absence was discovered, her ability to make it back to the hotel through the inevitable mobilization of security forces would be nearly nonexistent.

She grabbed the man's feet and dragged him toward an alley, and then heaved him into the narrow passageway, surprised by how thin he was beneath his uniform. Slick black forms scurried away from the reeking garbage bins that lined the alley walls, and Jet waited until the rats had left before hauling the cop to the nearest half-full container and unceremoniously dumping him in, stuffing a sack of refuse on top in order to conceal the corpse.

The blood was a problem, but given the streets were so empty, she hoped that it wouldn't be discovered until she'd searched the apartment and was on her way back to the island. She had no way of cleaning it up, so she couldn't worry about it – all she could do was conclude her mission before the city center went berserk looking for the killer. She didn't know much about crime statistics in North Korea, but after seeing the military presence and the cowed demeanors of the population, she guessed that violent crime against police would be somewhere near nonexistent, which would make the murder even more alarming and demand an immediate, substantial response.

A glance at the sky heartened her somewhat – a squall line over the Yellow Sea to the west pulsed with lightning, promising a chance of rain before the night was through. If the summer storm blew inland, it might wash away the blood, or at the very least keep people off the street until it passed. Jet checked the time and forced herself to stop obsessing over things that she couldn't control, like the weather. She'd lost precious minutes dispatching the cop and disposing of his body, and time wasn't her friend – she needed to complete her task. She could worry about the fallout later.

She peered around the corner of the building, frowning again at the bloody trail she'd left on the sidewalk, and then darted to the corner and across the street, only minutes from the apartment if she wasn't interrupted again. Jet made it to the end of the block, sticking to the shadows, and stopped at the intersection, head cocked, listening for approaching vehicles. Hearing nothing, she sprinted across the six-lane thoroughfare and continued to Sang-mi's building – a seven-story structure that occupied most of the block, the grounds modest but neatly trimmed and the windows dark as night.

Rami had learned that the apartment in question was on the third floor, but had no other intel on the building, the Mossad having no local assets in North Korea to scout the area. Jet backed into a doorway across the street and eyed the front façade. The main entryway was as black as pitch, and there was no sign of any guard at the glass security door. She knew from the satellite imagery that the building was a horseshoe shape built around a central courtyard with a play area and benches, but beyond that had been left to guess the best approach. Now, studying the main entrance, her instinct was to circle the building and see if there was a back way in – she didn't fancy having to pick a lock in full view of the street, with a cop's blood on her boots.

Jet walked slowly, painfully aware that she was the only thing moving and thus open game for anyone patrolling the area, and she kept her movements subdued so as not to draw attention if any insomniacs were gazing out their windows instead of counting sheep. She spotted a tall wall with iron spikes along the top at the corner that sealed the courtyard from the street – but scaling it was not an option, given its smooth surface.

Further along, the outlook improved when she spied a row of dumpsters along a gated access way. A fire escape leading up to the roof hung above them, with landings in front of oversized windows at each floor. She trotted to the dumpsters, studied the bottom of the fire escape, and considered the sheer brick façade. After testing the joints between the bricks, where the mortar had long ago worn away, she resigned herself to clawing her way up to the landing, inch by painful inch, using finger and toeholds.

Jet climbed onto one of the dumpsters and estimated that she only had to make it ten feet before she'd be able to grab the bottom of the fire escape and hoist herself the rest of the way up. If the platform had been just a little lower, she could have used one of her Parkour running scrambles, but she knew her limits, and given the height, that maneuver wouldn't work.

She felt along the bricks until she found a promising initial hold and, when her fingers were wedged in the gap, felt with her other hand until she found another, and then repeated the search with her toes until she was supporting herself using the wall. She reached higher and probed the surface and, when she had an adequate grip on the new brick edge, pulled herself up eight inches, her right shoe searching for a hold until she found an adequate depression and could do the same with her other hand.

The painstaking ascent took ten minutes, with two close calls when she almost fell into the dumpster, and by the time her hands locked onto the base of the ladder that extruded from the landing, her arms were trembling from the effort and her fingers were numb. She willed herself to a final burst of energy and dragged herself onto the landing, and then lay, panting, waiting for the lactic acid to seep from her muscles so she could continue.

When she'd recovered, a glance through the window confirmed that she was at the end of a long, unlit hall. She tried to open it, but it wouldn't budge, and she didn't want to risk breaking the glass if she could avoid it. Jet mounted the steps to the third-floor landing and tried again, but found it locked as well, as was the fourth floor and the fifth. She hit pay dirt on the sixth, where a broken latch rewarded her effort with a creak and the frame slid upward, and then she was through the opening, creeping along the hall toward the inevitable interior stairway that would provide access for the residents.

She turned a corner, noting the numbers on the apartment doors, and spotted an elevator with a stairwell to one side. Jet darted to the steps and hurried down them as fast as she dared in the nearly total darkness, keenly aware that the cop's body could be found at any moment. When she reached the third floor, she stopped and listened intently. When she heard nothing but her own breathing, she eased into the corridor, confident that the woman's apartment would be one of the last in the row on the right if the numbering sequence was the same as the higher floors. At the second-to-last door she paused, checking the number to confirm she was breaking into the right dwelling, and then knelt down and felt in her pack for the pick set, the bulge of the policeman's pistol at the small of her back a reminder that she was operating on borrowed time.

CHAPTER 33

Jet slipped a thin pick into the lock and then worked a flat one in, exerting steady twisting pressure while running the first pick along the tumblers. The lock succumbed to her efforts within sixty seconds. The click of the bolt releasing sounded as loud as a gunshot to Jet's ear in the empty hall. She stood, pushed the door open, and stepped inside, closing the door behind her and locking it again so she wouldn't be disturbed.

She removed the penlight from her pack and switched it on, and did a quick survey of the tiny apartment, which consisted of a kitchen, living and dining area, and single bedroom with an adjoining bathroom – the entire area no more than six hundred square feet, if that. She was surprised to see an ancient PC and workstation in a corner of the living room, and wasted no time powering it on, waiting anxiously as the clunky hard drive whirred through the boot process.

The logo of the North Korean operating system, Red Star OS, glowed on the screen, and after a pause, a crude graphical desktop blinked to life. Jet retrieved the sat phone, thumbed it to life, and connected it to the computer's only USB port with a thin cable. She selected an icon on the phone that would instruct it to read the contents of the disk and isolate anything that might match their criteria, and then went to work in the kitchen to begin the physical search of the apartment while the device performed the cyber version on the computer.

The freezer held only a few plastic-wrapped bundles of meat and vegetables, and the shelves of the refrigerator section were nearly bare, not many places to conceal a disk or a dongle. She dutifully emptied every jar in case the woman had hidden a flash drive inside one, but found nothing. Jet moved to the drawers and rummaged through them, using the flashlight to inspect the insides of the cabinets after pulling the drawers free, also to no avail. When she was finished with the carpentry she moved to the oven and then the cooktop, working quickly but efficiently, leaving nothing to chance.

Next came the bedroom, which posed no great challenge, given the dearth of furniture – just a bed and chest of drawers by a tiny closet with a handful of cheap garments dangling from wire hangers, awaiting an owner who would never return. She removed the drawers first, repeating her inspection from the kitchen, and then dismantled the bed, searching the mattress and then the frame, but found nothing but dust bunnies and a few dead cockroach husks.

The closet likewise yielded no trove, and a thorough search of the bathroom was equally fruitless. After inspecting the toilet tank and studying the bowl to confirm no monofilament dangled into its depths, she concluded with a frustrated exhalation.

"So much for this being easy," she whispered, and moved to the computer desk in search of something with which to unscrew the electric outlet plates – a common hiding place, she knew from her training. She found a letter opener that would do and slid the workstation away from the wall, but stopped when a photo dropped to the floor from where it had fallen down the back of the desk and caught on the lip. Jet held it under the flashlight beam and frowned. It was a photo of the daughter, maybe two years younger, smiling at the camera in bright sunlight, her cheap mirrored aviator glasses and form-fitting yellow top nearly jumping out of the frame.

A beep from the sat phone announced that the scan of the PC was done, and Jet pocketed the photo and checked the little screen, where the icons for three possible files with cryptic names had been downloaded. She double tapped the first and shook her head – it was the daughter's visa application. The second was a scan of the mother's passport and travel documents, also of no interest to her. But the third was pay dirt, as far as she could tell – a collection of official documents in Korean, the government logo clear as day on the headers.

Jet switched the phone off and did the same with the computer, and then killed the little flashlight to allow her night vision to return. After a few moments, she left the apartment and made for the sixth floor, unwilling to chance running into anyone on her way out or, worse, being captured by a surveillance camera. She hadn't seen any in the halls, but the lobby would be the natural place for them.

At the window, she powered on the sat phone and waited for it to acquire a signal and, when it locked in, activated the code that would encrypt and transmit the file via satellite to Mossad headquarters. The icon indicating the send was in process blinked and pulsed just as sirens began howling from nearby.

Jet froze at the sound and then tore her eyes away from the screen to scan the street and the access way below. The sirens grew louder and were joined by several more as they neared, confirming for Jet that the dead officer had been discovered – and her egress from the city was about to get much more difficult.

"Come on," she whispered at the phone, unwilling to move until the download had completed, but aware that every moment at the fire escape increased the odds of her never making it out of North Korea. The sound of male voices from down the street drifted to her as the phone beeped softly to confirm a successful transmission, and she switched the device off and pulled back from the open window when several pairs of boots thumped by the access way. She caught a glimpse of running policemen out of the corner of her eye and slid the window into place so it wouldn't draw any attention, her mind working furiously.

There was no way she could sneak down the fire escape now, which left her with only one option: she'd have to walk out the front door when there was nobody on the street and take her chances on making it back to the hotel. Failing that, she'd have to make it up as she went along – if she wasn't in her room by dawn, there was no point in trying to return; her absence would be noted when she failed to respond to the obligatory wake-up call the guide had indicated she'd receive at seven, and after the security team had checked the room, she'd be incarcerated for the duration while the authorities tried to figure out how and especially why she'd snuck out of the hotel. Eventually her hastily prepared identity would come apart, and then she would be as good as dead. The file that had provided background on the country had also had plentiful cases of tourists who'd been jailed for a decade or more for things as trivial as removing a sign from a public place as a souvenir. She didn't need much imagination to grasp that entering the country for unknown reasons under a fake cover would be treated as espionage, which she was certain carried a stiffer penalty than did vandalism or theft.

The only question in Jet's mind was how swift the response would be to finding the cop's corpse. If she moved fast enough, she might be able to evade any patrols, but that window of opportunity was closing, and she was on the wrong side of it.

She returned to the stairs and took them two at a time. At the lobby, she saw the distinctive mirrored dome of a security camera and turned her head away, hair hanging over her face as she walked to the door, her posture as relaxed as possible. If anyone bothered to go through the footage, they might well miss her if she looked like a tired resident going outside to see what the commotion was all about.

Jet paused at the glass door, eyeing the street, and after several moments cracked it open and slipped through the gap. The volume of the sirens was even louder at ground level. Blue emergency beams strobed off the tops of buildings near the alley a few blocks away, and she pressed against the façade as lights in the apartments above her began illuminating.

Jet edged in the opposite direction from the crime scene and was nearly to the corner when shouts from the intersection spurred her into motion. A whistle shattered the night and she bolted for the smaller street she'd been inching toward, head down and legs pumping as she willed herself to a burst of extreme speed, a chorus of yells following her, any hope of escaping unnoticed abandoned.

CHAPTER 34

Herzliya, Israel

The director rose wearily and rounded his desk, pausing for a moment before a window with double-paned, one-way mirrored glass, to prevent scrutiny or laser listening devices from detecting the vibration caused by speech, or snipers from taking a shot at him. It was night, and the lights of the surrounding residential area glowed with a warmth he didn't feel, his concern over the future overwhelming all else.

He tapped out his hundredth cigarette of the day and lit it without thinking. The habit was one he was powerless to quit; his iron discipline in all other matters for whatever reason served him poorly in this one. He took a deep drag, the familiar burn deep in his lungs reassuring in a perverse way, as the constriction of his blood vessels and increase in his heart rate signaled to him that for now, at least, he was still among the living. For how much longer, he couldn't say, and had long ago resigned his expiration date to Fate. The business of surviving occupied all his waking hours, crowding out any worries about his health, no matter how warranted. He'd given up getting physicals when his doctor told him the same thing for five years running – his blood pressure was too high, his cholesterol through the roof, his exercise regimen nonexistent, his caffeine intake dangerous, and his smoking so toxic that it was a wonder he was still breathing.

The director viewed his body as he viewed everyone around him: a tool for serving a purpose, nothing more. He felt no attachment to the degrading pile of flesh and bones he pushed through space each day, and found the entropic process of aging horrifically fascinating in the same way that one might find it impossible to turn away from the spectacle of an anaconda smothering a goat – but, oddly, not at a personal level. His disassociation from his body had been a lifelong phenomenon, and he was sure that detachment was the same that enabled him to make decisions others might balk at for moral or ethical reasons. The director had no such compunctions. He was mission-driven, as were his operatives, and he thought strictly in terms of outcomes, not process.

The cigarette sputtered in his hand, and the paper crackled as he took a final drag before extinguishing it in a crystal ashtray he kept on the windowsill – one of four scattered around his office. He blinked away his fatigue and checked the time, and with a final glance at the homes no more than rock-throwing distance from the anonymous building that had served as Mossad headquarters for decades, he walked to his office door, his steps as ponderous and measured as a death row prisoner's on the way to the gallows.

His senior analysts and advisors were already gathered in the meeting room three stories below ground level. Their faces spoke to days without sleep; one of the occupational hazards of protecting Israel from the myriad enemies who devoted their lives to its destruction. The director rubbed a weary hand across the stubble on his chin and sat resignedly in the chair at the head of the conference table. He eyed the gathering and nodded to a man in his fifties to his right – Daniel, one of his inner circle, and a career Mossad officer.

"What have you got?" the director growled.

"We translated the documents, and it's as we feared. They detail payments to banks in the Caymans and Panama from known terrorist accounts in Switzerland and Dubai. The total is in the tens of millions of dollars. Reading between the lines, the money ultimately flowed to interests in China and North Korea."

"Any way to track them at a more granular level?"

"With time. This is just what was flagged from known hostile and criminal syndicate accounts."

The director glowered at Daniel. "You mention time."

"Yes, that's the most alarming part of the intercept. It mentions a date only a few days away."

The director sighed. "What is the significance of that date?"

Jacob glanced at one of the other attendees. "We're still trying to verify our conclusion."

The other man, in his late thirties, cleared his throat. "There are mentions of coordinates in Iran. Also in China. As you know, the Chinese location was raided by our operatives, and evidence was found of a refrigeration system, which confirms what was hinted at in the first tranche of the Korean documents. This second part identifies several dates, a payment scheme, and a location in Iran. It also has language that leads us to believe – and this is preliminary – that Iran isn't the final destination for the weapon."

"Of course it isn't," the director snapped. "We know where they intend to deploy it. We're sitting at ground zero."

Daniel sat forward. "There's also a mention of a final payment once the goods arrive at the distribution point. The way it's worded, there's no other conclusion than that the location is the one in Iran." He paused. "We know the account that's flagged for the final payment instruction. One of the Cayman accounts."

"Can we monitor it for activity?"

"We intend to reach out to our American friends for some assistance in that regard. As you know, the NSA surveils everyone in the world. They can flip a switch and watch that account real time. We'll hear within minutes of when the final payment hits, which will tell us that the goods, as they refer to them, have arrived in Iran…for distribution shortly thereafter."

The director nodded, his face creased in thought. "Then we have a window where we will be sure where the bioweapon is – before it's deployed."

Daniel returned the nod. "Correct. An admittedly short one."

"And you know the target date? But not where it is until then?"

"That's right. We're assuming the weapon is in transit to Iran. There could be any of a hundred different ways it is to arrive. As you know, Iranian smugglers are remarkably inventive."

The director grunted. He indeed knew all too well. An entire network had arisen after the U.S. sanctions imposed on the country had gone into effect. Many of those in the trade now had been working it for decades; some were second and third generation dynasties that had made fortunes circumventing the sanctions, either through Europe, Africa, Asia, or Russia. It was a hackneyed joke that the only thing the sanctions had ultimately accomplished for Iran was a question of price, not availability, just as they were seeing in Syria, with the outflows of oil stolen by ISIS and then mysteriously transported to Turkey and, from there, to Europe and even to unscrupulous brokers in Israel. In that case, stolen oil could be had for a third of the price of legitimately obtained oil. In Iran's case, goods cost more, but availability was guaranteed if you could meet the asking price.

"Those bastards are going for the kill," the director said, to no one in particular. Iran had been a thorn in his side as long as he'd been with the Mossad, and it didn't surprise him in the least that forces within that country would be conspiring to massacre millions in Israel.

Another man spoke up. "It certainly appears that way. There aren't many other explanations."

"Do we believe this is a state-sponsored effort on their part?"

Daniel shrugged and exchanged another glance with his younger associate. "Impossible to know at this point. But we can't rule it out. Of course they would go to great pains to mask any involvement."

The director's expression hardened. "Of course."

Daniel's tone matched the director's. "The date is mentioned as a target, nothing more. Obviously to allow some flexibility in shipment. But we consider it reliable, given the number of mentions that coincide with the Iran coordinates."

The director sighed, his frown deepening. "How certain are we that we are dealing with a bioweapon? Is it mentioned as such in the document?"

"The terms *toxic* and *contagious* are used in two places."

Silence settled over the room as the director absorbed the news. "Not many ways to interpret that, are there?"

"When taken with the Freon canisters we found in China, no, sir. There aren't."

"Then we are in agreement this is an existential threat to the nation?"

The question was a formality the director had to ask before meeting with the government officials to whom he answered. Everyone knew it, and everyone nodded.

"Any dissent?" he asked, waiting. Nobody spoke. The director looked to Daniel. "Let it be memorialized that we are going to contact the Americans for assistance monitoring the Cayman account, and that our official position at this point in time is that a bioweapon intended for dissemination within Israel's borders is on its way to Iran, where it will be distributed to terrorists with us as the target. The conclusion is unanimous and will be formalized by tomorrow's afternoon meeting." He raised an eyebrow. "That give you enough time?"

"We'll do our best." It was Daniel's turn to pause. "Obviously, there is a limited range of options that can neutralize the threat."

The director rose, throwing a dark gaze at the room. "Obviously. We can discuss those once I've briefed the Security Council. I'm sure they can guess them."

"We'll have to strike decisively."

The director waved the comment away. "That is above your pay grade to consider. All we can do is recommend." He walked to the door and turned to the table. "I need you to work through the night on this. I'll schedule a meeting to brief the council in the morning. We have to be one hundred and ten percent sure of our facts before I break the news, is that clear?"

Daniel stood and spoke for the group. "We'll do whatever it takes."

The director nodded to himself and twisted the door handle. "See to it."

The corridor to the elevators seemed perceptibly darker than when the director had entered, and his brow was furrowed with thought as he waited for one of the conveyances to arrive. The worst nightmare of an intelligence director in any country was a hostile getting control of a WMD and deploying it against the civilian population, and that unthinkable possibility had just become reality in the blink of an eye. The elevator arrived, and he stepped inside and pressed the ground-floor button, his fatigued mind racing at hyper-speed as he pondered the unimaginable and how the scenario was likely to play out.

"God help us all," he murmured under his breath, and leaned against the wall as the car rose in a whisper-silent ascent to take him back to his office and the sofa where he'd spent too many of his adult years sleeping instead of having a life – a sacrifice that, if he wasn't successful in neutralizing this threat, would prove to have been in vain.

An outcome he would not allow himself to consider.

CHAPTER 35

Jet heard the police cruiser before she saw it, the engine a menacing growl that reverberated along the empty street. She ducked into a doorway moments before it swung around the corner and prowled toward her like a hunting dog. The faces of the officers inside glowed pale green from the dashboard lights. Jet pressed against the wall, trying to become part of it, the dead cop's gun in hand in case her effort at dematerialization failed.

The car slowed as it neared, and she flicked the safety off the semiautomatic pistol in readiness. The vehicle's side-mounted spotlight played along the sidewalk on the other side of the street, sweeping across to her side with the regularity of a metronome. She held her breath, her pulse hammering in her ears, and waited for it to wash across her doorway, hopefully missing her because of the angle – unless it shone straight into the entryway as the car passed directly across from her.

She heard a voice blare over the radio from the cruiser's open windows, and then the spotlight switched off and the car accelerated with a squeal of rubber on slick pavement. Jet waited until its brake lights had disappeared into the next street before inhaling deeply and engaging the safety on the pistol. The near miss was a harsh reminder of how precarious her position was, and the wail of more sirens in the distance announced that it wasn't going to get better anytime soon.

Jet was running out of choices as the minutes ticked by. If she couldn't evade increasing patrols, her only option was to find somewhere to hole up during the day and attempt to make it to the border at night – a prospect that was as unappealing as it was dangerous. The DMZ was mined and heavily fortified, with motion detectors and infrared a certainty. She'd be better served putting the cop's gun in her mouth and pulling the trigger; at least that would be quicker than months of torture in a North Korean prison.

She banished the negative thoughts and focused on getting clear of the neighborhood before any more police appeared. Even with her skills, it would be impossible to remain undiscovered for long if there were a cruiser on every block.

The rumble of a heavy motor greeted her when she turned onto the next street, and she threw herself behind two garbage cans as an old army personnel truck with at least a dozen soldiers standing in the rear roared toward her from a larger boulevard a hundred yards away, the driver pushing the heavy vehicle as fast as it would go over the potholed asphalt. She curled into a ball and kept her head down so her hair would cover her face lest her pale skin give her away to a vigilant soldier, as all the while the adrenaline coursing through her veins argued to run for it rather than wait for a bullet.

The truck bore down on her and she gagged at the pool of putrescence she was lying in, one of the cans leaking a viscous seepage that reeked of rotting cabbage and fish. The headlights wobbled and then the truck was past her, springs creaking as it bounced along, the men in the rear holding on for dear life. It slowed as it neared the next intersection and then careened around the corner, leaving a trail of exhaust in its wake.

Jet rose, her nose wrinkling at the stink rising from her clothes, and coughed before brushing the worst of the detritus from her shirt. She shifted her pack to a more comfortable position and resumed her run.

Fifteen minutes later it was obvious that the North Koreans were putting in serious effort to seal off the area, and she would need a minor miracle to escape the dragnet. She'd dodged three more police cars, each a near miss, and was losing hope with each encounter, as the sound of more heavy military trucks filled the night. On an even playing field she was anyone's match, but a thousand to one were odds too tall even for her.

She was nearing the end of another block when the sound of

another big truck approached from behind her, and she dodged into a doorway, guns in both hands, fearing that this was the point where her good fortune ran out. This vehicle was moving much more slowly, and she tensed as it neared, her jaw clenched so hard her teeth ached.

A clatter and a grinding rumble brought a frown to her face, and she peeked around the doorway edge. The vehicle was hard to make out in the darkness, but she could see the distinctive outline of…a garbage truck with a man hanging from the passenger side, riding on the running board. He leapt off and scooped up a brimming can, and the truck slowed further as he rounded the rear and dumped the contents in before returning to the running board. The crushing mechanism ground laboriously from the back, and the garbage man called to the driver with a laugh.

Jet waited for the truck to roll past her, the men oblivious to her presence, and when it sped up to get to the next cans, she secured the pistols in her waistband and bolted from the doorway. She was at the truck in moments and grabbed the bar handle that ran from top to bottom of the frame of the collection maw and swung up onto the flat rear bumper without missing a beat. A glance up revealed enough footholds to support her, and she pulled herself upward using the bar, barely making it to the top of the trash superstructure before it slowed again and she heard the collector jump to the pavement for another can.

She inched forward, counting the seconds, and then the truck increased speed again and the crushing mechanism went to work. Jet was able to remain in position, flat against the top with her fingers locked on the rim, out of sight of anyone on the street level as the truck crawled along its route.

Two blocks later it stopped, and she heard voices and saw telltale blue emergency lights winking in the darkness. The cops at the roadblock spoke with the driver and then waved the truck through, the stink of the cargo enough to make anyone sane want it moving downwind as soon as possible. Jet breathed through her mouth, refusing to give in to the urge to vomit, reasoning that the ordeal was still better than having her fingernails torn out or her skin seared off.

After two hours of stop and go and three more checkpoints, the truck picked up speed, barreling along at a blistering twenty miles per hour. Jet had no idea where it was headed, but as long as it wasn't the city center, she was ahead of the game. She dared a glance at her watch and saw that she only had a few more hours before dawn, so unless it was driving directly to her island, she would have to come up with an alternative plan that didn't involve her passport or the hotel.

What that was, she had no idea; but she'd gotten out of worse situations before and would find a way to do so again.

The road worsened, and single-story dwellings replaced the towering buildings of the city. Jet caught a glimpse of countryside in the darkness and a smattering of unpainted concrete bunkers, most with bicycles chained in front yards, no cars anywhere to be seen. That made sense given that fuel was nearly impossible to come by on the average North Korean's income, the country one that, like China of a generation ago, was powered largely by bike.

The truck bumped along a straight course and after forty-five minutes slowed at an intersection in preparation for the right turn onto an even more rutted road. Jet seized the opportunity, and when the truck was moving at running speed, slid down the bar and jumped off, barely managing to stay on her feet as she ran toward the squalid collection of homes they'd passed, a plan already taking form.

She stopped halfway to the string of structures and fished the sat phone from her pack and, when it had acquired a signal, pressed the second speed-dial number and waited while a phone rang in Singapore. Rami's voice answered on the third ring, his tone brusque.

"Yes?"

"I had to take out a policeman. I'm on the run – can't make it back to the hotel by daylight. I need an alternative."

"What kind of shape are you in?"

"I'm fine. But I need help. Now."

The long pause that ensued was more disconcerting than any words he could have spoken. "I'll call you back," he finally said.

"My ass is hanging out a mile here. I need a plan B, Rami."

"I understand. I'll call you back. I need to check a few things."

"How the hell am I supposed to get out of here without papers?" she snapped, frustrated.

"That's what I'm going to check. Give me ten minutes."

The line went dead. Rami seemed like a competent control officer, but there were practical limits to what anyone could do with no notice and no local help in place. Her instinct told her that she'd have to fend for herself, which meant making it to one of the borders under her own steam without being stopped by any of a thousand suspicious military personnel along the way.

Hijacking a truck or a ship was out of the question – there would be no way for her to know what the driver or captain said to anyone who intercepted them. That, and the file she'd read had underscored that the North Korean navy had myriad submarines and patrol boats, all committed to keeping traffic from crossing the DMZ line. And of course there were the mines that dotted the sea between the north and the south.

A truck would be no better; document checks were a certainty on any major road. With so few vehicles, each would be subjected to scrutiny, and she understood she wouldn't make it, tempting as the hijacking idea was. Same for hiding, as she'd done on the garbage truck. There would be no way to avoid capture once the sun was up – even the dimmest soldiers would be able to spot a woman on the roof of the truck in broad daylight.

That left an option she dreaded, but could see no way around unless Rami pulled a rabbit out of his hat.

The call, when it came, confirmed her worst fears.

"You're going to have to bicycle to the Chinese border and swim the river. There's no other way. It's apparently an easy crossing in the summer, provided it hasn't rained in the last couple of days."

"What then?"

"I'll work on getting a charter plane to the airport in Dandong, just across the river. If you can make it there, we'll get you out."

"You're confident you can do it?"

"I'll find a way."

"What can you tell me about the road to China? Patrols, roadblocks?"

"It will take a while for me to get intel. My advice is to steal some clothes so you look local, and do the same with a decent bicycle."

"I don't have a while."

"I can't create intelligence from thin air. Just keep your eyes open and stick to smaller routes. Your phone has maps on it. That should help."

"You don't have a forger anywhere in North Korea who can create some papers for me?"

"We have no assets, as you're already aware. It's bike or nothing. Sorry. It's only a hundred miles."

Jet shook her head in the dark. "Only?"

"Depending on how fast you ride, that's less than twenty-four hours, and most of the way is flat."

"You aren't joking, are you?" she said, and exhaled slowly. "I'll power this down and call back in a couple of hours."

"We'll try to have something for you by then."

Jet stabbed the call off and pulled up a map of the area. Her choice of roads was limited – there were only a couple that skirted the airport and ran north, and one was a highway, so she'd have to stick to the smaller road that paralleled it until Rami was able to give her some guidance.

When she'd memorized the route and located her position, she switched the phone off and went in search of a serviceable bike. She still had the lock picks in her pouch, so any padlock would pose no problem, but she suspected locating a bicycle in good enough shape to make it a hundred miles would be hard, given the miserable condition of the homes.

The only good news was that there wasn't a creature stirring, and she still had at least one more hour of total darkness in which to ride well clear of the city's farthest suburbs. Any approaching vehicle could be easily dodged, given away by its lights. Once day had broken, she suspected it would be harder, but since she had no choice, she opted to remain optimistic and trudged toward the homes. The stink wafting from her clothes provided all the reminder she needed to steal anything she could find to replace them, no matter how ragged or worn.

CHAPTER 36

Jet pedaled hard. The single-speed bike she'd stolen was a relic, the basket attached to the handlebars older than she was, but it had serviceable tires and minimal rust, though the seat was uncomfortable as any she'd sat upon. It had been the best of the four she'd scouted, the others appearing to be challenged to make it down the block, much less to the border. She'd picked the lock in seconds flat and left a few bills folded in the crack by the door – more than enough to buy a better replacement, she thought.

The pedals squeaked with each rotation, but she had managed decent speed in the predawn, estimating her progress at ten miles per hour, sometimes a hair more on downhill runs. Using simple math, and allowing for rest breaks, evading checkpoints, and taking a more circuitous route to the border, she would be there just after dark, which would enable her to scope out the river for a favorable crossing point.

When dawn lit the horizon with neon mango and cinnamon, she stopped by a tree and activated the sat phone. The position tracking put her at eighteen miles north of Pyongyang, a satisfactory distance for the amount of pedaling she'd done. Rami answered promptly.

"I have a bike," she announced.

"Good news."

"What've you got for me?"

"We're working on a flight. A check with the Americans, who keep North Korea under close surveillance for obvious reasons, gave us some valuable insights. There are checkpoints on the main road, but if you stick to the smaller back roads, you should be okay. There may be roaming patrols, but they don't bother with roadblocks on the rural stretches. Did you get out of the city?"

"Yes. I've only seen a few other riders, all coming the opposite direction, riding into town. Nobody looked at me funny, but it's still early."

"Any military?"

"Half the riders are in uniform."

"Check in again in a few hours and I'll have something more. But we located a pilot and plane big enough to get you to Seoul. Our station chief there is preparing another passport for you so you don't run into any problems with immigration. This one's Spanish."

"It won't be an issue in China?"

"We don't think so. That's part of the negotiation – the pilot can bring it. He's reluctant to fly to that part of China, given the tension with North Korea, but it's a matter of money, not ability or equipment. We'll work it out." He paused. "You have an ETA?"

"If all goes well, sometime late tonight or early tomorrow. A lot depends on what I run into on the way…and the river crossing."

Rami grunted. "Good luck. Call periodically."

"Will do."

Jet disconnected and checked the map for the smallest roads leading north. When she had the layout of the surroundings vividly in her mind, she switched it off, returned it to the pack, and jettisoned the cop's gun. Another pistol wouldn't do her any good if she was caught, and there was no point in incriminating herself with it in her possession. She wiped it clean, tossed it into the high grass, and felt in her pocket for a tissue. Her fingers found the photo she'd pocketed. She removed it and eyed it in the morning light. Ye-ji was smiling, the glow of youth on her face. Something in the image caught her eye, and Jet did a double take, blinking to clear her vision. She squinted at the photo and, after a long minute studying it, slipped it into the waterproof pack and sealed the pouch before cinching it back around her waist.

Jet swung back onto the bicycle saddle and returned to pedaling at a moderate pace, following the lead of the locals, who didn't hurry or push themselves on their bikes, likely due to the borderline starvation many outside the cities suffered from on a regular basis. The North

Korean diet consisted largely of rice and squid, the latter an abundant maritime harvest that was rich in protein, caught in the cold water off the coast. But neither had any fat, and nor did the population – everyone she'd seen had been rail thin and weathered from a harsh life at the mercy of the elements.

The temperature climbed uncomfortably as she rode, and her next rest stop was near a brook, where, after looking around, she removed her shirt and rinsed it until she'd removed the noxious stink. The garment dried in no time in the withering heat and took on a suitably wrinkled and worn shape that was more consistent with the tops the women she'd spotted had been wearing. Jet had deliberately chosen clothes that would blend in with the locals, knowing she'd be traversing the city at night to get to the apartment and wanting every advantage in looking anonymous. That bit of tradecraft was serving her well, because none of the riders that passed her gave her a second glance, her naturally bronzed skin darkening as the sun arced overhead.

Just before noon she spotted two soldiers in the distance, sitting at a guard post that more resembled a ramshackle outhouse than a military installation. She swung off the road, circled back the way she had come, and rode hard for a mile before she cut across a field and walked her bicycle north. A glance at her map told her that in a fair distance, another small road would cross her path, and she stayed low as she passed the guards on that road, their shack so far away that she could barely make them out.

The afternoon wore on, and as the hours passed, her stamina began to flag. To maintain her hydration Jet had drunk from streams that appeared unspoiled, but she hadn't eaten since the prior night, and the demands of the hundred-mile ride were weakening her. She didn't dare try to buy anything to eat, her lack of Korean being a surefire trip to a prison camp, so all she could do was pace herself, stopping more often and filling her belly with as much water as she could. She'd been through worse and would tough it out, but her endurance had been far better at twenty than at twenty-nine, even though she was in peak physical shape.

A call to Rami confirmed that a prop plane would be at the Chinese airport by two a.m. with a passport and a bag of protein bars and electrolyte drinks. The pilot was a seasoned professional who would wait until the following daybreak for her, but no longer. He didn't want to have to explain to the day shift why he was sitting on the tarmac or whom he was waiting for, and wasn't going to risk being taken to prison and having his plane impounded for any amount of money. China was a staunch ally of North Korea, and the authorities along the border cooperated with each other, even though officially they were adversarial; anyone suspect was automatically returned to the North Koreans, treated as an illegal immigrant rather than a refugee from a despotic, hostile regime that would incarcerate them, or worse, for daring to attempt to escape.

Jet removed the photo of Ye-ji several more times, trying to confirm her impression but unable to without a magnifying glass, her fatigued eyes ill-equipped for the task after days of sleep deprivation and the North Korean sun. She made a final check of the map as the last of the light seeped from the western sky, and calculated that she was only twenty-two miles from the river and, hopefully, the end to an episode that had been as trying as it had been dangerous. When she settled back onto the bike saddle, her bottom aching from the seat's chafing, she allowed herself a small pained smile.

If she never saw another bicycle for as long as she lived, it would be too soon.

CHAPTER 37

Jet waited by the Yalu River in the moonlight, the brown churn flowing faster than she would have liked. The lights of the Chinese town across its reach shone brightly in the darkness. Downriver, ghostly towers of vacant apartment buildings rose into the night along the waterfront, built for owners who would never live within a thousand miles of Dandong; the apartments had been one of the few authorized investments for a citizenry desperate to preserve its buying power, and the resulting rush drove a housing boom unlike any the world had ever seen. Thousands of empty units now sat dark in the gloom, the streets deserted without any sign of life, Jet could tell even across the half mile of water.

She'd considered attempting to mimic her North Korean trek beneath the bridge that spanned the river, but had decided against it after watching the area for an hour; the guards on her side of it made the idea impractical. Unlike their Pyongyang counterparts, these men seemed alert and watchful, and there was little chance she'd be able to slip by them unseen.

Which left swimming. She knew from the satellite image that the river was narrower the further north she moved, but after her all-day ordeal she didn't have the appetite for slogging many more miles along the bank to cut a few hundred yards off her swim. She was resigned to tackling the river at this point. The airport was another four miles on foot from the far shore, and the hike would be one that would sap the last of her energy and require everything she had.

Her stomach growled, a reminder that she was running on empty, and she methodically checked and rechecked the waterproof pack to ensure it was tightly sealed. Once on the Chinese side, she would have to avoid any patrols and find her way to the airport without being challenged – hopefully not as difficult as she'd found to be the case in Pyongyang.

Jet glanced down at the small pistol sitting beside her on the rocks, and patted it affectionately before tossing it far out into the water. She hadn't been forced to use it, and it had served as at least minor comfort on her trip; but now, its purpose served, it would be a liability if discovered by the Chinese.

She unlaced her running shoes, tied their laces together, and hung them around her neck, the better to swim without shoes creating resistance on her feet. After a final glance at her watch, she picked her way down the rocks and stepped into the water. The chill was expected, but still bracing.

Jet edged further into the river until she was submerged to her neck, and was surprised to find the current gentler than she'd thought. After a few deep breaths she pushed off the bottom and began taking measured strokes toward the far bank. A fueling platform loomed upstream, the bridge's outline clear against the stars as she pulled herself through the water, and her body fell into a rhythm designed to conserve her energy. Rami had assured her that the Yalu River was easily swimmable, according to the reports he'd found, but after fourteen hours of hard riding, she wasn't taking anything for granted.

She paused at the halfway point and tried to measure her drift while floating on her back, and found the current to be manageable. Her backstroke relieved some of the developing cramps in her shoulders and legs, and within another half hour she was scrambling up the gray rocks on the Chinese side, grateful that there, unlike their saltwater brethren, the stones were free of barnacles that might gash her bare feet. Jet stood dripping on the waterfront walkway and shook her hair out like a wet dog before stripping off her shirt and wringing it out. After another look around she did the same with her pants and then slipped her shoes on, ready to begin the final leg of her journey.

The shore was deserted, scores of darkened apartment blocks stretching as far as she could see. She checked her pack to ensure that its contents were still dry and then set out for the airport, at least an hour or two away. A massive circular office building that resembled a doughnut bisected at a horizontal angle loomed in front of her; the boulevard that ran toward it was easily ten lanes wide and empty as a glacier.

The sense of walking through a surreal alien landscape intensified as she passed the office complex and approached two huge sporting fields, the wind whistling through the stands. Her damp clothes clung to her frame, and even though the breeze was warm, she shivered involuntarily at the sense of being the only living thing for miles.

She neared an intersection and removed the phone from her pouch to check the map again. The airport was straight ahead, but there was no road that went directly to it other than a highway that jagged far to the right, taking her well out of her way. She zoomed in on the image and saw a smaller road that led to a collection of factories and what looked like traditional single-story homes, and was committing the route to memory when headlights swung from the direction of the highway and approached.

Jet shut off the phone and darted toward some brush by the side of the road. She threw herself flat against the ground as the car rolled toward the intersection, and peered from the scrub at a pickup with a bank of emergency lights on its roof and markings identifying it as a police vehicle or security patrol on its doors. Three armed officers sat in the bed as the truck meandered along the empty thoroughfare, and she ducked down to keep the light from reflecting off her face as it closed on her.

If the police were doing more than obligatory rounds, it didn't show, because the pickup continued past her position without slowing. She waited until the sound of its engine had faded and then moved quickly across the intersection, trotting toward the artery that ran through the factory district. Rows of industrial buildings of impossible size stretched along the equally improbably wide boulevard, and she stuck to the shadows on the same side of the street, moving cautiously, fearful of a night watchman spotting her and calling her in to the authorities.

The road she was looking for materialized from the gloom on her right. The landscape changed from sprawling skyscraper developments to modest homes with paint peeling from their façades. After forty minutes of navigating along the intersecting streets, the lights of the airport appeared in front of her, and she picked up her pace with a final burst of energy.

She neared the end of the runway, ran across the flattened grass stretch at the tip, and then was on the road that led to the commercial terminal and the series of modest hangars just before it that was her destination. Jet called Rami to let him know she had arrived, and after a long pause, he told her that the plane would arrive shortly and to stay out of sight until it did.

A half hour later, a single-engine prop plane dropped onto the runway and taxied to the hangars. Jet darted to it when it was in a dark area just before the closed private terminal and climbed into the cockpit. The pilot nodded to her and adjusted his headset and then murmured into the integrated microphone. Moments later, he turned to Jet and spoke in broken English.

"There is bag in back with items for you. We take off, yes?"

Jet allowed herself a smile at the welcome news and exhaled in relief as she reached behind her for the backpack, hunger burning in her stomach like an out-of-control wildfire, her body close to shutting down from being pushed past its limits. The plane returned to the end of the runway and she removed one of three bottles of energy drink and a like number of protein bars, pausing only to study her new passport and slip it into her pouch as the pilot pushed forward on the throttle. The little aircraft leapt forward on its takeoff run and Jet settled into her seat, the prospect of her first meal in over twenty-four hours almost as appealing as the idea of some shut-eye. She drained half a bottle in three swallows and unwrapped a bar with trembling hands, and if she'd ever tasted anything more welcome than the first chewy bite, she couldn't remember when.

CHAPTER 38

Herzliya, Israel

The director appeared even more glum than usual, and his dour expression and hangdog look clearly conveyed his foul mood as he entered the conference room reserved for the gathering of the Security Council. His second meeting with the six men chartered with responding to Israel's greatest threats in as many days didn't portend anything good, and when he took his seat and tossed his cigarette pack on the table beside an ashtray, it told everyone in the room that they were in for a long briefing.

"Gentlemen," he began, "thank you for coming so quickly. We have studied the material we obtained from the North Korean woman and have confirmed that this is a worst-case scenario. A bioweapon is on its way to Iran, where it will be deployed against us by a coordinated group of terrorists who we believe are working with, or at least are being allowed to operate by, the Iranian government." He paused, allowing the news to sink in. "There is no doubt of the threat. And we have only one way to stop it: a military strike within Iran."

Nahum Weisenthal, the chairman of the council, sat back in his chair when the director was finished detailing how he knew what he claimed to know. Everyone was familiar with the story from the prior meeting, but hearing confirmation was sobering, even though they'd all expected it.

"Which will correctly be interpreted as an act of war. A surprise attack, exactly like we did in the Six-Day War."

The director nodded. "That is correct. There is no other way."

Weisenthal shook his head. "There is always another way. Why have you ruled out an embargo? We, and our allies, can stop anything bound for Iran at its borders."

"No, they can't. The Turks are notoriously inept and unreliable, and Iraq is a bad joke, with most of the country out of control. Don't even get me started on Afghanistan, Armenia, or any of the rest. Those borders are so porous you could drive a cruise ship through them – not to mention that the agent could also be coming in by sea or air." The director paused. "All of this is well known."

"You are proposing we go to war with Iran."

"I am proposing that we save Israel from certain destruction. If we have to bomb a location in Iran, that isn't even a choice. We can furnish the proof after the fact to avoid escalation."

"The Muslim world won't believe it."

The director shrugged. "Not my problem. My job is to advise you of what we know, and recommend a course of action that will protect the country. I've done that."

Another man, with a gray complexion accentuated by thick black-framed glasses, sat forward and cleared his throat. "We know where they're going to receive the weapon. Any idea how they intend to deploy it? Perhaps we can intercept the agent on its way from Iran?"

"Gabriel, we suspect that they intend to use missiles to deliver the payload. We've received confirmation from the Americans of a number of coalition missile systems that were 'lost' in Syria, and a recent attack on a convoy bringing similar missiles to Turkey was a definite terrorist scheme – a successful one, I might add. That points to sophistication, and with the Iranian government's involvement looking almost certain, their use of missile technology to reach us with the agent is highly likely."

"That's a stretch. We would immediately track the trajectory. It would be justification for a nuke strike against them – suicide."

The director nodded. "You assume we're dealing with rational minds. Anyone who would unleash a bio-agent on a country isn't rational. They view dying while waging war against us as martyrdom and would embrace death if it destroyed us." He looked around the room. "Besides, they wouldn't need to have official backing. All they would need is a few compromised members of the military to help. A few black sheep, and the same objective is achieved."

"What about a commando raid? We could have men waiting to be helicoptered in. Something deniable."

"The Iranians aren't stupid. There will be no denying they were attacked, so suggesting less effective ways to handle this will only reduce our chances of success. Politics has to take a backseat to survival."

Weisenthal interrupted the exchange. "Yes, yes. We all agree that however we react, it first and foremost has to be guaranteed to be successful. The question in my mind is, can we alert the Iranians just before we strike? Perhaps they will take care of the problem once they realize we're onto them."

The director shook his head. "It won't happen. Our only advantage is surprise. Eliminate that, and they'll simply move the agent and deny everything. I would argue that a surgical strike by a fighter group is the best approach. Laser-guided ordnance. Only hit the target, and limit collateral damage as much as we can. Then we can reveal what we know to the world, and our actions will be vindicated."

One of the uniformed men, the highest-ranking general in the armed forces, nodded slowly. "Are we sure about when the weapon will arrive in Iran, and where?"

"We have a date mentioned as that of 'the great triumph.' And the Americans are monitoring the bank account where money will be sent once the agent has been confirmed as having arrived safely. So we have a window. Which is why I recommend you have fighters waiting for the go-ahead. They can be there in an hour. That's the most secure way of handling this."

"What about a missile strike?" Weisenthal asked.

The general shook his head. "As a backup. But planes having a visual on the target are the best route to avoiding any missteps." He hesitated for a moment. "And Iran has purchased the latest technology Russian and Chinese missile defense systems, and there's some question how many of ours would make it through."

"Then what good are they?" Weisenthal snapped in frustration.

"We aren't sure about the effectiveness of the newest defense systems. There's disagreement among our experts, and the Russians aren't talking. Recall the American strike in Syria – a significant percentage of the missiles fired at the airstrip didn't hit their targets, and nobody's talking about why. We don't want to learn the hard way we've been outflanked."

"Have we ascertained what's at the location in question?" Weisenthal asked the director.

"An abandoned school of some kind."

"A school? Are you sure it's abandoned?"

"Satellite imagery shows no signs of life going back several years."

The men continued the discussion for two more hours, nobody happy with the outcome, least of all the director. He understood the risks to unilateral action all too well and had spent most of the night in meetings with his advisors, looking for a way out. In the end, there was none. They would have to put birds in the air and bomb the site after the payment hit the account. Allowing for reasonable latency for the NSA to alert them of the payment plus flying time, they would have no more than a couple of hours of slack.

Hopefully that would be enough.

Then again, the director had found that hope was a lousy strategy for anything that mattered, and so left the meeting with an even longer face than when he'd entered, his pack of cigarettes nearly empty and every bone in his body aching from fatigue and stress.

CHAPTER 39

Istanbul, Turkey

Cezar paced in the hallway outside a waiting room in Turkey's most prominent hospital, his craving for a drink and a cigarette nearly overwhelming. He had gotten leave two days ago, extenuating circumstances justifying the unexpected time off with his superior because of his brother's condition, and had flown to Turkey when word of the surgery had reached him. Now, he, his mother, and one of his other brothers were in Istanbul, awaiting the outcome of the transplant that was the best chance of saving his brother's life.

The facility was far cleaner than he'd expected, the floor tiles spotless, the rooms painted gloss white and smelling of antiseptic, and the staff was plentiful and courteous, unlike what he was used to in Romania, where chronic shortages and surly dispositions were the norm. The building was modern, all mirrored glass and steel, and even the ambulances seemed new, validating the center's reputation as state of the art. The surgeon was a specialist in transplants who had performed hundreds with a high degree of success. Everything that could be done for Gavril had been – the stranger who'd bummed a light in Romania had delivered as promised.

Cezar preferred not to think about what he'd had to deliver in return. The price had been high, but he'd had no choice. It was his brother, after all.

When he couldn't stand the anxiety of waiting any longer, he returned to the surgery wing's waiting room, where his brother Bogan was comforting their mother, who looked like she'd aged ten years in the last month. Watching her firstborn slowly degrade and waiting for the news of his death had taken its toll, and Cezar's

191

difficult decision was validated again when he saw her.

"I'm going outside for a smoke," he said. His brother and mother nodded, his brother texting on his phone, his mother reading from a Bible, her lips moving slightly as she recited prayer after prayer. Cezar resisted the sudden urge to tell her that wasn't how things worked, that a God he'd never believed in wasn't responsible for Gavril's newfound good fortune – that it was he, Cezar, who had moved heaven and earth. Instead, he retraced his steps, smiling at the pretty desk nurse who'd seemed flirtatious earlier, and exited the surgery wing, moving through the lobby to the street half in a trance, still only half believing he was in Turkey and his brother was being saved.

He stepped out into the parking lot, most of the cars shining and new in the late morning light. The surgery had begun at dawn; time was of the essence once the donor organ had arrived, and now, more than six hours later, there was still no word on the outcome. He had been told the procedure could take considerably longer, depending on a variety of factors, but had tuned out when the surgeon had explained what they were – his brother would either live or he wouldn't. How long it took and why was of only cursory interest; although Bogan had paid rapt attention, his engineering background better preparing him for the concepts than Cezar's experience in the armed forces.

The smoke calmed his nerves, steadying him, and he swallowed the knot that had been threatening to choke him since he'd arrived the prior day. There was nothing he could do to reverse the strange course events had taken for him nor erase the crushing guilt he felt every waking moment. He'd heard the news of the attack on the missile convoy several hours after it had happened, when the base had been put on high alert. He and many of his companions had been trucked south to assist in site control and later the manhunt that had ultimately turned up nothing but the charred remains of a handful of stolen vehicles painted as police cars.

Cezar certainly felt guilty about his role, but only to a point. He was a soldier, a fighter, trained to kill, and though he wished his fellow soldiers hadn't had to die, he would have done the same thing all over again to save his brother: providing his new friend with a few dates and times and the convoy's route had seemed a small price to pay, on balance. He might live out the remainder of his existence wishing there had been another way, but he refused to allow remorse to consume him. What was done was done, and no regrets would bring the dead back to life.

He dropped his cigarette onto the pavement and crushed it beneath his boot, and then lit another one, reluctant to return to the hospital just yet, where the walls bore down on him and the cloying air and unfamiliar jabber of the locals frayed his nerves. He was halfway through the smoke when his brother burst from the exit, excitement animating his features.

"He's done. He's out of surgery," Bogan said.

Cezar flicked his cigarette away and was halfway to the door when his brother caught up with him.

"We can't see him yet," Bogan warned.

"When can we?"

"Soon. That's all the nurse said."

"But he made it," Cezar stated.

"So far…"

Cezar frowned. "You left Mom alone?"

"She'll be fine. She has her Bible. I told her to stay there and wait for us."

They arrived back at the waiting room a minute later, where a nurse was helping their mother stand. Cezar moved to her and finished the job, and then hugged her for a long moment, her body frail in his arms. Tears streamed down the lines in her face, soaking a spot on his chest, but he didn't care. The joy and relief she was experiencing was palpable – and he'd brought that about.

They were standing in the hall when the surgeon appeared in green scrubs, obviously tired, with the woman who'd translated for them in their preoperative meeting at his side. He shook hands with the family, accepted a hug from Cezar's mother, and then turned to Cezar to field the questions he knew would be forthcoming.

"How did it go?" Cezar asked.

The translator did her job, and the surgeon spoke in a soft voice.

"It was complicated, due to his condition, but the surgery went as well as can be expected. He's relatively young, so his prognosis is good for this type of procedure."

"When will you know whether he's out of the woods?"

"The next three days will be critical. Presuming he doesn't develop an infection or some other complication, every day thereafter, his odds improve."

Bogan interrupted. "Doctor, you've done a lot of these, haven't you?"

The translator conveyed the question, and the doctor turned to him. "Yes. That's right."

"What do you think? Your honest opinion. We can handle the truth."

A tired sigh greeted his request. "He's very sick, but the organ was in good shape, there were no unexpected issues during the surgery, and now, his recovery is in God's hands. If he doesn't reject the organ, he could live a normal life – although no alcohol."

"What next? When can we see him?"

"You won't be able to go into his room, but we have a special suite set up where you can watch his recovery through a window. His immune system is precarious and will remain that way for some time due to the drugs we have to give him to reduce the likelihood of rejection."

"That's a real risk?" Cezar asked.

The surgeon nodded, his patience obviously wearing thin after the marathon procedure. "Yes. I'm sure my assistant can explain more." He hesitated. "I'm sorry, but it's been a long morning, and I need to get some rest. I'll be back to check on the patient in eight hours. Don't worry, the attending physician is very good. Your brother will receive good care."

The surgeon said something to one of the nurses hovering in the background, and then shook hands again and retreated into the surgery area. The nurse led them down another hall into a recovery suite and indicated a thick plate of glass with blinds over it. She raised the blinds and there was Gavril lying in a bed with his head resting against its raised back, eyes closed, pale as a cave dweller, oxygen nubs in his nose and an IV dripping into his arm – but alive, his chest rising and falling with each breath as the vital signs monitor's jagged wave traced his heartbeat.

Cezar's mother wailed and resumed crying, and this time it was his brother's turn to comfort her. The woman sobbed quietly, and Cezar turned away from the window, his eyes also welling with moisture.

"I…I'll be back," he said, and pushed through the door, a panicked expression clouding his face. He saw a restroom sign and made for it, and barely reached the sink before he vomited the contents of his nearly empty stomach, heaving and retching, bile burning his throat and nose.

Two minutes later he'd regained control of himself and, after blotting his face with a paper towel, retraced his steps toward the recovery suite, stopping abruptly when confronted by four uniformed officers with somber expressions.

"Cezar Moliyev?" the lead officer asked, mispronouncing Cesar's last name, the syllables unfamiliar to his Turkish tongue.

Cezar looked from soldier to soldier before meeting the officer's eyes. "That's right," he said with a nod.

The man barked an order, and two of the soldiers grabbed Cezar's arms while the third snapped handcuffs on his hands.

The last things Cezar registered before he blacked out from shock were his mother's and brother's faces standing in the doorway of the recovery room, watching him being dragged away like a side of beef by grim men with murder in their eyes.

CHAPTER 40

Seoul, South Korea

The hotel, only five hundred yards from the Israeli embassy, was one of the nicest Jet had stayed in while in Asia. One of numerous high-rises in the center of town many stories below her window, it was upscale bordering on lavish. Loren, the Seoul station chief, had arranged for the room, and she'd paid with the wad of won that had been one of the items in her goodie bag along with the food and passport. After a long hot shower, she'd tumbled naked into bed and slept for six hours before being awakened by the jangling of the phone on the nightstand beside her.

She rolled over and held the handset to her ear. "Yes?"

"The pilot told me you could use some clothes," the station chief said. "I'm calling for your size."

She told him and looked over at her shoes. "And a pair of Nikes. Black. Or Doc Martens. Your call."

"I'll leave those up to you once you've got something to wear."

"Fine. And I need some underthings."

"I'll have my secretary get them. Stay put. I'll send her by in an hour or so."

"I'll order room service. It's on you."

"Her name's Sarah."

"Have her bring a magnifying glass. And a tablet computer, and charger for my sat phone."

There was a pause. "Anything else?"

"Twenty grand in unmarked bills."

This time the pause was longer. "Are you serious?"

"At the prices this place charges, what you gave me won't last long. Local currency's fine."

"I'll do what I can."

"I'm good for it. If you have a problem, call the director."

The line went dead and Jet smiled. She stretched like a cat and yawned, and then rose and made her way to the bathroom to brush her teeth and freshen up. She luxuriated in another long shower, enjoying the expensive-smelling, rich-lathering house shampoo, and when she finished, wrapped herself in one of the robes hanging from the wall hooks and settled back on the bed.

A call to room service resulted in an omelet, juice, and a pot of tea delivered in thirty minutes, and Jet devoured the food, her caloric count still well short of what she'd burned on a hundred-mile bike ride and at least a ten-mile run. Finally satiated, she moved to her pack and withdrew the photo she'd saved and studied it intently.

An hour later the phone rang again, and the front desk announced she had a visitor. Jet told the desk to send her up, and went to check her reflection in the full-length mirror by the bathroom door. All things considered, she could have looked worse; although her face and neck were badly sunburned, she knew from experience that it would become a deep golden tan within another day or so, courtesy of her genetics.

She answered the knock at the door with the knife from the room service tray in hand behind her back, the serrated blade sharp enough to inflict major damage, and stepped aside so the young woman in owlish glasses and a smart pantsuit with two plastic shopping bags could enter.

"I'm Sarah," the woman said. "Where would you like this?"

"Bed's fine."

"Sorry I'm late. It took a while to get the cash and computer you requested. Forms, and then a bank run before the computer store."

Jet nodded. "And the charger?"

"Everything's in there," she said, indicating the bags. "Two changes of clothes. Charger, computer, money, magnifying glass."

"Excellent. Thanks for bringing it."

"No problem," Sarah said, and then backtracked to the door. "I've got to get back. Loren asked you to call as soon as you can. The number's in the bag."

Sarah let herself out and Jet dumped the bags. In the first were the clothes, muted dark colors in keeping with Mossad field norms, and a bundle of dollars, euros, and won thick enough to choke a pony. In the other she found the tablet, charger, magnifying glass, and underwear, along with some deodorant and other odds and ends Sarah had thoughtfully included.

Jet plugged the cable into the phone and sat at the table as it charged, with the magnifying glass in hand. She studied the photo for a long beat and then set it down, frowning. When she rose, she made straight for the bags and found a business card at the bottom with a handwritten local phone number scribbled in pencil.

She debated calling the station chief and then sat back down and switched the sat phone on, holding it by the window. When it acquired a signal, she pressed the speed dial number for Rami and waited as it rang. He answered on the second ring.

"Yes?"

"We need to talk."

"It's not a good time."

"I can call the director."

A sigh. "What is it?"

"The Korean woman. The mother. What's her background?"

"Why?"

"How deep did you go?"

Another sigh, this one impatient. "Deep. What do you think?"

"So what is it?"

"She was a secretary at a sensitive location."

"Military background?"

"Negative. Had a heart murmur."

Jet hesitated. "You're sure?"

"I ran the check myself."

"What would you say if I told you I had a picture of her in a Korean army uniform that looks like officer rank?"

"I'd say that it might have been a costume. Or a gag. Or she was trying it on for a laugh. She was never in the military."

"It's a reflection in her daughter's glasses, Rami. Doesn't look like a gag to me."

The line was silent for several seconds. "Is there anything else?"

"Why would she lie about her background?"

"She didn't. It checked out. Did you not hear me? How much sleep have you had?" He paused. "There's probably a simple explanation. But I don't have time to find it right now. Things are...escalating."

"How?"

Another pause. "Sorry. Need to know."

"I'm calling the director."

"Suit yourself. Our business is done."

Her next call was to the director's private line, which she knew by heart. His familiar abrasive voice answered.

"What is it?"

"It's me."

"I know. But I can't really talk."

"Make time. Two minutes. You have a problem."

The director sighed. "Things have heated up."

"What does that mean?"

"It means that your find confirmed our suspicions, and now we're trying to save the world."

"Can you be more specific?"

"No."

"I need to understand what the document said and what you're planning to do."

"Why would I tell you any of that?"

"You used my daughter as leverage. I almost got killed getting you that information. And I believe you have a major issue. Is that enough?"

The director hesitated. "What is this issue?"

"I have a photo of the Korean woman wearing a military uniform. Officer, from what I can tell. Only she was never in the service, per your Singapore control. That's a disconnect."

She could almost hear the director's mind whirring at lightning speed. She pressed the point. "I can take a high-res shot with my tablet and send it to you for analysis. You'll see I'm right. Give me an email account and I'll do so. But I want the translation of the woman's info."

"Why?"

"Something's off. I don't know what, but it's off."

"How much sleep have you gotten? I read the report of your phone debriefing."

"Enough. I'm not imagining things."

"Fine. Here's the address. I'll have an analyst look at it. And I'll send you the translation. Not like you don't have the original on your phone."

"It'll save me the time typing it into the translator."

"You're stubborn."

"I'll send it in a minute," she said, and hung up.

CHAPTER 41

The report arrived twenty minutes after she sent the photograph, and Jet pored over the translation, pausing when she recognized a familiar name. When she was done reading it, she called the director back.

"Did you get the photograph analyzed?" she asked.

"It's been, what, less than an hour?"

"You should make it a priority."

"I appreciate your counsel on how to run things," he snapped, sarcasm clear in his tone. "There are limits to my patience."

She ignored him. "I see coordinates. I checked them on my tablet. Inside Iran?"

"You also saw a date. It's tomorrow."

"Is that confirmed?"

"We're confident it's a drop dead date. Might be earlier."

"No identification of the agent, though."

"North Korea has chemical and biological programs. Use your imagination."

"The shipping company mentioned? It's the triad's."

"So?"

"They're connected to this."

"I'm not surprised. A natural middleman for the devil's work."

"That's how Zhao knew."

"We already figured that out," he snapped. "Now I have to get back to other matters."

"You need to send someone after him. If he's still alive."

"He is. But there's a problem you're not taking into account."

"Which is?"

"I don't have any assets I can spare. Everyone within the area at a high enough level was in your operation. So there's nobody to do it. At least, nobody competent."

"You can fly someone there."

"It would take me a day to get someone from here to Beijing. At a minimum. Take another look at that date and think through why that won't work."

"You don't have anyone in Korea?"

"I wouldn't have sent you in if I did. Not with a level of expertise that has any chance of success. You're talking about a highly protected target in a fortified compound. We looked at an intrusion before settling on snatching him at the wedding, and it's as close to impossible as you could imagine. A waste of time. Which we're out of."

Jet made a face. "The uniform doesn't fit with any of this scenario."

"Assuming that's her. And that there isn't an alternative explanation. Now if you don't mind, I've devoted as much as I can to you for one day."

"I risked everything. And I'm telling you, something stinks."

The director's tone hardened. "You know as well as I do there are always unanswered questions after an op. Sometimes we put the pieces together. Other times, we don't. Solving your puzzle isn't possible in the time we have left. That's it."

Jet took a deep breath. "I can go after him."

The silence was deafening. "Have you forgotten that it was all we could do to extricate you the last time? With a trail of bodies a mile long left behind?"

"I'm in the area. I can be there in a few hours. Get me a visa and I'll go in."

"I have no resources I can support you with. You want to do this, you're on your own. I'm sorry. We can't afford distractions, and that's what this is."

"You're wrong."

"Maybe."

"You mentioned that you'd considered going in after Zhao, but rejected it. Why?"

"He's got a mansion in Beijing. Guarded, of course, with alarms, motion detectors, security cameras. There was no way to get in and grab him."

"For a team, you mean. What about one person who has no interest in taking him out alive?"

The director paused. "I don't know. Levi handled the research. The usual in-depth vetting. The conclusion was it wouldn't work. I don't remember all the details."

"I want to talk to Levi."

"Why?"

"To understand what I'd be walking into, and figure out if there's a way to pull it off."

She heard the director light a cigarette. "I suppose I can arrange a call with him. He can reach you at this number?"

"Yes."

"Give me a couple of hours to reach Loren and have him gather the files so he can speak intelligently. In the meantime, I'll see about the visa. But that's as much as I can do. I have to get back to work."

"How long will the visa take?"

"Ask Loren. I have no idea."

The click of the call terminating was loud in her ear. Jet set the phone down so it could continue charging and gathered her new clothes. She selected a pair of pants and a top, tore off the tags, donned them, and inspected herself in the mirror. It would do.

She would give Loren an hour and then call him. Meanwhile, she would check flight schedules. Beijing was a highly traveled route from Asia, so she anticipated no problem there. Jet switched on the tablet and navigated to a popular agency, and quickly confirmed dozens of flights that day, departing regularly.

She glanced at the time. If she was quick, she could dash out and buy some decent shoes and be back before her call. She pocketed the Korean won, put the dollars and euros in the room safe, and went in search of a shop that could accommodate her needs.

When she returned to the room, wearing a pair of Doc Martens boots and toting a black nylon backpack to hold her new acquisitions, she settled into the chair by the window and called Loren.

"Where are we?" she asked.

"It takes four days to get a Chinese visa for a Spanish passport unless you're part of a special tour, which we can't do on this short a notice."

"That won't work."

"I know. We have a contact with the Chinese embassy who can get one processed in a few hours – for a price. I've contacted him and am waiting for timing and cost."

"Will it stand up to scrutiny?"

"It will be legit."

"I want to be on a plane today."

"I understand the urgency, but there are practical limits. You might be able to catch a flight by this evening. That's our hope."

Jet scowled. "Is there anything I can do to speed up the process?"

"Nothing, I'm afraid. We're limited by our contact's response time and the logistics of putting a visa through the system and ensuring it's registered, stamped appropriately, and signed by the correct party. All of which takes time to walk through, no matter how motivated you are."

"So offering to pay more wouldn't accelerate that?"

"Not in my experience. If we can get it by this evening, that's a win."

"I also need someone in Beijing who can provide low-level logistical support."

"What kind?"

"A weapon, any supplies I need. The usual."

"We have several freelancers who are dependable. Call me in a few hours and I'll get you their info."

Jet hung up and considered what she'd signed up to do: travel to a country where she was wanted for kidnapping and murder, albeit under a different alias, and penetrate a triad stronghold about which she knew nothing. It seemed mad, but her gut was telling her that there was something badly wrong with the scenario that had developed – she just didn't know what. But with the bioweapon delivery to take place at some point tomorrow, assuming they'd interpreted the document correctly, she had to do her best to find out. A big part of her wanted to fly back to Israel, gather up Hannah and Matt, and be on the first plane to anywhere, but the director had been right – it wasn't just her daughter at risk, it was an entire nation of little boys and girls like Hannah who were facing devastation.

The ringing of the sat phone pulled her from her thoughts, and she punched the line to life.

"We need to make this quick," Levi said.

"Perfect. The director says you considered an alternative plan to the wedding?"

"That's right. And discarded it as impractical."

"Walk me through it."

"There were a number of moving parts that caused us concern. The largest of which was how to get the target out of the hot zone without getting everyone killed. That was why the helicopter lift seemed like a better way to go."

"And we know how that turned out."

"What do you want to know?"

"Take me through it from the start."

Fifteen minutes later, he finished.

She started in with her questions. "How in-depth was your research?"

"We cut no corners. We have everything. Plans of the house. Security system. Guard shift patterns. Even the personnel involved. We ran surveillance for a week."

"What about the executable to shut down the systems?"

"Four lines of code."

"How did you get the plans?"

"He used an American architectural firm to design it and supervise the construction. We hacked their server and downloaded it."

"You're sure they represent what was actually built?"

"To the best of our knowledge. The Americans handled all of the equipment sourcing and ordering. Apparently Zhao didn't trust his countrymen to do it correctly."

"Can you send me the entire file? Including the executable?"

"The director told me I was to give you whatever you wanted."

"A list of materials I would need to shut down the transformer would also be helpful."

"No list necessary. We were going to use thermite."

Jet had made the material before. It was quick and easy to manufacture with a few common ingredients, and inert until exposed to a white-hot flame, at which point it easily melted through metal.

They spoke for a few more minutes, Levi answering her operational questions, and after committing again to sending her the file as soon as he hung up, she terminated the call.

Jet needed to read the details to confirm, but at least on the surface, with a few modifications, the plan might be workable.

Only without the objective of getting the triad boss out alive.

CHAPTER 42

Arbat, Iraq

A cloud of flies so dense it seemed practically solid buzzed around the field latrine at the edge of the refugee camp, one more condition that with the 120-degree heat served to make the miserable conditions unbearable for the residents. Rows of tents roasted in the bright sun; the surrounding green hills offered little comfort to the dusty tenements, their rolling slopes so different from the dry patch of beige dirt the tents occupied as to be on another planet.

The camp was overflowing to the bursting point, thanks in large part to the battle against ISIS in nearby Mosul and the ongoing war in Syria that were driving anyone who could to escape the war zones. With nowhere to turn, many unfortunates wound up in the camps, living hardscrabble in deplorable conditions where disease and malnutrition were endemic. With no prospects and no understanding of what had befallen them or why their homes were under constant attack, they had run, often with only the clothes on their backs and what they could carry. The resultant humanitarian crisis was of monumental proportions most of the rest of the world remained ignorant about until European cities swelled with those who could reach them, the resultant culture clash as ugly as any in history.

A geriatric school bus sporting a patchwork of rust and peeling paint shuddered to a halt at the camp gates, its siding rattling against the chassis like the frenzied clattering of castanets. The guards remained beneath the tarp that sheltered them as the bus door groaned open and a man descended from the bus's depths and approached them. He offered a greeting, and the guards returned it in kind, and then cash changed hands and the bus was waved through, the chain-link gate rolling shut behind it.

The bus, its tires bald and cracking, creaked to a stop beside a water tower, and the driver killed the engine. Three of the camp denizens waited by the tower, and more discussion and an exchange of money took place. Two of the refugees hurried away, and a few minutes later, eight boys and girls, none older than ten, returned with them and filed toward the bus. The man who'd paid the refugees offered the children water bottles that were accepted as though rare treasure, and then the children were directed onto the bus while the men said their farewells and the driver and his companion returned to the cab.

The engine stuttered to a rough idle, and then the heavy vehicle executed a slow circle and headed back to the gate, the only sound other than its motor the sough of an arid wind as hot as a blast furnace blowing through the water tower's beams. When the bus picked up speed and rolled from the camp, the men returned to their tents to spend the remainder of the day broiling on the hardpan, and the dust cloud from the bus's passage trailed it like a beige ghost as it disappeared from sight.

The bus stopped at three more camps before pulling behind the gates of a walled compound on the outskirts of the nearby city of Sulaymaniyah, whose mosque towers and high-rises shimmered in the heat. The children were herded off the bus to a common area, where a man waited with an electric hair clipper. He sheared the boys' locks an inch from their skulls and trimmed that of the little girls to a foot in length. When their grooming was complete, an old crone pointed them to a common shower area consisting of a concrete slab, where they were told to shed their clothes so they could be hosed down – a welcome interlude after the roasting conditions inside the bus. Four women with pecan complexions and the no-nonsense expressions of nuns scrubbed each in turn with brushes and soap, and then a grinning man with a hose sprayed away the beige suds and hair, smiles and giggles greeting the warm stream of water.

The sun dried the children quickly, and another man instructed them to stand in line to get undergarments and clothes. An older man with no teeth sized up each of the urchins and then handed them a parcel that would fit their approximate size, and then they were told to don the clothes in the far corner, after which they would be fed.

An hour later, the children sat at crudely built wooden tables with bowls of bean-based gruel before them. They ate ravenously; the tasteless slag was nevertheless an improvement over what they'd been fed for months in the camp. The lot in life of war orphans in Iraq was harsh and unforgiving, and any food at all trumped the constant hunger they'd grown up with. Music played from a portable radio by the cooking pots, and a few tentative smiles greeted offers of second helpings. Dusty and hot as the setting was, it was better than the camp, and whatever good luck had resulted in them being chosen for this treat was appreciated by all of them.

One of the matrons ordered them to use the bathroom before they got back on the road – a series of holes in the ground behind stacks of rotting pallets to create a modicum of privacy. When all had relieved themselves, they were herded back onto two buses in the courtyard, both of which now bore the insignia of a relief organization emblazoned over fresh, roller-applied white paint.

The engines started with coughs of exhaust, and a man climbed on board each, carrying a bundle of papers and a bag of dates. The buses backed from the compound as the gloaming painted the desert sky lavender and salmon, the few puffs of high clouds neon cotton against the glowing celestial backdrop, and then it lurched onto the main road, receiving only a few curious stares from pedestrians braving the swelter as the sun sank into the western hills.

The men and women who'd attended to the children lined up for their pay, and upon receiving their dinars, made for the street after a few words of warning from the paymaster. None questioned the odd spectacle they'd participated in; the unintelligible and nonsensical was a routine feature of life in a country plagued by war, first with neighboring Iran and then with the Americans and now with each other, as well as with assorted collections of native mercenaries and murderers. To be offered a day's work in an economy teetering on the brink of collapse was not to be dismissed as anything but a stroke of good fortune, as was the opportunity to care for some of the children, innocent casualties of systematic brutality that was older than any of them, and the only thing most of them knew.

By the time night fell, the compound was completely dark, the gate padlocked shut, and there remained no trace of the day's events other than a smoldering barrel with the ashes of the children's clothes in it at the far edge of the courtyard. A scrawny dun-colored dog poked along the wall, sniffing for any evidence of food scraps, drawn by the reek from the crouch toilets evaporating in the heat, and after vainly probing the gate for an opening, loped away in search of more promising fare.

CHAPTER 43

Jet sat at the hotel room table, poring over the materials Levi had sent to her secure inbox, having protected the data with military-grade encryption and a onetime password he'd given her before signing off. He hadn't been exaggerating when he'd described his research on the triad boss as thorough, and she was impressed by the amount of information he'd amassed and its level of detail, given the short period of time he'd had to conduct surveillance.

The gangster had a sumptuous home by Beijing standards, located on the outskirts of the city in a relatively new area where successful entrepreneurs and celebrities had gravitated, the neighborhood largely unknown to any but the rich and their servants. Levi had both satellite photographs as well as covert shots of the wall surrounding the property, presumably taken by one of the local assets.

The main house was over fifteen thousand feet of ostentatious nouveau riche excess, with six master suites on the second floor and a small pond replete with pet swans. The perimeter wall was ten feet high and topped by electric fencing with bright yellow warning signs dangling from the wire. Motion detectors and an alarm system protected the house, with an emergency line that would summon police in the event any of the windows or doors was breached, all of which was described in detail in the architectural plans hacked from the famous American design firm's server.

Jet read with interest the breakdown of the hardware used to control the alarm system, surveillance cameras, detectors, and climate control, the CPUs located in an underground vault with its own cooling system. Access cards were required to enter any of the secure areas, which included the equipment rooms and all the entries to the house, which had card readers mounted beside each door.

Zhao had a retinue of sixteen armed guards at all times, working three eight-hour shifts, their coming and going scrupulously documented by whoever Levi had directed to stake out the home. Each shift had a team leader, and all the men were hardened triad soldiers, undoubtedly killers who had earned the privilege of protecting the crime boss and his family. Most were equipped with submachine guns, and all knew how to use them.

She scanned the leaders' backgrounds, their modes of transport to their duty, even their home addresses, and shook her head in wonder. After two botched operations, it was nice to see that a thorough situational assessment could still be done by her group. It was as complete as she'd have performed if she'd been chartered with planning such a mission, and she was impressed by Levi, even if his bedside manner left much to desire.

Jet next turned to the description of the executable code he'd sent as a self-loading program. It would freeze the security system CPUs and force them to reboot continuously, appearing to the men watching the monitors to be a glitch or hardware fault. Far more elegant than simply shutting down the network, the glitch would appear to be organic, and the program would erase all trace of itself after a half hour of starting and stopping. None of the devices connected to the network would function, but the manner in which the cameras and sensors had been shut down would alleviate suspicion of foul play, and even when a technician checked it, he would find nothing.

The only problem being that the network wasn't connected to the Internet, so it couldn't be hacked remotely. To upload the program, she would need to access a terminal connected to the network, which would require defeating the fencing, detectors, and cameras to access the port.

Which was where the thermite would come in.

It was ingenious, she had to admit. The entire plan was. Its only flaw was that it was completely worthless if the objective were to remove Zhao from the grounds without being mowed down by triad gunmen.

But if you were a lone wolf whose imperative was to gain access without being detected, locate Zhao within his own home, and beat or torture the truth out of him, it could work. Of course, she'd still face the same hurdles Levi had described when she tried to leave, but a single fast-moving operative had a decent chance, whereas a team saddled with a reluctant captive would have been dead meat.

She understood why they had shelved the plan, but for her purposes, it was still impressive. Given the short time frame she had to work with, she would never have been able to cobble together anything like it, especially the results of the week-long surveillance. The trick now would be in the execution, not to mention getting out of the compound without getting killed.

With a frown of concentration, Jet studied the make and model of the backup natural gas generator that would kick in when the power cut off. The transfer switch was programmed to activate after thirty seconds without juice from the street to avoid constant false stops and starts from the area's intermittent brownouts, especially during the rainy season. That was the Achilles' heel of the entire system – assuming you could cut the power without arousing suspicion, breach the wall, and then make it past the cameras, motion sensors, keypads, scanners, and armed thugs, all before the generator kicked in.

If someone had changed the default program, the plan wouldn't work.

If she couldn't run the gauntlet of obstacles and make it to an entrance before the generator began operating, it wouldn't work.

She could think of a dozen other reasons it might not work.

None of which fazed her.

Jet was used to pulling off the impossible. It was what she did, and she was the best. This, however, would test every one of her skills, and the slightest misstep or miscalculation would be fatal.

She smiled to herself. "So what else is new?" she whispered, and moved to the blueprint to commit the floor plan to memory, humming tunelessly as she zoomed in on areas of interest, the challenge of the mission fully engaging her in a way she sometimes missed.

When she called Loren again, she was sure she'd be able to at least get into the compound, if without any guarantee of getting back out. That would be up to a host of uncontrollable variables she'd have to deal with as they arose. But she was confident she could at least get to Zhao, which was farther along than she'd been that morning.

"We'll have the visa by four," Loren said.

"And the contact in Beijing?"

He gave her a cell phone number and a name. She repeated it back to him and then paused. "Only one number?"

"The other contact didn't answer."

"Did you already speak to this one?"

"Yes. I told him you'd want a handgun, and he indicated it wouldn't be a problem, even on short notice. There are plenty of weapons lost from military sources every year. Not unusual."

"Perfect. There's a flight at six. How do I get the visa?"

"Sarah can deliver it."

"Perfect."

Loren paused, and when he spoke, his tone was softer. "Good luck."

"Let's hope I don't need any."

CHAPTER 44

Kermanshah, Iran

A beige Toyota Land Cruiser twisted up a dirt trail in the hills overlooking Kermanshah, the peaks of the Zagros Mountains like jagged shards of broken gray glass along the pale blue horizon. Abu Azim rocked back and forth as the vehicle struggled up the incline, a recent rockslide having made the final stretch all but impassable. His hawk-like eyes scanned the slope ahead, a permanent frown reflecting his mood, even now, as the hour of victory neared. Azim was a pessimist by nature and would believe that his people would finally obtain justice when it happened, and not before. Too many years of bitter disappointment had forged his nature for him to be optimistic, even though everything was on schedule and all the parts had fit neatly into place.

The track veered sharply left, and when the Toyota rounded the bend, four men toting Kalashnikov AK-47s blocked the route, barrels pointed at him. Azim braked to a stop and the tallest of the gunmen approached. When he saw who was driving, his face broke into a grin.

"Ah. Sorry. We weren't expecting you for another hour, at least," he said.

"I made good time. How is everything going?"

"We are ready."

"Good. Show me."

The man called out to the others, who turned and made their way up the hill, and then rounded the hood and climbed into the passenger seat, his face sun burnished and dusty. The truck lunged forward, tires spinning on the gravel until gaining purchase. Azim glanced over at the gunman and returned his eyes to the trail as he spoke.

"Have you had any unexpected visitors?"

"No. Few are out during the day this time of year, as you predicted."

Azim grunted. "How much farther?"

"Perhaps a hundred meters."

Another curve brought them to the end of the track, where camouflage netting covered four surface-to-air missile launchers freshly painted beige to match the terrain, their markings erased by the coating of color. Azim managed a small smile as he stepped from the vehicle. Perhaps this time, things would indeed be different.

The gunman accompanied Azim to the missile launchers and stood by the nearest one, hand on the guidance module.

"These fit like a glove," he said.

"The technician verified they are all functioning correctly?"

"Yes. As far as he can tell without launching them."

The frown was back. "What does that mean? Is there a chance they won't work?" Azim growled.

The gunman shook his head. "No. He tested all of the connections, inspected the microprocessors, and said they are all good."

Azim gazed off at Mount Parau in the distance. Its peak shone white with the snow that capped it year round. "We can't afford any errors."

"There will be none."

"See that there aren't," Azim ordered, his tone ominous. "And the rest of the gear?"

The gunman looked down at a building at the edge of the city. "It is already in place."

"The men are not showing any signs of weakness?"

"No. They are ready for their sacrifice. They understand their role and will do what they must."

Azim walked to another piece of equipment – a mobile radar array, its wheels chocked in place, the screen covered with a protective piece of plastic. "I am proud of all of you. This is a great thing. You will make history. The beast will be dealt a death blow. They will know what it is to suffer, as we have for so many years."

"It is an honor to be a part of this. We wouldn't have it any other way."

Azim nodded. "The batteries are fully charged?"

"Yes. And we have test run the generator. We will start it when you give the signal. There is sufficient fuel and power to last six hours."

"That's more than you'll need."

"We thought it best to be over-prepared."

"Always wise," Azim agreed, and glanced at the others. "Where are the technician and the missile operator?"

"We have them in a house in the city. Three of my most trusted men are with them to ensure nobody has a change of heart. They will return in a few hours."

"You think that's necessary?"

"I am trying to anticipate anything that could interfere with our success. Such as a last-minute display of weakness."

"Let us hope that they are as committed as we are."

"They are, but they also are doing this for pay. That makes them less reliable than those whose commitment is total."

Azim nodded approvingly. "It is a prudent step." He strode back to the truck with the gunman, his brow ridged with thought. When he reached the driver's door, he paused. "The cargo will arrive this evening. We will effect payment when everything is in place. I will remain in contact to keep you informed should anything change."

The gunman patted the satellite phone in his pocket. "I will wait for word from you."

"If all goes well, I will return before the show begins. I want to be here to see it."

The gunman nodded. "This is a once-in-a-lifetime event. We will expect you, then."

"I wouldn't miss it for anything. And the mullah will want a real-time report of the launch."

"I look forward to it."

Azim climbed back into the truck and started the engine. "You have done well."

"*Allahu akbar.*"

Azim reversed in a half circle and then began the long ride back down the mountain to the mosque in Kermanshah that was giving him shelter, his mind searching for anything that could go wrong. The planning had been painstaking, the mullah having presided over every aspect, right down to the funding. The normal problems that Azim would have expected due to the unorganized and amateur nature of many waging jihad had been eliminated by the mullah, whose background lent itself to detail.

And it was his money and, more importantly, his pride on the line. He had invested not only a small fortune in carrying out the strike but his honor by associating his name with the operation. The mullah had spent the better part of the last three months arranging the world-shattering events, and Azim knew he had left nothing to chance.

But there was still a knot in his gut as he navigated the trail back, watched by his men until he became a speck against the brown cliffs, the SUV the only thing moving on the forlorn hillside.

CHAPTER 45

Beijing, China

Jet moved toward the immigration area in the Beijing Capital International Airport amidst a swarm of other travelers, four flights having arrived at roughly the same time. The passport lanes were all open, however, due to processing time built up by the backlog of passengers, many of whom had traveled from Europe and India on long flights – to the point where the ventilation system was struggling to keep up with the throng and the area was redolent with the cooking wool smell particular to humans after extended time in planes.

She quelled her impatience at the sluggish progress, keenly aware of the passage of time she didn't have but unable to do anything to speed the process along. After an agonizing hour it was her turn, and she handed her Spanish passport and newly minted visa to a stone-faced woman with acne scars and a mannish haircut, who scrutinized the passport like she was checking for counterfeit banknotes before moving to the visa and looking it over with similar care. After a long pause, she reached for her phone and placed a call, and moments later a tall man approached and nodded to Jet.

"Purpose of your visit?" he asked in fluent Spanish.

"Pleasure," she responded.

"Where will you be staying?"

"I haven't decided on a hotel. Can you recommend one?" she asked, stressing the sibilance of her *s* in the Castilian fashion.

The man looked her up and down and then turned to the woman and said something in Cantonese before returning to Jet. "I'm afraid we aren't allowed to. There are information booths in the terminal."

The woman passed Jet's passport and visa back to her and signaled to the next person in line. Jet shouldered her backpack and beamed at the man. "Thanks anyway."

"Enjoy your stay in Beijing."

"I plan to."

She faced another excruciating wait at customs and forced herself not to check her watch every few minutes. When she had cleared that hurdle, she hurried to the high-speed rail station that would carry her to the Sanyuanqiao district, and paid the fare. The thirty-minute ride ate yet more time, and by the point she stepped out of the train, she was as agitated as she allowed herself to get.

On the street, bright with neon and streetlights, the air heavy with pollution and the sidewalk teeming with humanity, she withdrew her sat phone from the backpack and powered it on. Her Beijing contact answered, his English reasonable.

"I'm off the train," she said.

"There's a coffee shop two blocks south. The Beanery. I'll meet you there."

"What are you wearing?"

"Jeans, a black shirt, and a baseball hat with a white Mercedes logo. You can't miss me."

"Perfect."

"See you in five."

The coffee shop could have been anywhere in the world, from Buenos Aires to New York, except that the clientele was entirely Chinese. She entered and looked around the faux living room seating area, with its comfortably distressed furniture of an urban, bohemian style, and spotted her contact sitting at a two-top table with a steaming cup in hand. She walked over and sat across from him, her face a blank.

"Ken," she said, the name a statement, not a question.

"That's right. And you are?"

"Kim."

"You want some coffee or tea?"

"No, thanks." She slid a pen from her pocket and began writing on a paper napkin beside Ken's cup. When she was finished, she sat back and waited for him to read it. He leaned forward and did, his eyes giving away nothing. When he was done, he offered a fleeting smile.

"That's quite a shopping list."

"Our friend said you already have some of it."

Ken nodded thoughtfully. "That's right. I'm just thinking about where I can find the metal powder at this hour. Not to mention a clean motorcycle." He took a slurp of his coffee and eyed her. "When do you need this by?"

"Yesterday. And the bike doesn't have to be clean. It just has to not show up as stolen for twenty-four hours. After that it won't matter."

Ken studied her. "You'll probably want a helmet, too."

"Put it on my tab."

"Will first thing in the morning work?"

"I need the sap now."

He laughed and then realized she was serious. "Really?"

"I have a date at midnight I don't want to miss."

His eyes narrowed. "Lucky man."

She held his gaze. "I didn't say it was a man."

"None of my business." He removed a slim cell from his pocket and held it to his ear, spoke almost inaudibly into it for a few minutes, and hung up. "I can have it in an hour. The rest will have to be tomorrow."

"That won't fly. I need it all before...eleven thirty." She leaned forward after glancing around to ensure nobody was paying them any attention. "Our friend said you were good. Time to prove it."

"That only gives me...three hours."

"I'll double your pay."

The grin came back. "You convinced me. Meet back here?"

"What time does it close?"

"It doesn't."

"Then I'll see you at eleven thirty. No later."

Ken knocked back the rest of his drink and stood. She watched him walk to the entrance and leave, and surveyed the crowd for signs of anyone showing any special interest in her. A Caucasian man she'd missed upon entering glanced at her from where he was waiting at the bar for his drink and looked away. Jet rose and made for the door, the hair on the back of her neck prickling.

The man stepped in front of her and she relaxed. No pro would confront his target. She immediately understood that his interest wasn't related to her work.

"You're not from around here, are you?" he asked in English tinged with an Australian accent. She smiled and shrugged to indicate that she didn't understand. He switched to Chinese and got the same uncomprehending look. Jet brushed past him and ignored the feel of his hand on her bottom, refusing to give in to the urge to break every bone in it as a lesson against groping. Instead, she continued to the exit and hurried out the door, the threat posed by a masher unworthy of even considering. If he insisted on following her, he'd get the most unpleasant surprise of his life, but she wouldn't tempt fate by waiting around to deliver it.

Fortunately for him, he remained in the shop, and she moved into the crowd, just another young woman among millions on a hot summer street, invisible as long as she kept her hair hanging in her face and her head down. She paused at a shop window fifty meters from the coffee shop to confirm that she wasn't being tailed, and when she was sure she was clean, went in search of a restaurant where she could load up on protein before what could well be the longest night of her life.

After she'd found a promising eatery and settled in, she checked the time and calculated the difference in Tel Aviv – five hours behind Beijing time, so 3:40 p.m. at home. She took out a burner cell she'd acquired on the street and tapped in Matt's cell phone number. The warbling ringtone reminded her of how far she was from those she loved, and when he answered, his tone puzzled, her heart caught in her throat.

"Yes?" he said.

"How's Hannah doing?"

A pause. "Is it really you?"

"In the flesh."

"She wants to know when her mama is coming home. So do I."

"A couple more days. Things got complicated."

Matt had been in the life long enough to know better than to ask for any detail. "But you're okay?"

"Never better. How about you?"

"Bored out of my skull."

"You should take a trip. I hear Cyprus is lovely this time of year."

Static hissed on the line as Matt processed what she'd said. "Is it? I hadn't realized."

"Hannah would love it. A nice spontaneous surprise. I'm sure there are still flights today."

He didn't miss a beat. "That's an excellent idea. She's tired of being cooped up, that's for sure."

"I'll call later, when I can. Let me know where you'll be staying."

"Of course. How long have you heard is enough time there to see all the sights?"

"I'd keep it open-ended. You might fall in love with the place."

"I've been known to do that. Hate to leave the valuables here, though, if we're going to be gone for any length of time."

"Keep them close to your heart. You'll be fine." The stash of diamonds that comprised their emergency fund was still in the leather pouch Jet had worn around her neck during their travels. She hoped Matt would read between the lines, and was relieved when he did.

"Sure thing. Do you need anything?"

"Not at the moment. Is Hannah there?"

"She's down for her nap. Should I wake her?"

Jet desperately wanted to hear her daughter's voice, but didn't want to disturb her. "Just tell her Mama loves her. And you too."

"I love you too." He hesitated. "Stay out of trouble."

"I'll do my best. Best to check flights sooner than later."

"I'm already on it. Take care of yourself."

"You too."

Her voice cracked on the final word and she signed off, her

message delivered. She was sure the Mossad was monitoring Matt's cell traffic, and the director might be furious with her for tipping Matt that he should get out of Dodge, but if she wasn't successful tonight, or something happened… She wasn't going to take any chances with her loved ones. That was off the table.

A waitress arrived and placed an English menu before her, Jet's features announcing her as a foreigner to the natives, and Jet quickly read it and pointed to the dishes she wanted. The woman bowed slightly and rushed off to process the order, and Jet was left to mull over how she was going to proceed once Ken delivered the goods. Her instinct was to wait not an instant longer than she had to. She'd requested a number of items in addition to the weapons and motorcycle: a sap, a box of sparklers, a disposable lighter, a small ceramic planter, a box of coffee filters, a set of lock picks, a measuring cup, and a few other necessities she felt might come in handy. If Ken was true to his word, she'd go in tonight, well ahead of the deadline on the Korean document – which was tomorrow.

The waitress set her meal down on the table, and Jet picked at the steamed fish and sipped her tea, taking her time, unable to do anything until she had her supplies, thinking of Matt and the horror of a bio-attack, visions of a laughing Hannah running in the spring sunshine at the forefront of her thoughts.

CHAPTER 46

Herzliya, Israel

The director's desk phone buzzed at him and he looked up from the satellite imagery he was studying on his computer monitor and stabbed the line to life, the handset on speaker mode.

"What is it?" He had left instructions not to be disturbed, and had lain down on his sofa for a catnap but been unable to rest, and so had gone back to eyeing the terrain around Kermanshah and zooming in on the building that would be targeted in the raid. The city was one of the oldest in Iran, home to almost a million people, densely populated and only partially recovered from the devastation wrought during the Iraq-Iran war, when it had been largely destroyed. As he'd told the council, jets were the preferred delivery system for the strike, due to the accuracy with which they could pinpoint their payloads, minimizing the potential for collateral damage – although to completely destroy the building's surroundings in such a fashion that any bioweapon would be neutralized would be impossible, and depending on what nightmare was in the building, a cloud of it could easily blow downwind, affecting hundreds or even thousands.

It was his assistant. "Sir, you need to come down to conference room A-2 immediately."

The director's blood chilled at the words. There were few things too sensitive to discuss on a secure line to the director's office, and right now, there was only one he could think of that would prompt the call.

"I'll be down shortly. Have the others been contacted?"

"Yes, sir. They're on their way."

It was as he suspected. The Security Council had been summoned, which could only mean the worst.

"Are the feeds ready?"

"Of course, sir. As you instructed."

"Very well. When will they arrive?"

"ETA is ten minutes for the last of them."

"I'll be down in eleven." He paused. "Send your briefing to my computer so I can come up to speed when I speak to them."

"It's already done, sir."

An icon in the corner of the screen pulsed red at him. "Good."

The director hung up and reached for his cigarettes. He lit one, switched his monitor from the sat feed to his desktop, and clicked on the icon. A data file appeared and he read it quickly, noting the times on it, the substance of the report already known to him. He reread it a final time and then deleted it from his drive, stubbed the cigarette out, and stood. The moment he'd been dreading had arrived; the point of no return reached.

When he stepped into the conference room, the only member of the council missing was its chair, Nahum Weisenthal. Hurried footsteps sounded from the hall as the door closed behind him and moments later Weisenthal entered with an expression like he'd drunk battery acid. The director nodded to him and then the others.

"Nahum…gentlemen, you know why we're here. The Americans alerted us the moment it happened. Twenty-two minutes ago, the account in the Caymans was credited the final payment amount. So the weapon has been delivered to the target."

The men nodded as one. Weisenthal's complexion was sallow. "We're out of time. Are we all in agreement? Anyone have any last minute doubts they want on the record?"

Nobody did. The general eyed Weisenthal, who sighed. "Very well. Give the order."

"The secure relays are in place. You can use that," the director said, pointing at the red handset beside a more innocuous white one. "It's a direct line to command."

The general reached for the phone and lifted the handset to his ear. "This is Beta Six. Order the birds into the air. Repeat. Order the birds into the air." He waited for confirmation and then hung up and faced the others. The director sat forward.

"What happens now?"

Weisenthal blinked several times, and when he answered, his tone was hard. "It will take just over an hour for the planes to be within range. They will scramble and be in the air in ten minutes. So in…an hour fifteen, tops, we will be at war with Iran. All of our troops are on the highest alert, and we're ready for any of a number of reactions, from diplomatic to military. Our missile defense systems are active, and the Americans have been notified that they are to regard the area a hot zone and to refrain from any coalition flights until the situation has stabilized. We can't be sure of the Russian response, or how Iran will react, but we have to expect the worst."

"We have the dossier prepared for release immediately following the strike," Gabriel said. "It will go to the Americans, the Russians, and the Iranians. We believe that will cause all concerned to stand down, and the attack will be seen as legitimate self-defense – a preemptive strike necessary for our survival."

"Of course Iran will deny it," the director said.

"The Americans will corroborate it," Weisenthal said. "The Russians will have no choice but to back off from any overt military action in the face of their confirmation. Without Russia's backing, Iran won't dare retaliate. They'll make noise, but in the end they will want this to go away just as badly as we will."

Gabriel didn't look convinced, but held his tongue. His expression drew Weisenthal's ire, though. "What is it?"

"We have no indisputable evidence of any bioweapon. That's the problem in all of this."

"We've been over this a dozen times," Weisenthal snapped. "This isn't Iraq, and we aren't the Americans or the British. We would never attack Iran on false pretenses. Nobody in their right mind would believe that. The risk to us is too great. There could only be one reason, and that will be clear from the dossier."

"We'll take heat for it. We all know that."

"Heat will fade over time."

"Not in the Arab world."

The director shrugged. "They hate us now. They'll still hate us after. What will change?"

"I'm not arguing," Gabriel protested. "I'm just pointing out the obvious hole."

"It's a nonissue," Weisenthal said.

Gabriel nodded. "I hope you're right."

The director grunted. "We have set up real-time monitoring in the next room. We'll be able to watch the progress through the plane and pilot cameras." He pushed his chair back. "Gentlemen?"

The men trooped out, all clearly troubled, the weight of what they had just done already a burden they would carry to the grave. For the first time as a nation, Israel was going to attack Iran, whom it had been accusing of being a dangerous aggressor for generations. The international ramifications were seismic, and nobody believed that their problems weren't just starting, regardless of any dossier or data proffered.

Like it or not, they had authorized an overt act of war against the most dangerous adversary in the Middle East, and not a one of them doubted that, justified or not, there would be hell to pay.

CHAPTER 47

Beijing, China

Liu Bo yawned as he waited at the bus stop amidst six other unfortunates, the hour, at fifteen minutes past midnight, late. He lived in a district on the other side of the city from his master Zhao Yaozu's palatial spread, in a more modest area of working-class Chinese. But Liu was anything but working class – rather, he was a career criminal in the employ of the triad, for whom he'd handled everything from extortion to slavery to murder for hire. Now, as the head of the evening security shift for Zhao, he was on easy street, his life more predictable, his hours unvarying even as the duty was uneventful. Which allowed him time for side businesses that padded his salary considerably: drug dealing and enforcement work in his neighborhood. If you had a problem with a business rival or suspected your wife of cheating on you, he was also available, all outside of his arrangement with the triad.

Another dull eight hours of tedium under his belt, protecting his boss from nothing, he patted his growling stomach, which had grown more ample since he'd taken over what was really a desk job three years earlier. It was boring work, watching the feed in the home's security suite and monitoring the patrols to ensure everyone was doing their job, but he'd adapted to the hours and the steady pay, which after thirty years of sporadic feast or famine from criminal endeavors he'd grown to appreciate, if not depend upon.

He ran a hand across his face, which was underscored by a knife scar just above his chin that traced his jawline. His features were sharp and cruel, accurately reflecting his nature. Liu had killed his first man at fourteen and had taken the lives of so many since then he

229

didn't bother to keep count. It was a job, like any other, and he was a professional who was good at what he did. That was how he viewed it, and he slept as well as anyone in the city, untroubled by guilt or doubts. He enjoyed an unsurpassed stream of paid talent to keep him company whenever in the mood, ate well, and consumed conspicuously for his station in life. That he lived in a modest home was by choice – he could have owned an expensive car and a desirable apartment in one of the swanky high-rises the new money favored, but he preferred a low profile. Even in China, where the triads had substantial sway, it didn't pay to flout your wealth – unless you were at his boss's level, in which case there were no rules; as the head of a powerful triad, Zhao Yaozu was virtually untouchable.

The bus arrived, and Liu waited for the rest of the grunions to trudge up the steps before following them inside. He took a window seat in the half-empty cabin and settled in for the thirty-minute ride back to reality, eyes closed, sprawled across the entire bench to discourage anyone from sitting beside him.

Four more passengers loaded on at the next stop, and he barely stirred at the vibration when the bus picked up speed again through the mostly empty streets. The cabin filled with the rumble of the engine, nobody talking, and he rode in comfortable silence, his stomach growling occasionally lest he forget that he hadn't eaten dinner yet, his body on a different schedule than most.

Jet watched the back of the triad enforcer's head from three seats behind, having boarded the bus at the stop after his once she'd watched him mount the bus steps at his stop. She'd gunned the motor of her newly acquired 250 cc motorcycle and arrived with plenty of time to spare, parked it in the shadows, and made her way to the bench to await the bus's arrival. She'd debated following it on the bike but had decided to err on the side of caution rather than risking being pulled over or being unable to park at his end point without attracting attention, and figured she would be able to return in about the same amount of time it would take on the motorcycle, the buses moving at a fast clip on the deserted boulevards.

She knew Liu Bo's entire history from the dossier and could have waited at his apartment building for his arrival; but again, didn't want to risk his taking a detour to a night spot. There was only one sure way to know where he was at all times, and this was it. She shifted on the uncomfortable plastic seat, her backpack beside her, her thoughts on the operation to come, Liu a footnote in the series of difficult maneuvers that would be required to pull it off.

Twenty-three minutes later, Liu yawned and stirred, and she stiffened. He reached for the button that signaled the driver to stop at the next corner, and stood. Jet remained seated, pretending to text on her burner cell phone, as half the riders were likewise doing. If Liu noticed her, he didn't give any indication, and he brushed past her seat without glancing in her direction.

Jet waited until he'd stepped from the bus and begun walking before rising and following him out the door, and then waited for the bus to pull away, as though planning to cross the street behind it. Liu was oblivious to her subterfuge and walked briskly in the direction of his building a block and a half away, she knew from the dossier.

When he turned the corner, she sprinted after him, the soles of her boots silent on the sidewalk. She withdrew a black baseball cap and pulled it on backward, changing her appearance from a late twentysomething going home from work to a university student leaving a party.

Liu slowed as he neared his apartment, a ten-story affair built fifteen years earlier during a period of runaway expansion, and lit a cigarette. He had food in his refrigerator but was tempted to buy takeout to save cooking time, until he remembered a container of lo mein from the prior day that would go bad if he didn't finish it. He exhaled a thick cloud of smoke and picked up his pace. The sidewalk empty in front of him except for another pedestrian ahead, striding in the same direction.

He turned into the walkway that led to the glass doors of his building, and then slowed, sensing someone behind him. He spun, but relaxed when he saw that it was only a young girl busy on her cell phone. She nearly ran into him, so occupied by her texting was she, and he smirked to himself at the kids these days, living in a bubble, experiencing life through a screen instead of in high-definition reality.

Liu continued to his door and never saw the blow that dropped him like a sack of bricks.

Jet swung the sap, a leather pouch filled with lead grapeshot that was attached by a heavy spring to a wooden handle, and struck the triad killer in the temple. The blow was carefully calculated to cause maximum damage; the momentum of the strike created by the combination of the lead and the spring was enough to kill in a single blow without any visible sign of trauma if delivered correctly. She didn't care whether it was lethal or not – at the very least, he would be down with a concussion for the duration, and at worst, the world would be no poorer for the elimination of a predator.

She knelt beside his inert form and frisked him, removing his wallet, then his cheap watch, and finally, his keys, exactly as a mugger might. Jet was finished with the task in twenty seconds and glanced around as she straightened. Secure that she was in the clear, she pocketed Liu's possessions and the sap, and returned to her fascination with her phone while retracing her steps to the bus stop, in no hurry, just another self-involved tech junkie completely immersed in her virtual world.

CHAPTER 48

Tel Aviv, Israel

Four F-16 Fighting Falcon fighter jets sat on the tarmac of the military airstrip while their crews loaded the air-to-ground missiles that would be used on their mission. The pilots unsealed their orders and read them with disbelief, faces clouded with concern. Their commanding officer entered their quarters and they stood and saluted.

He motioned for them to sit. "You understand the objective?"

They nodded. One of the pilots raised his hand. "We're seriously going to strike a target in Iran?"

"That is correct. We're confident it is harboring biological or chemical weapons that pose an imminent threat. This is not a drill. You will be flying low to the ground in order to avoid triggering early warning systems. You have the coordinates and your orders. We will be monitoring the flight real time at the highest levels, and you'll be maintaining radio silence the entire way. It's a stealth strike, exactly like you've been trained for. Should be a milk run for boys of your skill."

The pilots smiled, all of them in their late twenties to mid-thirties, and the best Israel had to offer.

The commander saluted them and glanced at the clock on the wall. "You have five minutes to suit up. Good luck. Dismissed."

The men scrambled for their flight suits, expressions hard, the mission a simple one at its core – fly across the entire country just above the natural terrain, as well as half the Middle East, and then obliterate the target with ordnance that could be guided to within a few feet of accuracy, all while evading detection by hostile forces that would shoot them down in a heartbeat when they didn't respond to any queries as to what the hell they thought they were doing.

Just another day at the office.

Once dressed, the pilots loaded into an electric cart that drove them out to the planes, where the ground crew was finishing their equipment checks and fueling. They wasted no time boarding their fighters and ran through their preflight checks with studied calm, their course already plotted on their flight computers. According to the briefing paragraph that had accompanied the mission orders, they would fly over Jordan, skirting Saudi Arabia, cross Iraq, and then dogleg north, heading into Iranian airspace at Qasr-e Shirin before continuing to their target. The dicey part of the entire proposition, if launching a strike that would be an act of war against the most powerful military in the region wasn't sufficient, would be sticking close enough to the mountainous terrain once on the Iranian side without smacking into the side of a cliff.

Their checks complete, the turbines spooled up and the flight commander taxied to the end of the runway. The other F-16s followed close behind, their lights extinguished as per their instructions. After requesting and receiving clearance from the tower, the first jet rolled onto the runway and accelerated at blinding velocity, becoming airborne in seconds and streaking upward at a radical angle.

The rest of the pilots followed at half-minute intervals, and in no time were flying in formation a hundred meters above the ground, invisible except for the roar of their jets, keeping to subsonic speed to avoid creating sonic booms.

The ground crew retreated to the hangars, and the commanding officer stood staring at the runway, his chiseled features set in a scowl. This mission was a first in his twenty-five years in the service. His aide waited beside him with a neutral expression. When the sound of the planes had faded into nothingness, the commander spun on his heel and faced his assistant, his face softening somewhat.

"I hope the brass knows what they're doing."

The aide remained silent, no response required. The base was now on the highest state of alert, and the other fighters were being readied for a full-scale attack; the plan was to be in the air when the strike was launched in case incoming missiles destroyed the base.

The commander exhaled and strode to the administrative offices, his assistant in tow. The mobilization of the entire Israeli air force now required his undivided attention, the fighter formation a cause set in motion that would do what it did, and his duty now was to prepare for the aftermath.

CHAPTER 49

Beijing, China

Jet switched off the motorcycle's engine and walked it a block to leave it behind a hedge near Zhao's mansion. She'd ridden around the area several times and felt like she knew it cold from the dossier, which had diagrammed and contained photographs of everything from the location of the transformer to promising trees that could be used for cover to the hedge.

Once the bike was out of sight of the street, so no police would be tempted to ask what an unfamiliar vehicle was doing in the upscale neighborhood, she locked it and slipped the key into her pocket, leaving the helmet dangling from one of the handlebars. She looked around the darkened street a final time and set off for the transformer, which was around the corner and down the block, by Zhao's grounds.

She knew from the advance intel the location of the security cameras, which on the exterior of the property were located at the service and main entrances, so she had no fear of detection as she went to work on the transformer. When she reached it, she ducked down behind the green metal housing that protected it from the elements, removed her backpack, and set it beside her. She withdrew the small clay flowerpot and fit a coffee filter into it, and then retrieved the measuring cup and two bags of metal powder, one containing iron rust and the other powdered aluminum.

After measuring out roughly 75% rust to 25% aluminum, she inspected the nearly full pot and nodded. That would do the trick. She set the pot within easy reach and, after a glance down the sidewalk to ensure she was still unobserved, went to work with the lock picks on the padlock that held the cowling in place. The padlock yielded to her efforts in less than a minute, and she replaced the picks in her bag and felt for a small oil can. She squeezed a liberal amount on the pair of hinges on the other base of the housing and then replaced the can in her bag and lifted the heavy weather shield open.

The transformer hummed steadily from the current pulsing through it. After inspecting it, she located the thick cable that supplied power from the street, and then eyed the nearby tree that rose three stories from the sidewalk. Jet nodded to herself and moved to her backpack, removed the box of sparklers, and selected ten. She twisted the wire bases together and stuck the bundle into the powder at an angle, so half of its length was hanging over the edge of the pot, and then placed the container onto the oversized bolt that secured the street power cable to the transformer.

After another look around, she sealed and replaced the bags of metal powder and the sparkler box in the backpack and slipped the pistol from it, chambered a round, and wedged the gun into her waistband, pocketing the two spare magazines. Finished with her preparations, she slid the backpack on and felt for the disposable lighter in her pocket. When she had it in hand, she leaned toward the flowerpot, flicked it to life, and held the flame to the sparklers.

The bundle caught after several seconds, and Jet quickly swung the cowling closed and snapped the padlock back into place, smiling at the glow that emanated from the slotted vents on either side. Now that the homemade fuse was lit, she estimated she had a minute, possibly less, to make it up the tree. She ran to it as fast as she could, her belt in hand, and wrapped one end around the trunk. She gripped both ends and slid the belt as high up the bark as she could reach, and then pulled herself up, gripping the trunk with her knees before repeating the maneuver twice.

Once she was perched on a thick branch, she cinched the belt back in place around her waist and eyed the top of the wall, a gap of eight feet between her and the electric fencing. The mansion glowed fifteen meters beyond it. She held her breath as she counted seconds in her head, watching the gunmen on the inside gathered by the entrance, smoking and talking in hushed tones. She forced her heart rate to slow and began breathing again once it was within a normal range, her body tense as a steel spring in anticipation of the power going out.

A few moments later, a loud hiss like water through a fire hose sounded from the transformer, and a blinding flash of white flame shot from the vents along with thick clouds of smoke. Several beats later the grounds went dark, every light in the house blinking off in unison. The guards cursed in confusion, and Jet threw herself from the tree to the wall, sailing through the night like a bat, arms extended in front of her.

She hit the top of the wall hard enough to knock her breath from her, but her fingers latched onto the edge, preventing her from falling. Precious seconds she didn't have ticked by, and she was finally able to gasp and haul herself up and over the wall, squeezing below the bottom wire of the electric fence, which was positioned so it would have fried her had current been running through it.

Jet dropped to the ground and was instantly in motion, sprinting for the service entrance at the rear of the house. She reached it just as the backup generator sputtered to life, and the lights winked back on with an audible snap. After pausing to remove the key card she'd lifted from Liu's wallet, she held it against the scanner mounted by the door and the lock clicked once. She twisted the handle and eased the door open, and then she was in.

Her next obstacle was to locate the terminal she needed before a guard happened across her and the game got ugly. She knew the layout cold from her study of the blueprint, but didn't see the terminal. She swore under her breath and made for the stairs that led down to the basement server vault, where there was another terminal – unless they had removed that one too. Eyes on the door to the stairs, she groped for the butterfly knife in her back pocket and flipped it open; if there was anyone guarding the vault, she would have to dispatch them silently, or the entire exercise would have been in vain.

Wen, the graveyard shift supervisor, leaned forward and surveyed the bank of blinking lights on the panel in front of him. His assistant, Dong, frowned and moved to the wall, where the security camera monitors had come back to life.

"Power outage," he said. "We're on the generator."

Wen nodded. "I can hear the damn thing all the way in here."

"Worked like a charm, though. We're back in business."

"We need to call the power company and find out what the problem is."

A handheld radio crackled from a charger on the credenza behind them, and Wen reached for it and held it to his lips. "What happened?" he demanded.

One of the guards' voices answered. "There's a ton of smoke coming from the transformer at the street. Something must have blown or caught fire."

Wen and Dong exchanged a glance. "Send a man out and inspect it. I'll call the power company."

"Will do."

A minute went by, and then another, and the guard's voice called from the radio. "Looks like it blew."

"Is the cover in place?" Wen asked.

"Yeah. Still locked. It's the transformer, though. It's still smoking."

"All right. I'll make the call."

Wen set the radio back in the holder and lifted his cell phone to his ear. He waited as it rang, and then thumbed through an automated attendant menu until he was put through to a live operator. He explained the problem and gave the woman their address, listened as she gave him an estimated time of arrival of two to three hours, and ended the call with a shake of his head.

"Hope the boss doesn't wake up from the damned generator noise."

Dong made a face. "He's been taking enough dope to sleep through cannon fire. I wouldn't sweat it."

Both men chuckled, although nervously. Zhao was still one of the most powerful men in the city, and to enjoy a bit of humor at his expense carried with it more than a little danger.

Jet reached the server vault door and used the key card again to unlock it. Inside, the temperature was at least thirty degrees cooler than in the hall, thanks to a powerful climate control system that pumped glacial air through grates at the top of the far wall. She closed the door behind her and switched on her flashlight, and swept the room with the beam until it settled on a terminal next to a rack of servers.

She crossed the floor in five steps and withdrew a USB drive from her front pocket as she sat at the terminal. After a moment's study of the terminal, she inserted the drive into one of the ports on the front of the server and powered it on, waiting impatiently as it booted up. When the screen blinked to life, she watched as a menu alerted her that a new program was trying to run an executable program, and asked if she wished to proceed or abort. At least that was what she believed it said – all the words were in Chinese.

Jet closed her eyes and envisioned her own system, and which side of the query was always the proceed button.

The left, of course, she thought, and was reaching for the mouse before stopping herself.

What if in China the menu was reversed? She had no reason to believe it was, but second-guessed herself. Cars drove on the right side of the road, just like in most countries. It stood to reason that they would have kept the menu the same.

At least that was her hope.

She selected the button on the left, hovered the mouse over it, and clicked it once.

The drive blinked five times and went dark.

She retrieved the drive and pocketed it, and then moved to the servers, staring at them with enough intensity to power a small city.

And smiled when they all stuttered and rebooted.

Wen gaped at the bank of monitors, which had suddenly filled with gray static.

"What the hell?" he exclaimed, and turned to his terminal. The screen indicated that the system was rebooting, and he cursed long and hard, the oath comparing the computer manufacturer to the nether regions of a none-too-hygienic pig.

Dong shrugged as he watched the sequence start, run through the boot process, and then shut down before booting again.

"Generator probably screwed something up. Either that or the transformer," he said.

"Crap. You know how to troubleshoot the servers?"

Dong shook his head. "Not unless kicking them would work."

"Might be worth a try. Any of the others know about computers?"

"Very funny."

"Thought it was worth asking."

Dong frowned. "I could go down and disconnect them, and see if plugging them back in does anything. That's what I do with my modem at home when it quits."

Wen sighed at how his night was going so far. "Might as well. Can't see how it could hurt."

Dong nodded and hooked one of the handheld radios on the way to the door. "Maybe try peeing on them if that doesn't do the trick?"

"You'll probably just fry yourself. If restarting them doesn't fix the problem, I'll call a tech."

"Who will no doubt be awake at two in the morning, just in case we need anything."

"There's probably a night watchman or something at the alarm company. Maybe they have somebody on call."

Dong rolled his eyes at the optimistic idea, but decided to hold his tongue when he saw Wen's expression. Instead, he checked the time and reached for the doorknob.

"Let me go take a look."

CHAPTER 50

Samuel, the flight leader, banked gently to port and climbed slightly as his plane sliced through the air over the Syrian desert, the landscape pitch black beneath him. He couldn't see the other planes, but his radar had them in tight formation behind him. He checked the time and saw that thirty-eight minutes had passed since takeoff, which based on their current position would put them over the target in about another half an hour.

A turbulent spell from a thermal updraft rising off the hot sand buffeted the jet, jostling Samuel against his harness, and he automatically performed a quick read of his gauges to verify all was well. The planes were flying at a third of their top speeds, the experience uneventful except for trying to adjust so they didn't plow into the ground. He knew it would get more difficult once they were over Iraq, but was untroubled by the prospect of an additional challenge – a clandestine night run like the one he was leading was the sort of thing that he'd dreamed of when he'd signed up to be a pilot. Now, in the reality of the moment, he realized that little about it was exciting other than the basics of low-altitude, high-speed flight, and his thoughts turned to his wife and young daughter at home in Tel Aviv, no doubt worried about why Daddy had been called away without explanation.

Samuel prayed silently that the mission would end not only successfully but without initiating World War Three – not knowing all of the information upon which the brass had made their decision, the only thing he was sure of was that he was about to perform a clear act of war without Israel having been attacked. The idea didn't give him pause; the thought of his family at home, potentially being exposed to the consequences of his actions – that was the part of the equation that troubled him.

His altitude alarm blinked and he adjusted again, pushing the thoughts from his mind. He had his duty to perform, and it wasn't his place to question orders from the top. If there was a clear and present danger to his homeland, he would take quick and decisive action on its behalf, and the diplomats could sort out the pieces once the threat was neutralized. The missiles he was carrying would fly straight and true to the target, and what happened from there would be out of his hands.

Another bout of turbulence slammed the plane around, and he focused on the task at hand, confirming they were still on course.

It wouldn't be much longer now.

Jet was pulling the server room door closed when she heard the steady approach of footsteps from above. She looked around, knife instantly back in her hand, and spied a storage room door to her left. She barely had time to ease it open and slip inside before the heavy clomping of boots descending the stairs greeted her, and she inched the door closed, unperturbed by the total darkness that enveloped her.

The footsteps rang out on the basement level and she tensed, ready to plunge the blade into whoever opened the door. She felt along the knob in case there was a locking mechanism, but there wasn't, the architects not foreseeing the need for one. She heard the server vault door open and close, and debated trying to sneak by whoever was inspecting the servers – upon reflection, an eventuality that was completely predictable. She'd simply waited too long in the room; a critical error that could be her undoing.

Sweat ran down her spine. The temperature in the small space was stifling, and the air musty and stale. Her eyes slowly adjusted to the darkness, and she could make out a thin band of light seeping beneath the door. She pressed her head against the panel and listened patiently, battling the urge to make a break for it while whoever was checking on the servers was occupied. She almost gave in to her impulse, and then froze when the vault door reopened. A radio squawked, and Jet heard a male voice speak in rapid-fire Chinese only feet from the storeroom. Another voice answered, and then the footsteps resumed, this time ascending the stairs, leaving her sweat-soaked in the confined space.

She waited two minutes, forcing herself to watch the luminescent dial of her watch rather than go by her gut. When she didn't hear anything more, she pushed the door open and stepped into the basement hall. Jet took a deep breath and made for the stairs, more confident now that her brush with discovery was over. The house was large enough that she should be able to make it to the second floor without being spotted, and then all she had to do was find Zhao's room and interrogate him without the sound of their session drawing guards.

Jet inched past the main stairway, an obviously newly installed elevator system mounted to the steps evidence that his leg hadn't healed well. She continued to the kitchen and sidled into the adjoining butler pantry, which was dark as night. She paused, hyperalert, and when she was sure the coast was clear, crept up the service stairway that led from the pantry to the second floor and stood motionless with the door cracked a half inch, listening intently for any hint of movement in the hall. After half a minute of silence, she moved to the wall fader and dimmed the hall lights till they were barely illuminated, wary of waking anyone in the bedrooms with their glow.

She pressed her ear against the first door and, after a few moments of hesitation, slowly turned the ornate antique knob and entered the room, head cocked to the side. Faint moonlight streamed through the window, and at a glance she could see that the bed was empty. She retraced her steps to the hall and made her way to the next door and eased it open.

This room had been set up for a child. She could make out posters of pop bands on the walls and a four-poster bed with Hello Kitty sheets, clearly the mobster's young daughter's. Her forehead crinkled at the sight of another empty bed, and the realization that she had no way of knowing for sure he was in town struck like a piano dropping on her head.

If he was at another one of his homes, the entire exercise would have been futile, and she'd have risked everything for no reason. The thought caused her throat to constrict, and she swallowed hard. There was no point introducing distracting doubts now. She would search every bedroom, and if Zhao wasn't there, slip out the same way she'd come in, with no one the wiser.

Stepping from the little girl's room, she walked silently to a third bedroom and tried the knob, which was unlocked. A sound from the lower floor spooked her, and she twisted the knob and pushed the door open faster than she'd intended.

Jet found herself staring at a figure seated by a massive gray marble fireplace in air-conditioned coolness, flames crackling in the hearth in defiance of the heat outside. The brocade and gold velvet curtains were closed, and a single lamp was illuminated for reading. The woman looked up from her book, obviously startled, and then her eyes locked with Jet's and recognition flashed across her face. She stood, allowing the book to fall from her hand, and glared at Jet with an intensity so powerful it was like a blow.

"You," Sang-mi hissed, and rushed at Jet in a blur.

CHAPTER 51

The Korean woman moved so fast Jet was taken off guard, her impression of the woman's age dispelled by the unexpected burst of speed. Sang-mi collided with her and they fell to the hardwood floor together. Jet turned her head just as the woman tried to blind her with hands curled into claws. The Korean's nails tore the skin of Jet's cheek, and then Jet landed a strike against the side of the woman's head, stunning her long enough for her to roll away.

Sang-mi was back on her feet with surprising agility, and Jet regained her footing as the woman rushed her again. This time Jet was ready for the move and parried it with a judo hold, twisting the Korean's arm and using her momentum against her. Sang-mi slammed into the wall with a grunt but recovered almost instantly, again taking Jet by surprise. Any assumptions about the woman's age that Jet had allowed to cloud her judgment were obviously in error – she had the strength and speed of a younger woman, her reflexes fast as a snake, her moves skilled.

They circled each other, each feinting to throw the other off guard, and Jet recognized the woman's probable hapkido and taekwondo training by her stance. Knowing the martial arts' strengths and weaknesses afforded Jet her first advantage, and she waited for an opening she was sure would come. The Korean was breathing heavily through her nose, a trickle of blood running from it to her mouth, and she licked the crimson thread away without expression, fully focused on Jet, her hands outstretched in an unreadable posture Jet knew was the precursor to another onslaught.

When the flurry of strikes came, they did so with a fury that took Jet's breath away, and she struggled to parry them and deliver blows of her own. One strike to the side of the woman's throat hit home, and her knees buckled. But she regained control in an instant and transitioned the fall into a sweep kick Jet barely avoided, landing hard against the floor but cushioning the fall with her elbow.

Sang-mi's deafening scream signaled that she realized she was outmatched, and Jet knew that it would draw gunmen, the door inadequate to muffle the cry. Jet kicked her with all her might, but she blocked it with her forearm and tried to punch Jet in the groin, missing by scant inches only when Jet turned her hip at the last second. The blow numbed Jet's left leg for a moment – long enough for Sang-mi to scream again and then spring to her feet and press the attack with another series of punches and elbow strikes, which nearly felled Jet as she regained control of her leg and managed to block the most devastating of the blows.

The Korean woman continued her assault by again trying to blind Jet with her nails, but this time Jet was prepared and surprised her by stepping into her arms and head butting her as hard as she could. Sang-mi stumbled to the side, and Jet grabbed both sides of her skull and gave it a brutal wrench as the older woman fought to stay upright.

The snap of the Korean's vertebrae was as loud as a slap, and Sang-mi collapsed like a rag doll, her limbs twitching spasmodically. Jet stared down at her for a moment, and then the meaning of the woman's presence in the triad boss's mansion hit home and she stepped back like she'd been struck.

"Oh, my God…" she whispered, and looked around the room for anything she could use as a distraction to occupy the guards. Interrogating Zhao was forgotten, her only goal now to escape and call the director before events spiraled out of control. Her eyes settled on the fire, and she saw her chance.

Jet ran to the curtains and tore them from the rod, and then rushed to the fireplace and lit them. She tossed the burning bundle onto the bed and hurried to the window, but that was no good – two of the guards were pointing up at the room and shouting.

Her best avenue of egress blocked, she'd have to take the direct route through the house, unappealing as that was. Jet whipped the pistol free, flipped the safety off, and moved to the door, where she hesitated at the sound of feet pounding up the main stairs. Out of time and with no other choice, she threw the door open as the flames behind her consumed the furniture and licked at the walls. She knew the house had been built from sheetrock and wood frame, and equipped with a state-of-the-art fire protection system – which was controlled by the servers in perpetual reboot downstairs. Within a few minutes the fire would spread to the entire top floor, hopefully causing enough chaos on the grounds for her to slip away in the confusion.

Jet stepped into the hall, the heat and smoke following her out, and was turning to bolt for the service stairs when she heard the crash of one of the bedroom doors being flung open behind her. An incoherent bellow of pure rage echoed down the hall, and then a large-caliber handgun began firing as she tucked and rolled away, the rounds shredding the walls around her.

When she came to a stop near a baseboard, she swung her pistol up and fired three times at the shape she could barely make out through the smoke that was now billowing from the Korean's room – Zhao Yaozu in a wheelchair, a Desert Eagle .50-caliber pistol trained in her direction. One of her bullets hit him in the stomach, and he exhaled with a shocked, "Oof," and stared at her in disbelief. She was readying to put another round through his chest when she shifted her aim at the last moment and squeezed off five shots in rapid succession, dropping two guards who had appeared on the far landing.

Zhao tried to bring his gun to bear on her again but didn't have the strength to steady his aim, and when he got off another shot, it went wide. Smoke occluded the hall as the blaze burned through the roof and the walls, and Jet held her fire, the ruby stain spreading across the front of the mobster's white silk pajamas signaling that any further shots would be a waste of valuable ammo. Instead, she leapt to her feet and zigzagged down the hall toward the service stairs, followed by a wounded howl that resembled nothing human.

Then she was turning the corner and taking the stairs two at a time, the hellish tableau behind her left to play itself out. The inferno would put a fitting end to the triad boss's reign, consumed by fire in the castle he'd built as tribute to his invincibility. Whether the stomach wound claimed him or the flames didn't matter. Jet's imperative now was to get away without being gunned down – a task that had gotten exponentially harder with the first of the mobster's shots.

When she got to the ground floor, she stopped and peeked around the corner. Three gunmen were charging down the hall from the main entrance, submachine guns in hand. She didn't hesitate and emptied her pistol at them, the closely grouped targets almost impossible to miss. Jet was ejecting the spent magazine and slapping another into place when the gunman at the back, who'd only been clipped by her fire, opened up at her, and she crouched down as a stream of lead tore through the plaster only inches from her skull. She flattened against the floor and waited until the man had emptied his magazine, and when she heard the snick of the bolt locking, rewarded him with four more shots, two of which caught him in the chest.

He fell back and she ran toward the dead men, pausing only to scoop up one of the submachine guns before reversing and tearing down the hall. She was almost to the rear service entry when another gunman appeared from one of the side rooms with pistol in hand. He fired at her, but she was moving too erratically even at the close range, and she loosed a dozen rounds at the corner he'd ducked behind after he saw her level the gun in his direction. A shriek of pain told her she'd hit at least some part of him, and she increased her speed as she ran past the room and squeezed off another three rounds at the shooter, who was slumped in a ball on the floor in a lake of red.

She reached the service door, held the key card to the sensor, and then was outside, running in a crouch toward the generator enclosure. The guards were concentrated at the front of the house, leaving her time to reach it without being seen, their attention drawn by the vision of the mansion engulfed in flames.

Jet opened the enclosure and eyed the generator, the sound deafening even after all the gunfire. After a quick assessment, she reached into the tangle of cables and gave one running to the spark plugs a powerful jerk.

The generator abruptly froze and the grounds plunged into darkness save for the orange glow from the flames licking at the night sky. A cry from her left was followed by the rattle of machine-gun fire. Divots of grass fountained into the air around her, but she was already in motion, a dark shadow sprinting out of sight toward the rear wall, the bulk of the house between her and the gunmen – at least long enough for it to matter.

She made for the corner, where the side wall met the rear, and didn't slow as she neared the intersection, instead running laterally halfway up the side wall with two powerful steps before pushing off and launching herself at the rear edge, arms outstretched. Bullets pocked the brick beneath her as her hands locked on the edge, and then she was squeezing through the gap at the top of the wall while the gunfire intensified from the house.

Ricochets whined as she scrambled over the top, chips spraying her face from near misses. She pulled herself the rest of the way beneath the electrified fence and dropped to the ground outside as the shooting waned. With a glance around to orient herself, she bolted toward the motorcycle, the spire of fire and smoke behind her lighting her way. A half minute later she was at the bike and fumbling for the key, her fingers still numb from the abuse she'd subjected them to with the Parkour wall vault. In the distance, ululating sirens announced the approach of the fire brigade.

Key in the ignition, she kick-started the motorcycle to life and slipped the helmet on just as headlights swung onto the street from the mansion grounds and the throaty growl of a muscle car greeted her. She didn't wait for the shooting to resume, instead slamming the bike into gear and wrenching the throttle, redlining the engine as she sped away with her lights extinguished. The car accelerated after her, but even with its overblown motor it was no match, and she leaned into a hard right turn and gave the bike more gas, leaving the pursuing car's headlights and the echo of Hail Mary gunshots behind as she raced into the stygian Beijing night.

CHAPTER 52

Kermanshah, Iran

Abu Azim sat in a camp chair by the radar array, a tablet computer in his lap, watching a live transmission from the building in the city below. The mullah's scheme was reaching its apex, and if his predictions about the Israeli response were correct, at any moment now fighters or missiles would come streaking over the horizon to destroy the structure. Azim smiled at the thought of using the paranoid nation's energy against it. The mullah deserved his reputation for brilliance.

A "journalist" was reporting on a feed that was also being taped for later dissemination. The tiny faces of a hundred children, their small hands holding candles, peered from the screen, the voice of the reporter providing the narrative.

"Every year the orphans of the Kermanshah shelter hold a candlelight vigil in solidarity with the children who have died in Palestine at the hands of their oppressors. For these children, many of them refugees who have fled the American aggression in Iraq or the CIA-sponsored terrorism in Syria, the vigil has special meaning."

The camera panned in on a little girl, her eyes big as a puppy's, clutching a candle in an aluminum foil base. Somebody said something off camera, and she smiled at the lens.

Azim set the tablet aside as the leader of the terrorist cell approached and squatted beside him. Azim offered a grin.

"Well, my friend, the hour is finally at hand," Azim said.

"My heart is soaring like an eagle."

"The mullah has cornered the devils. They have no choice now but to destroy the orphanage, which will be captured on film. The images will ruin them in the eyes of the world, and they will be revealed to be the bloodthirsty monsters they are. Imagine the horror as the footage is broadcast to the West: Israel attacking innocent children who are holding a vigil. There is no way the country can recover from it. Their allies will desert them, and Muslim nations will rise up as never before to rid the earth of their kind once and for all."

"They believe a chemical weapon is inside?"

"Yes. That was the entire strategy: working with our Chinese contact to find a plausible way for them to make the discovery. One that they would believe to be genuine so the information wasn't questioned. The North Korean was paid well to defect and to leak the information, and her faked injury during the kidnapping made it all the more believable. We knew they would have to send someone in to locate the rest of the planted report. They would have no option but to go after it – we provided sufficient clues so they would know it was in the woman's apartment."

The terrorist shook his head in wonder. "It is like playing chess, is it not? The mullah will become a legend. He has outfoxed the hounds."

"Indeed. I never doubted he would. Sacrificing millions of euros on the bank accounts to convince them the plot was genuine was a master stroke. It enabled us to time their aggression to the minute."

"It is a shame about the children."

Azim waved the sentiment away. "They are the offspring of infidels in Syria. They are of no consequence."

"Are we sure the jets are on their way?"

Azim checked his watch. "Forty-seven minutes ago, our contact in Israel confirmed jets taking off from their base. Exactly as the mullah said they would."

"Allah is favoring us tonight."

"Yes, and may He guide our missiles to their targets once they have attacked the building."

The terrorist frowned. "But will the devils not reveal the Korean report in their defense?"

"Nobody will believe them. Their intelligence service is known to lie about everything as a matter of course. It is their motto to achieve their ends through deception. The report will be denounced as a fake – and we know that it is, but they will be blamed for its creation. All records of the Korean woman have been purged from the computers, so it will look like a typical false flag, like so many of the attacks in Europe."

"It really is perfect. He must have received divine inspiration."

"I believe that he has." Azim retrieved the tablet and resumed watching the broadcast. "Get ready. It will be any time."

"The camera crew are great men to make this sacrifice."

"They are martyrs whose reward awaits them in Paradise."

"As it should be."

The reporter was holding a microphone up to a shy four-year-old, the corners of his mouth crusted with icing from a cake that the children had been served earlier.

"Do you wish everyone would stop fighting?" the journalist asked.

The little boy nodded vigorously and fixed the camera with a wide-eyed stare. "Yes."

Azim slid his sat phone from the pocket of the camp chair and placed the call he had been waiting all day to make. The mullah answered after one ring, his voice excited.

"I am watching the broadcast," he said. "You have done an excellent job."

"Thank you, Mullah. We are all indebted to you."

"Nonsense. This is a battle where there can be no middle ground. We are on the side of right. It could be no other way. You owe me nothing. It is I who am honored to have played a small role."

Azim nodded at the typically humble words. "A great day. The devils should be here within minutes."

"Then I will let you attend to things. We will talk afterwards. Good hunting."

"I will call when it is done."

CHAPTER 53

Beijing, China

Jet guided the motorcycle into an alley and removed the satellite phone from her backpack. She switched it on and waited as it hunted for a signal, the icon flashing to indicate it was searching. She'd lost her pursuers and ridden at high speed for half a mile before slowing and looking for a suitable place to make her call.

The phone locked onto a satellite and she dialed the director's cell phone number. It clicked twice and forwarded to an operator.

"Nobody is available," a dispassionate female voice announced.

"Find him. I need to speak with him immediately."

"I'm afraid he can't be interrupted."

"Get him on the phone. Tell him an emergency call from China must speak with him now. It's a matter of national security. He gave me this number for a reason. This is the reason."

"My instructions were clear."

"If you don't get him on the phone, the worst tragedy to ever hit our country will be your fault."

The operator said nothing for a beat. "Let me see if I can interrupt."

Jet waited, fighting back the impatient anger she felt swelling in her. When the director's gruff voice came on the line, he'd never sounded more annoyed.

"I can't talk," he growled.

"Listen carefully. The North Korean woman is alive – or was. She was staying in a suite at the triad boss's house. Whatever you think this is, you're wrong. Whatever you're doing because of that leaked information is wrong. It's all a lie. You've been set up."

255

The director's voice was tight as a drum skin when he spoke. "You can't know that. We can't take the risk."

"The woman was supposed to be dead. She wasn't. She also was ten years younger than we were led to believe. I just had the pleasure of fighting her. She was almost as strong as I am. Everything you think you know is a lie. If you go forward, you're doing exactly what these people want. It's all misdirection to achieve that – don't you see? It's the only thing that makes sense."

"Why would the Chinese–"

"Don't assume it's them. They're involved in the heroin business through Palestine and Egypt, remember? Ask yourself why their friends there might want you to carry out whatever you have planned, and there's your answer."

The director sounded strangled as realization hit home. "Oh, God...I have to go."

Jet held the phone, which had gone dead, and frowned at it before switching it off with a shrug.

"You're welcome," she whispered, and then dropped it into her backpack and felt the bump on her forehead with a wince – a souvenir of her fight. The scratch marks on her cheek had already begun to scab over but they stung like fire, and she made a mental note to find an all-night pharmacy so she could buy antiseptic ointment so they wouldn't get infected, as well as cover-up so she could mask the wound. Her last call on the burner cell was to Ken, to whom she gave the whereabouts of the motorcycle, and then she busied herself hiding the pistol, unused magazines, and butterfly knife under the seat compartment for him to dispose of. Finished with her cleanup, she set off on foot toward downtown to locate stores to buy her necessities, and an Internet café so she could book the first flight she could find to Cyprus, regardless of the cost.

The director returned to the ad hoc war room, his complexion white. "We have to abort."

"What?" Weisenthal blurted. "Have you lost your mind? They're almost on top of the target!"

"There's no time to argue. Our intelligence was flawed." He gave a twenty-second summary of his call, and by the time he was done, the faces of the others were equally blanched.

The general looked to Weisenthal, who nodded assent, and the soldier lunged for the phone. After a brief exchange he hung up and closed his eyes, his forehead beaded with pinheads of sweat in spite of the chill in the room.

"Well?" Weisenthal asked.

The general, his nerves shot, ran a hand through his hair. "It will be close."

Abu Azim leaned into the radar array monitor and grinned at the sight of the four glowing blips that had appeared moments before, flying in formation toward the building.

"How long until they are in range?" he asked.

"They're already in range."

He nodded. "Excellent. Remember, we don't shoot them down until they've destroyed the building."

"I know." The operator glanced at Azim. "How did you know there would be four planes?"

"The mullah. He said for this sort of operation, his sources confirmed they would send no more than four fighters." Azim's eyes narrowed as he studied the screen. "What are they doing?"

The technician blinked as though confused. "I... It must be some sort of stealth maneuver. Maybe they're splitting up for their final run?"

"Perhaps," Azim said, frowning. "But..." He stepped back from the screen and turned to where the lead terrorist was standing by the missile launchers with his men. "Launch the rockets!"

The terrorist looked confused. "They haven't hit the building yet!"

"They're turning around. Launch, dammit! Now, or they'll be out of range!"

The terrorist shouted instructions at his men, and they moved from the array. The four missiles streaked from the launcher into the night sky, trailing fire as they sped at Mach 1.5 toward the Israeli planes. Azim spun and glowered at where the missiles had appeared on the radar screen, traveling from the center toward the outer edge of the monitor, where the planes were now moving away.

"Come on…come…on…" he hissed between clenched teeth, his fingers white on the edge of the console and disbelief in his eyes.

Samuel glanced down at his threat alert and immediately spotted the inbound missiles. He debated breaking radio silence to warn his men, but instead followed orders to maintain radio silence and hit his afterburners, accelerating from five hundred miles per hour to nearly triple that, in spite of the low atmosphere. He pulled the nose of his plane upward, climbing, the prospect of a collision with the ground at more than the speed of sound unappealing, and prayed that his men had been warned by their alerts or, at worst, had seen his plane rocket away.

His radar told him that they had, and they followed his trajectory, the danger of detection insignificant compared to the certainty of being hit by the missiles on their tails. He leveled out at two thousand feet above the terrain, eyes glued to the radar screen, watching the drama behind him play out as the missiles kept coming.

Azim's muttered plea to the missiles changed to a string of curses that increased in volume as seconds passed. For several moments, the blips looked like they were going to converge, and then the planes shot away, the distance between the missiles and the jets remaining constant until the planes vanished from the screen.

"Change the range on the radar," he snapped at the operator, who obliged by punching a button and then looked away from the monitor, already knowing what it would show. Azim continued to watch as the gap between the missiles and the planes began to grow, and after several sweeps of the cycle, stepped from the array, his expression dark.

"Get everybody out of here," he called to the terrorist leader. "We've been blown."

He didn't wait for a response, instead raising the sat phone to his ear and pressing the recall button to let the mullah know that his plan had come to nothing.

CHAPTER 54

Larnaca, Cyprus

Jet shielded her eyes as she stepped from a taxi into the nearly blinding sunlight reflecting off the cobalt waters of the Mediterranean. Her sunglasses were inadequate against the intense glare, but the sun's warmth on her skin was refreshing after countless hours on planes. She looked around at the tourists walking along the waterfront, mostly couples and small families enjoying their vacations, and felt a pang of envy at the normalcy of the scene. She could pretend to be one of them and certainly would do her damnedest to enjoy her getaway with Matt and Hannah, but if she wanted a reminder of how different she actually was, all she had to do was brush her fingers against the scabs where a North Korean killer had tried to blind her.

The flight from Beijing had been anticlimactic, her departure from China a nonevent; the immigration clerk who processed her paperwork was uninterested in her, even with the gauze taped to her cheek over the wound from the woman's nails. She'd booked a ticket on the first flight out in the morning to Paris and had gratefully sunk into the plush seat in business class and been asleep within minutes of the jumbo jet taking off. A connection in France had her on the ground for four hours, and then she'd winged her way to Cyprus, her excitement building at having finally concluded her duties and the chance to see her family again.

She'd called the director from Paris, and he'd told her in his usual terse manner about the aborted flight, keeping the details to a minimum in his customary deference to the Mossad's "need to know" ethic.

"There was no blowback from any of the countries you overflew?" she'd asked when he finished.

"No. Nothing from anyone. Which is reassuring." He'd hesitated. "We came very close to Armageddon. And we have you to thank for stopping it. Israel owes you its thanks, as does the world."

"Any further word on the heroin?"

"Levi and Moishe are working it. But it's no longer your concern."

Jet paused. "Someone went to a lot of trouble to bring you to the brink."

"That didn't go unnoticed."

"Any chance of learning who?"

"We've got feelers out. But as you know, there are practical limits to how certain circles cooperate with us."

"I can imagine. At least with Zhao gone, the trafficking is likely to stop for a while."

The director grunted. "He'll just be replaced by someone else. It's a vicious cycle."

"Sounds like it."

"Again, you have my heartfelt thanks. Anything you need, just call."

"No offense, but I hope I never hear your voice again."

"None taken. I'm sure I'd feel much the same if the situation was reversed."

"I'm dropping off the radar for a bit."

"Enjoy the beach."

Of course he'd tracked Matt and Hannah to Cyprus. She hadn't even been surprised, just punchy from her travels.

"Thanks."

Jet walked toward the hotel Matt had selected, a four-star affair right on the sand, rock-throwing distance from the swankier but higher visibility Four Seasons. She paused to watch an old woman and a towheaded young boy feed a kit of pigeons, the toddler screaming in delight each time he shotgunned a fistful of seed at the birds and they scurried to retrieve it with much wing flapping and cooing. A particularly aggressive male with his chest puffed out punctuated his feeding with a display of strutting and open-winged ducking and swooping, to the obvious interest of several of the nearby females.

Jet smiled at the sight and glanced at several teenage couples on the surrounding benches, embracing and kissing. Even as evil men worked to bring down civilization, the world continued turning, and biological urges ensured the species would survive, if not prosper. She wondered how many close calls like the one she'd prevented took place each year around the planet – tense near misses over Syrian airspace between coalition forces and Russian, or provocations in the South China Sea, or soft coups engineered by clandestine agencies to advance murky agendas.

She was sure there were many – too many. All it would take was one to go bad, or to come to fruition, and everything could change for the worse. Human history was a litany of savagery and oppression and grand schemes gone wrong, of the few conspiring to control the many; and now, as before, the most malevolent always seemed to invest the most effort in dominating the rest.

The hotel lobby was impressive if shopworn, the polished marble floors and heavy Corinthian columns dated. Nobody gave her a second glance as she crossed the lobby and walked to the elevators. The bank of clocks displaying the time in six cities served as a reminder that nothing remained static and that all was relative. One of the brushed stainless steel slabs slid wide with a whoosh, and she stepped into the elevator along with a pair of businessmen in tropical weight suits, who were discussing weighty matters in Greek with the earnestness of those with something to lose. She tuned them out and concentrated on the blinking floor indicator until the car halted at hers, and pushed past them into the hallway, excitement rising in her core.

The room was the last on the corridor on her right, facing the ocean. She rapped on the door and waited, and after a small eternity it flew open and Matt stood silhouetted by sunlight streaming from the balcony. Hannah pushed past him with a squeal of excitement and threw herself at Jet's legs, pure joy radiating from her face, her face all the reward Jet could have hoped for.

"Mama!"

ABOUT THE AUTHOR

Featured in *The Wall Street Journal*, *The Times*, and *The Chicago Tribune*, Russell Blake is *The NY Times* and *USA Today* bestselling author of over forty novels.

Blake is co-author of *The Eye of Heaven* and *The Solomon Curse*, with legendary author Clive Cussler. Blake's novel *King of Swords* has been translated into German, *The Voynich Cypher* into Bulgarian, and his JET novels into Spanish, German, and Czech.

Blake writes under the moniker R.E. Blake in the NA/YA/Contemporary Romance genres. Novels include *Less Than Nothing*, *More Than Anything*, and *Best Of Everything*.

Having resided in Mexico for a dozen years, Blake enjoys his dogs, fishing, boating, tequila and writing, while battling world domination by clowns. His thoughts, such as they are, can be found at his blog: RussellBlake.com

Visit RussellBlake.com for updates

or subscribe to: RussellBlake.com/contact/mailing-list

BOOKS BY RUSSELL BLAKE

Co-authored with Clive Cussler
THE EYE OF HEAVEN
THE SOLOMON CURSE

Thrillers
FATAL EXCHANGE
FATAL DECEPTION
THE GERONIMO BREACH
ZERO SUM
THE DELPHI CHRONICLE TRILOGY
THE VOYNICH CYPHER
SILVER JUSTICE
UPON A PALE HORSE
DEADLY CALM
RAMSEY'S GOLD
EMERALD BUDDHA
THE GODDESS LEGACY
A GIRL APART

The Assassin Series
KING OF SWORDS
NIGHT OF THE ASSASSIN
RETURN OF THE ASSASSIN
REVENGE OF THE ASSASSIN
BLOOD OF THE ASSASSIN
REQUIEM FOR THE ASSASSIN
RAGE OF THE ASSASSIN

The Day After Never Series
THE DAY AFTER NEVER – BLOOD HONOR
THE DAY AFTER NEVER – PURGATORY ROAD
THE DAY AFTER NEVER – COVENANT
THE DAY AFTER NEVER – RETRIBUTION

Made in the USA
San Bernardino, CA
09 May 2020